T0068252

Praise for *The Worthy*

"Swift, funny and sometimes horrendous, a perfect book for a lazy afternoon."

—Kit Reed, *Hartford Courant*

"Compelling and savagely humorous . . . Clarke's balance of structure, attention to detail, and sublime cast of characters make *The Worthy* a fine American novel, reminiscent of the introspection of Ken Kesey and the biting humor of Chuck Palahniuk."

—Sean Reynolds, *Entertainment Today*

"Not unlike a savvy, bastard offspring of *Ghost* and *Animal House.*"

—Mike Shea, *Texas Monthly*

"Clarke paints an amusing and jaw-dropping (but only slightly exaggerated) picture of a life treasured by generations of beer guzzling food fighters."

—*Kirkus Reviews*

"Readers are in for one of those roll-around, guffawing kind of laughs."

—Alison Kothe, *Longhorn Living*

"[Clark will] win fans of readers who appreciate the absurd, the enthusiastically profane and the supremely satisfying idea that karma not only wins, it bites."

—Joy Tipping, *Dallas Morning News*

"There's a time, in college life, when it all seems like 'life is just one big beer-chugging, backslapping moment.' *The Worthy* both remembers that dumb fun and provides a bit of a corrective."

—Susan Larson, *New Orleans Times-Picayune*

"A clash of good spirit versus bad spirit, and it makes for a pretty spirited, quick read."

—Martin Zimmerman, *The San Diego Union-Tribune*

"*The Worthy* . . . practically begs to be turned into a movie . . . It's got young people, beautiful people, sex, murder, possession, blood and revenge."

—Cary Darling, *Fort Worth Star-Telegram*

Praise for *Lord Vishnu's Love Handles*

"*Lord Visnhu's Love Handles* has a plot so twisted that to encapsulate it, leaving out Clarke's shrewd, deadpan exposition, is to rob it of its brusquely winsome charm."

—Liesl Schillinger, *The New York Times Book Review*

"For sheer zany chutzpah you can't beat *Lord Vishnu's Love Handles* . . . Will Clarke writes in surreal Kurt Vonnegut–Monty Python manner."

—Fredric Koeppel, *The Commercial Appeal*

"The most peculiar mystery novel of the year . . . in all its manic, insane, profane, funny but inevitably confusing glory . . . a promising start."

—Les Roberts, *Cleveland Plain Dealer*

"Clarke is adept at pushing all the buttons—middle-aged angst, religious yearning, a careening, breakneck plot—which should endear him to Christopher Moore fans."

—*Library Journal*

"Chaotic . . . amusing first novel."

—*Kirkus Reviews*

"I loved *Lord Vishnu's Love Handles*. It's a great and unashamed page-turner, full of fabulous characters. I just wish remote viewers really were that interesting."

—Jon Ronson, author of *Them* and *The Men Who Stare at Goats*

"*Lord Vishnu's Love Handles* is mind-boggling and wonderful. It's the wackiest, craziest, genre-defying, can't-put-it-down book I ever read. Will Clarke is part David Sedaris, part Dave Eggers, part Charlie Kaufman, Hunter S. Thompson, Tom Robbins, and Kurt Vonnegut . . . and a 100 percent original Will Clarke."

—Sara Pritchard, author of *Crackpots*

"A twisted, hilarious, amphetamine-fueled parable for our time."

—S. R. "Rob" Bindler, writer/director of
Hands on a Hard Body

"*Lord Vishnu's Love Handles* is an entertaining and gritty journey into the supernatural, full of wit and surprises at every turn."

—Tony Hawk, world-champion skateboarder
and author of *Hawk: Occupation: Skateboarder*

Also by Will Clarke

Lord Vishnu's Love Handles: A Spy Novel (Sort Of)

The Worthy

A GHOST'S STORY

Will Clarke

SIMON & SCHUSTER PAPERBACKS

NEW YORK LONDON TORONTO SYDNEY

SIMON & SCHUSTER PAPERBACKS
1230 Avenue of the Americas
New York, NY 10020

This book is a work of fiction. Names, characters, places, and incidents
either are products of the author's imagination or are used fictitiously.
Any resemblance to actual events or locales or persons, living or dead,
is entirely coincidental.

Copyright © 2006 by Will Clarke
All rights reserved, including the right to reproduce this book
or portions thereof in any form whatsoever. For information address
Simon & Schuster Paperbacks Subsidiary Rights Department,
1230 Avenue of the Americas, New York, NY 10020.

First Simon & Schuster trade paperback edition July 2007.

SIMON & SCHUSTER PAPERBACKS and colophon are registered trademarks
of Simon & Schuster, Inc.

For information about special discounts for bulk purchases,
please contact Simon & Schuster Special Sales at 1-800-456-6798
or business@simonandschuster.com.

Designed by Davina Mock

Manufactured in the United States of America

1   3   5   7   9   10   8   6   4   2

The Library of Congress has cataloged the hardcover edition as follows:
Clarke, Will.
The worthy: a ghost's story / Will Clarke.
p.   cm.
1. Greek letter societies—Fiction. 2. Baton Rouge (La.)—Fiction.
3. Louisiana—Fiction. 4. Revenge—Fiction. I. Title.
PS3603.L38W67 2006
813'.6—dc22   2005058139

ISBN-13: 978-0-7432-7315-2
ISBN-10:   0-7432-7315-X
ISBN-13: 978-0-7432-7316-9 (pbk)
ISBN-10:   0-7432-7316-8 (pbk)

FOR MY BROTHERS

There are things way worse than death.
—LSU sorority girl overheard on bid day

The Worthy

one

I f you ignore what I have to say, it really won't surprise me. I've
come to find that most people ignore the dead. If you do
choose to hear me, listen closely, because what I have to tell
you is a story of unholy proportions. Hopefully, if I can make you
hear what I am supposed to tell you, I can finally break the ties
that bind me to the secret letter society of Gamma Chi.

But before we get started, let me tell you about myself. My
name is Conrad Avery Sutton III, and I am dead at age nineteen.
When I was alive, I won't lie, I had it pretty good—the Porsche, the
pretty girls, and a trust fund full of oil money. When I started as a
freshman at Louisiana State University there was no question that
I would rush. My daddy had been a Gamma Chi as well as his
daddy and all the men in the Sutton clan. Well, there was one exception, my cousin Barrow, who got blackballed and now he's got
one of those rainbow stickers on the back of his truck. God, my
daddy and uncle were so embarrassed; they still don't talk about it.

I went through Rush and I of course got a bid. I'll admit I
thought I was the shit with my navy jersey and gold letters. Next to
my Porsche, those letters got me laid more times than I can remember. Of course it was all fun and games in the beginning—one
endless keg of cold beer and blunts on command. But this mixture
of chronic booze and blood oaths turned into a bitter, stinking
mess.

Busted lips and broken beer bottles were all part of my pledge
training. I was cocky, and the brothers saw fit to divest me of this
character flaw. So I scrubbed urinals with a toothbrush to the beat
of someone punching my kidneys. I served meals to my brethren
walking only on my bloody knees. And when a spit cup was not

readily available for an active brother, I learned to offer my hand as a spittoon. I even learned the fine art of acting. I was given the starring role in Gamma Chi's video reenactment of the "Wasabi-up-the-Nose" scene from *Jackass: The Movie*. I never could smell right after that.

By the end of my first semester, I had learned to be a good pledge. I could recite all fifteen hundred words of the pledge creed—backward even. And for the amusement of the active chapter, I was asked to perform this dyslexic feat for their dinnertime entertainment. It's amazing how a knuckle upside the head can force you to learn even the most boring crap.

So I find it almost poetic that this bright April morning, the brothers will dedicate their new library and scholarship fund to me. The Conrad Avery Sutton III Memorial Library is a beautiful addition to the big old Gamma Chi house. My new library is full of polished woods, brass lights, and leather-bound books. Daddy went all out for his dead son. It was his way of dealing with my death. He worked while others cried. It obviously paid off; the construction crew completed the job in less than two months. And that's no small task, considering how rainy South Louisiana gets in the early spring.

You know, it's weird being dead. You're everywhere but nowhere all at once. You can sort of hear people talk before they speak, but you can't speak yourself. Or at least, you can't make people hear you when you speak. On rare occasions some folks have actually heard me. But most people are too busy with their own thoughts to pay any attention to mine. There is, however, one perk to being dead: The living are like open books that you can read without turning the pages of a conversation. Only thing is, most of the books in this stupid old house are full of blank pages and cheap porno. So I guess it's really not as cool as it sounds.

I mostly find myself following around Ryan Hutchins. He lives on the third floor and he's the biggest coke-snorting asshole you'll ever meet—and I'm not just saying that because he killed me.

When he's not busy killing innocent people like myself, he's beating his beautiful girlfriend, Maggie Meadows. He knocks her around quite a bit, and the saddest thing is that she never really fights back. I rage and scream something horrible when he does this to her, but Ryan is deaf, dumb, and blind to me and I can't do anything to save poor Maggie.

These are the things that you should know about Ryan Hutchins—not that he teaches poor kids to swim at the Y or that he donates blood every month because he's got that universal blood type. No, the real truth is what you need to know about him. That's because to everyone at LSU—and I mean *everyone*—Ryan's this big, bright, rising star. But truth be told, he's really the darkest black hole you'll ever meet, and nobody seems to realize this. Which profoundly annoys me, considering the psycho pretty much murdered me in cold blood. Of course, Maggie Meadows knows Ryan's a complete head-case, but she'll never tell anyone. She's too ashamed or in love or scared or I don't know what to ever tell.

Speaking of Maggie, her bruises are covered with makeup today and she stands there with her pretty blond hair in my library, greeting alumni as the sweetheart of Gamma Chi. Ryan stands by her side looking so sad and full of compassion that it makes me sick. You would have thought his best hunting dog got run over by a truck.

"He was a great guy." Ryan keeps nodding and shaking off tears.

It's the same morbid song I heard at my funeral, and everyone's singing the second verse here today:

"His parents are devastated."

"They had to check his mamma into one of those Charter hospitals."

"His dad sure didn't waste any time building this place."

"Or money."

"He was a cool guy. He let me borrow his Wilco CD."

"Kimbrough found the body."

"What did it look like?"

"He won't talk about it."

"Conrad was a real Gamma Chi."

This grief-fest has me ticking like a time bomb. I want to go off and punch someone. However, I can't: I'm no longer the owner of a pair of fists and that makes it kind of hard to hit anything.

But something weird is in the air today. Maybe it's the fact that everybody's gathered here concentrating on my memory, but for some reason, I feel almost alive again in this library.

I wonder if I could muster up the energy to do a real haunting on these bastards. You know, like spell out "Ryan killed me!" in blood on the walls or something real *Poltergeist*-like. But, no, I've actually tried that before and I just can't seem to get it to work.

"What you doing in here, boy?" Miss Etta, Gamma Chi's house cook, looks up at me as she lays out her buffet spread.

"You can see me?"

"Get on back to heaven! You dead now—shoo!" She flings her long crooked hand at me. "Go and be with the Lord now."

Everyone glances at crazy Miss Etta and dismisses our conversation as her obvious senility. I follow Miss Etta back to the kitchen as she hobbles away from me.

"Hey, wait a second, Miss Etta."

"I don't talk to the dead." She shakes her head. "You need to go back to heaven 'fore you upset folks."

"Hey, I can't go back." I point to the library. "Something's keeping me here."

"That's your problem. Let me alone now." She opens the big stainless steel fridge and pulls out a vat of Swedish meatballs.

"But Ryan killed me!"

"Listen, boy, you think that's going to make a difference if I march in there and tell them white folk that?" She shakes her spatula at me. "I know he killed you and I know he be beating on that pretty girl in there too. But ain't nobody going to listen to me." She scoops brown gravy and lumps into a serving dish and lights a Sterno can underneath it. "Now get out this house and go back to heaven."

For some weird reason, those words alone build up this pressure around me and push me out of the house. I find myself outside looking through the windows of my wood-paneled library as Ryan stands at the podium.

"Conrad was not only an outstanding scholar and pledge, but most importantly he was our friend and our brother." Ryan sticks out his bottom lip and slowly nods his head.

There goes Mamma boohooing again, and Daddy just sits there not knowing what to do with his hands. And here comes Miss Etta with the meatballs. She sneers at Ryan, but nobody seems to care. She's right; nobody would believe her.

"It is a great honor"—Ryan holds his mighty gavel in his right hand—"that I, on behalf of the men of Gamma Chi, dedicate this library and scholarship fund to the memory of Conrad Avery Sutton, the third." Ryan pounds the table with his gavel like he used to do my face on so many an occasion.

It's the same gavel that I heard rap the night I swore an oath to this brotherhood of lying bastards. It was my pledging ceremony—the night that Gamma Chi's first secrets were revealed to my pledge brothers and me. We were bound, blindfolded, herded, and punched into the back of a flatbed and driven out to the woods. They unloaded us like sacks of rocks into the dirt.

"Get your sorry asses up!" an active slurred at us. I felt someone's Red Wing boot kick me in the side and then the heel fell swift on my back. The force pushed my face into the cold earth. I was such a chicken shit that I was too afraid to spit, so I just swallowed the blood and dirt.

"Sutton! He said get up!" some weasel-ass active yelled.

I struggled and writhed against the rope and finally stood upright. Once we were all standing, they filed us into rows.

The brotherhood swarmed around us and shouted, "Worthy-worthyworthy! Worthy!"

Then it was silent except for the crackle of a few twigs underfoot. A match scratched and I could smell the gasoline and sulfur and then an all-encompassing red glow filled the blackness.

"Remove their blindfolds."

"Hold still," an active growled in my ear, and the black rag was jerked from my head.

I squinted. The fire was too bright and too hot and I was too close. My eyebrows were nearly seared off by a twelve-foot burning cross.

"Behold! The Fiery Cross of Gamma Chi!" Ryan barked from behind a velvet-covered card table as he read from what looked like a hymnal. "The omen revealed first to the mighty Emperor of Rome before battle is now revealed to only the Worthy." Ryan was all decked out in a black devil-worshiper-looking robe and hood. There was a large gold cross on his chest.

"Neophytes!" he sang like some psycho TV minister. "The men of Gamma Chi ask if you are worthy. Are you worthy?"

At least a hundred hooded Gamma Chis swarmed and hollered, "Worthyworthyworthyworthyworthy!"

"Before we proceed"—Ryan hesitated as he turned the page— "I, the worthy Chalice Keeper, charge you, the pledges of Gamma Chi, to take a solemn blood oath before our Father, the Lord Almighty, and the Holy Brotherhood of Gamma Chi, that from this moment forward you will never speak or transcribe the sacred rites that you are about to witness."

The flaming cross was beginning to die down and the smoke made me sneeze, which caused Ryan to lose his place. He glared at me, and then fumbled to the next paragraph. "Please respond nay if you are willing to betray the sacred, or if you are worthy, repeat after me: This blood that I spill is my own."

Everyone repeated all sing-songy and I felt a sharp sting at the base of my neck and the drag of skin opening up. The actives stood behind each one of us cutting a small cross into the backs of our skulls with a buck knife. The blood ran down my neck and soaked crimson into the white Lacoste shirt that Ashley, my ex-girlfriend, had given me for my eighteenth birthday.

"And with this blood"—Ryan stumbled over the doctrine while we followed in a choppy unison—"I am washed free of my sins and will sin no more. I will seek to be Worthy, and I pledge before God never to betray the favor of the Worthy, and if I do break this covenant, may I walk in the Valley of the Shadow of Death with no one to call me brother."

Ryan rapped the gavel on a block of wood and the active chapter snapped its fingers in approval. That snapping now disintegrates into the steady claps of applause that are now filling my newly dedicated library.

Ryan takes a seat near the podium with his halo on so tight that I wish it were a noose. He smiles at my parents as one of the new pledges presents them with this cheesy wood and brass plaque with my picture laminated on it. Mamma runs her hand over my picture; she cries for this boy with crazy black hair and a smart mouth.

Anyway, everyone stands and consoles one another over their grievous loss. And then they all form a line at Miss Etta's buffet. But not Ryan; he makes a beeline for the door. I follow him outside to the porch of this white-columned prison where Maggie's standing by herself, staring up at the swaying oak trees.

"What are you doing out here?" Ryan forces a smile.

"Nothing, just getting some fresh air." Maggie folds her arms and rubs her bruised triceps. Ryan lights a cigarette and exhales the smoke through his nose. Maggie coughs as he puts his arm around her waist.

"It's sad, isn't it?" Maggie cuddles up to him.

"Yeah." Ryan rests his smoke in the corner of his mouth. "Did you see his mom in there?"

"I know. Total basket case. I felt so sorry for her." Maggie tucks a piece of her hair behind her ear and looks back up at the trees.

"What would you do if that happened to me?" Ryan whispers.

"Don't talk like that."

"Why not?"

"Because I don't want to think about it."

He hugs her. "You'd date someone else, wouldn't you?"

"That's not going to happen."

"But if it did . . ." He tokes on his cigarette.

"*You killed me,*" I spit in his ear.

"What?" He looks around. "Did you hear that?"

"Hear what?" Maggie steps out of his arms and faces him.

"I don't know." He moves her out of the way and peers at the trees to see if someone's hiding behind one. "Never mind. I thought I heard someone."

He clenches his sweaty palms into fists.

"Are you worthy, Ryan?"

"Shut up!" he yells out at nothing.

Maggie hides behind a column. "Ryan, are you okay?"

He throws down his cigarette and loosens his tie.

"I need a drink."

"Worthy, worthy, worthy, Ryan."

Two

"Use a toothpick, baby." Miss Etta slaps a rushee's hand as he tries to snag a piece of cheese off her buffet table. "Your mamma raised you better than that, I know."

The freshman immediately grabs a frilly toothpick, holds it up for Miss Etta's approval, and then begins jabbing at the buffet.

It's been almost three months since the dedication of my library, eight months since my death, and Gamma Chi hasn't really missed a beat. It's now mid-August and time for a new set of victims. It's Rush. It's also hotter than two rats screwing in a wool sock. Baton Rouge is just one big sweat stain this time of the year. But it's kind of pretty in a primordial sort of way with its mossy oaks and palmettos.

The LSU campus is particularly nice to look at. It's all tropical plants and arched stucco walkways, surrounded by these enormous fraternity and sorority houses. They're southern mansions, really—white columns, Confederate flags, a broken window or two, and the occasional BMW. Gamma Chi's house is the biggest on the row. It's this three-story red brick job with white columns bigger than Dallas, and with oak trees even bigger. Most of the rushees are making their way up to the house now. They're all wide-eyed and intimidated. I remember how it felt. You feel very small standing in front of that big old house. Meanwhile, all these actives, in their Sunday best, look like grown men, while you, who are fresh out of high school, feel like you just hit puberty. You want to be cool like them. You want to be a man.

As I look out from my library at the rushees standing in the yard waiting for their next Rush party to begin, there's one rushee who catches my attention. His name is Tucker Graham, and he's a big guy, about six-ten, three hundred and something, with bright red hair. I can tell by the look in his eyes that he wants this. He wants all the keg parties, all the sorority girls dropping their panties for a Gamma Chi jersey. Even though most of these rushees have this same look, there's something different about Tucker. When all the other freshmen are huddled together, Tucker stands alone. And the weird thing is that he seems comfortable doing this.

"Dude, go away. Go pledge Sigma Chi or KA or Deke!" I yell at him.

Tucker stops in his tracks, looks around, and wipes the sweat from his forehead. I think he hears me. He pulls out his Rush map from his back pocket and opens it.

"Listen to me. Go away!"

"Gamma Chi. First party," he reads while moving his lips. He looks up, smiles, and continues up to the house. Like I said, it's easy to ignore the dead.

Tucker isn't what you'd call a "face-man." He's not one of these hotshots who would steal your girl or screw your little sister, but he'll be a top rushee anyway. He's a good old boy, the ultimate drinking buddy. And aside from his size, he's the standard of mediocrity next to which all big men on campus can shine. He also looks like he can fight like a pit bull, and I bet you he can hold his liquor pretty good.

"Hey, big guy," Ryan Hutchins greets Tucker at the front steps of the Gamma Chi house. You can't help but notice Ryan's teeth; they're unnaturally white and straight. I think his daddy must be an orthodontist. He's vainer than a girl too, works out all the time; he even sits in a tanning bed. Ryan's main goal in life is to be one of those models in a Ralph Lauren Polo ad—all athletic, Anglo, and rich.

"Hi." Tucker lumbers over to Ryan and shakes his hand. You can tell Tucker is thinking real hard about how to shake hands. A bad handshake is the kiss of death during Rush.

"I'm Tucker Graham."

"Ryan Hutchins, President." Ryan flashes a fluorescent smile. "We've heard a lot of good things about you, Tucker. You're from Vidalia, right?"

"Yeah. Vidalia."

"Come on inside and let's get you a name tag and get you around."

They enter the foyer of the house. Everything is sparkling clean; the woodwork is sugar white and ornately detailed like the icing on a wedding cake, and big houseplants, stolen from the parking lot of the Wal-Mart, are everywhere. The grand stairway—the one that I allegedly fell down drunk—is all carpeted with brand-new blue carpet. There's still the faint smell of stale keg beer and dirty old socks, though.

"Man, nice house."

"Yeah, we're pretty proud of it." Ryan's voice bounces around the high ceilings as he looks around. "Part of it burned down in 1979, so our alumni saw that as a chance to rebuild it a little bigger, a little better."

"I bet y'all have thrown down in this place." Images of wet T-shirt contests and floating kegs dance in Tucker's head.

"Hey, we weren't named the most partying fraternity by *Playboy* for nothing." Ryan scribbles Tucker's name on one of those Hello-my-name-is stickers and slaps it on Tucker's chest.

"Whoa, are you serious?" Tucker's mouth drops to the floor.

"You know somebody has to be the best. That's my motto."

They both laugh—Tucker out of obligation, and Ryan because he actually thinks he made a funny. Ryan leads Tucker into the chapter room to meet his inner circle.

The rest of the week is one continuous handshake for Tucker. He meets and greets all the top dogs of Gamma Chi, and come bid night, he's going suicide Gamma Chi.

Bid night, the night of ten thousand drunken lays, the night you become a man, or at least a pledge, which is one step closer to being a man than you were a week ago. And Tucker is ready. He stands in a massive line at the Student Union to pick up his bid, shifting from one leg to the other like he has to piss or something.

Some ticky little guy standing in front of Tucker turns around and introduces himself with a blistering enthusiasm, "Hey dude, I'm Randall. And I am pledging Deke!"

"Cool." Tucker smiles.

"So what are you pledging?"

"Gamma Chi." Tucker smiles even bigger.

"They're the best! Congratulations, man!" Randall puts his hand up for a high five.

Tucker slaps Randall's hand and they bump fists. And while this one moment between relative strangers would seem like nothing, it's not. It's a major turning point in the fate of Tucker Graham. See, poor Randall's envy has just confirmed Tucker's biggest dream—the dream that there's a house full of honest-to-God brothers waiting for him with a pledge jersey and a keg truck. Randall's admiration will be the evidence that Tucker will hold on to when things go bad later on in the semester. This one stupid compliment will be compounded with hundreds of others from parents and girls and even some teachers. These kind words will keep Tucker Graham believing—believing in a future full of beer and easy shags. However, the cold, stark reality is that Gamma Chi pledgeship means getting the shit kicked out of you on a daily basis. This crooked math is what will keep Tucker and all his pledge brothers from quitting. It's a simple equation, actually: you pay money to Gamma Chi so they will beat you senseless. Oh, yeah, and you get to wait on them hand and foot.

But when you're eighteen and alive and never going to die, you don't know enough calculus to figure this out. So you pledge and you believe what you need to believe and everything usually adds up somehow when you get initiated.

Tucker finally gets up to the front of the line. The Greek Council guy flips through this computer list, highlights Tucker's name, and hands him a bid.

It ever so proudly reads:

The men of Gamma Chi cordially extend
Rushee Tucker J. Graham a bid for pledgeship.

"Yes!" Tucker throws his fist in the air. He runs out of the Union, down fraternity row with all the other newly minted pledges.

Through the parade grounds and under the big oaks, past the Deke house, past the Kappa Sig house, past KA, past Theta Xi, and past Sigma Chi, Tucker Graham runs until his sides feel like they will bust. But he keeps on running to that big red brick house at the end of the row.

Tucker finds the front lawn of the Gamma Chi house transformed with floodlights, mud pits, hay bales, and keg trucks. He dives right in. Some active, a blond soccer player with cornrows, greets him with a high five. Tucker slaps his hand off. He then spots his new best friend, Ryan Hutchins, and lunges at him. He wrestles Ryan to the ground. And then stands up all muddy, shaking his stupid fist and shouting, "Woohoo! Gamma Chi!"

Then bam!

Tucker's face is in the mud and Ryan is on top.

Ryan tries to rip the shirt off Tucker, but Tucker throws him, and the two wrestle standing up. A couple of actives jump in when they see that Tucker is getting the best of their leader. It takes five actives to take Tucker down. Three of them to hold him and the other two to tear his shirt off. Tucker snakes around, causing the drunken brethren to slip and fall in the muck. He stands up huffing and puffing, covered in Indian burns and mud.

Ryan puts his arm around Tucker's neck and hands him a blue and gold jersey.

"You're going to be fucking Gamma Chi, man!"

Tucker wipes the blood dripping from his eyebrow with the shirt and puts it over his head. Ryan grabs Tucker by the neck of his shirt and forces him under the tap of the keg truck. Ryan opens the tap and Tucker Graham drinks from it like a newborn calf sucking on a teat.

"Come on, champion, drink up."

The beer floods out of his mouth and he tries to get out from under the tap, but Ryan jerks his head back into place.

"You ain't full yet, champion."

Tucker's face swells red and the beer rushes out his nose. He pulls back gasping for air. Ryan pushes him back under the tap, but Tucker with all his heavy-weightiness throws Ryan to the ground. Cold beer and puke spew from Tucker Graham like a fire hose.

Ryan laughs as if this is the funniest damn thing he has ever seen. Tucker stands up, holding on to the beer truck and then he pukes some more. Ryan lights a cigarette and takes a drag. "Are you done yet?"

Tucker nods his head yes and coughs.

"Naw, I don't think you're done yet." Ryan grabs him by the collar and pulls him back to the truck.

Tucker pulls away. "No, man! No more!"

"Come on, don't be such a pussy! Just one more time. Come on." Ryan smiles.

"I can't do it again, bruh." He shakes his head; his eyes are already glazed.

"Look Tucker, it's my job tonight to get you wasted and then to get you laid. So I'd be seriously letting you down if I didn't put you back under that truck." Ryan puts his arm back around Tucker. "And I don't want to let my new little brother down."

"Just one more time?" He wipes the slobber from his chin.

"Just one more time"—Ryan tokes on his cigarette—"and then I'll set you up with"—Ryan exhales—"one of the sweetest lays you have ever had, just right up those stairs."

He ashes on Tucker's arm.

"Ouch!"

"Sorry about that, bud," Ryan chuckles.

It takes just a few more backslaps from Ryan and Tucker finds himself back under that keg. Except this time he's got quite an audience: all his new pledge brothers, all these cute sorority girls, as well as the entire active chapter. All eyes are on Tucker Graham as the crowd chants, "Drink-a-beer! Drink-a-beer! Drink-a-beer!

Drink-a-beer! If you can't drink a beer like a Gamma Chi can, then what the hell are you doing with a beer in your hand!"

I must admit Tucker impresses us all. He sits under that tap and Milwaukee's Best flows straight from that keg into his stomach. Not one drop is spilt in vain. Everyone is in awe of this superhuman display of mind over gag reflex. After a minute or so, Tucker stands up and tips the lever. A tiny drop lingers and then falls from the tap. The crowd cheers with amazement. The keg is empty.

Ryan throws down his smoke, picks up Tucker's arm, and raises it over his head.

"Gamma Chi!" Ryan roars.

The drunken mob chimes in. Tucker is smiling like he just swallowed a canary, not half a keg. And as sad as this may sound, I do believe this may be Tucker Graham's proudest moment.

Now, Ryan keeps his promise and Tucker ends his bid night on the third floor of the Gamma Chi house with this French Quarter hooker named Cherie-Elise—the same hooker I got with my bid night. I didn't do her, though. I was too scared. So I acted like I passed out. That way, she still got paid. And just for the record, that's about as close to a good deed as I probably ever came when I was alive, but I figure it's got to have counted for something.

Cherie-Elise has got these watermelon-size tits, and she sort of looks like an older, rougher-tougher version of Cindy Crawford, except with bigger hair; she's even got that little mole thing going on. They only pay her two hundred bucks a lay—which for someone like Cherie-Elise, with her freak show titties and all, I don't see why she doesn't charge more. But she and her friends Kanday, Cherry-Pop, and Coco service the entire Gamma Chi house every bid night. It's like a tradition or something, and if you want to get down to the real nitty gritty, it's also why Gamma Chi charges a four-hundred-dollar pledging fee. I guess you could call it a college experiment in pimp daddy economics.

"So, you next?" Cherie-Elise sits in the middle of this ratty old single bed with nothing on but a stolen Xi Omega jersey—cut off just at her tits—bright yellow thong panties, and red high heels.

"Yeah." Tucker holds on to the doorframe as his eyes and head are pulled by the sheer gravitational force of Cherie's gigantic knockers.

"Okay, shuga, come on in and shut da'doh."

"Huh?" His eyes roll back in his head. He catches himself on the doorframe and starts unbuttoning his pants. He staggers over to the bed, but the pants around his ankles are in complete confederacy against him; he falls flat on his face.

"Shuga, you okay?"

"Goddamn pants!" Tucker wrestles against his slacks, but for whatever drunken reason, he can't get them off. So he pulls them back up and stands.

"Come on, shuga, I ain't got ah fuckin' night."

But now, not only are his pants working against him, so is the earth itself as it spins faster on its axis. He falls on top of Cherie-Elise and passes out.

"Aw, shit!" Cherie-Elise struggles to push his heavy ass off of her. Tucker's body lands in a thud on the floor. And you know what? I don't think the bastard's breathing. Piss puddles up all around him, and having died myself, I do believe he's given up the ghost, kicked the bucket, and bought the farm. But I don't see his spirit anywhere around here.

So I reach down to check his pulse, and damned if I don't fall in. Everything is black as pitch in here and all I can hear is what sounds like a swarm of bees. I'd try to get out, but there's no direction to move in.

I'm stuck inside this meat cage!

All of a sudden there is light. But it's not Jesus or nothing; it's just the light hanging from the ceiling. I focus on these long legs that stretch all the way up to this head full of wild hair, fat red lips, a big black mole, and bright green gum.

"Sorry, I got ta go." Cherie-Elise smacks her gum as she slings on her street clothes. "Little Miss Rumpshaka's got betta tangs ta do with h'self dan to clean up yo' sick-shit."

"Please! Get me to a hos-urggff!!" Vomit wells up and forces itself out of my nose and mouth.

"Here's da' phone, babe. Call dim y'self." She drops the receiver on my head and I see the glimmer of her ankle bracelet disappear behind a slamming door.

I try to force these fingers to punch out 9-1-1, but Tucker's
body falls back into a coma before I can jump-start his flooded
brain. As consciousness is extinguished, I float back up to the ceiling and stay the hell away from Tucker's body.

Three

The Sunday sun comes up all pink and mean, hollering at everybody in the frat house. The morning rays stick in Tucker Graham's eyes like needles from a heart-crossed lie. That son of a bitch is lucky he's not dead, but right now he wishes he were. He's covered in puke and piss, and now he's alive and awake and hating it. We're talking major alcohol poisoning, an alcohol-induced coma, and lucky for him—"Urgffhhh!"—or maybe not so lucky, he's woken up, boggling all over the place.

I tell you, I would be pissed off if I hadn't gotten out of his body when I did. I hate hangovers. I'd rather be dead.

Besides, this possession thing ain't for me. I guess the best way to describe it is it's like sitting on a public toilet seat or something. It's not like your toilet at home where you'd like to be, but somebody else's. And using it makes you feel sort of dirty, like some kind of herpes or crab might jump on you if you stay too long. It's just not a good feeling. Besides, I haven't met God yet, but I don't think he'd look too kindly on me being a body snatcher. If He sends people to hell for something, I'd think that would be a pretty good reason. And now that I'm dead, I've got to start considering that sort of thing.

I've nursed enough hangovers in my day and watching Tucker boggle one more time isn't going to help him or me, so I leave. I go to Ryan's room.

In the red glow of Ryan's clock radio, Maggie very quietly tiptoes around his room naked, looking for her clothes. Being a sorority girl and all, she's not supposed to sleep over in the house. So she sneaks out the back before any of her sorority sisters, who also spent the night, can catch her and turn her in to her sorority's standards committee.

She sprints to her car, a black VW Beetle with plates that read MAGPIE. She gets into her black gumball of a car and looks in the rearview mirror. She wipes the sleep and makeup away from her eyes. She starts the car; Dave Matthews's "Crash Into Me" blares over her speakers, and she starts to cry. She's tired of that damn old song, tired of being the sweetheart of Gamma Chi, tired of the rules, and tired of the bruises that nobody sees.

She shuts the radio off and drives around the Campus Lake sobbing. Looking up at the big houses that line it, she wishes she could fast forward her life to where she was away from Ryan, and married to a rich husband, living happily ever after up in one of those big homes. Then as she turns the corner around the lake, she looks out over it and wonders what it would be like to just keep that wheel turning right into the smoky water. But she's much stronger than that, and like a good girl, she follows the road to Chimes Street, just outside the main campus gates, and drives to Louie's Twenty-Four-Hour Cafe for some breakfast.

Maggie pulls up to Louie's. She wipes her face with a Kleenex and lets out a sigh of relief; the place is empty. She hasn't eaten anything but an apple in two days, and for some reason, she has a mighty appetite this early morning. So she puts on her happy face and goes inside.

"Hi, come on in." A purple-headed, dog-collared waitress opens the door for Maggie.

Maggie's eyes dart all over the diner, and she tries very hard to smile approvingly at all the waitstaff's tattoos and piercings. The purple-headed waitress brings Maggie a menu and a glass of ice water.

"How about some coffee, ma'am?" Purplehead asks with a surprising niceness. Purplehead is actually quite a friendly girl, and she smells sweet and earthy. I think it's that stuff most of the freakers on Chimes Street wear, patchouli.

"I would love a cup of coffee." Maggie opens the menu and smiles. "And I already know what I want . . . if that's okay?"

"Sure, shoot." Purplehead pulls a pencil from behind her steel-studded ear.

"I want a three-egg 'Mitchell' omelet, with a side of hash browns and a strawberry-banana smoothie, and a small stack of banana pecan pancakes, and can I have some whip cream on that? And some bacon too." Maggie folds her menu and hands it to Purplehead.

"Okay, I'll have that right out."

"Thank you." Maggie smiles, and then takes a sip of water. She looks around and catches eyes with a mohawked busboy. He sticks his pierced tongue out at her and then shoots her a peace sign and a grin. She just waves like a sorority girl and politely looks away.

You know, even though these people are a bunch of Chimes Street freaks, Maggie feels at home here. I guess she has more in common with them than you would think. I mean, Maggie's got just as many bruises and mutilations as they do. She just wears hers where nobody can see them. In fact, she's a little envious of their freedom to be so public about their pain.

Maggie's food arrives and, rightly so, all her attention is now focused on her omelet, hash browns, pancakes, and bacon. If there's one thing I miss about my life, it would have to be Louie's hash browns. If there is a heaven, I would imagine that's what it would smell like—all warm potatoes, red pepper, garlic, and butter. But at least I can say that I didn't die before I got my fill of "Mitchell" omelets. They're so damn good. They're this huge glob of melted cheddar cheese, running over mountains of hash browns, mushrooms, and Cajun sausage. This is all rolled up into this monster egg burrito thing. You wash it down with their strawberry-banana smoothie.

God, I wish I was alive right now.

Anyway, halfway into her meal, Maggie's cell phone starts screaming from her purse. She looks at her watch. It's six-thirty in the morning. It's got to be Ryan. She hurriedly swallows her hash browns and fumbles through her purse for her phone.

"Hello?" Maggie sings.

"Hey Magpie, where are you?"

"Louie's," Maggie half apologizes and half smiles.

"Louie's? What are you doing at Louie's?"

"Eating breakfast. I'm starving, sweetie."

"Really . . . Who with?"

"I'm by myself, Ryan."

"Oh . . ."

"Ryan, I'm all alone." Maggie tucks her blond hair behind her left ear. "I was on my way home and all of a sudden got really hungry. I'll bring you some if you want."

"Naw, no Louie's for me, too many carbs."

"I just got a fruit plate and some egg whites." She tucks her hair behind her other ear. "Why are you acting like this?"

"I'm not acting any way. Just call me when you get home."

"Okay." Maggie looks down at her watch.

"Hey."

"What?" Maggie bites her bottom lip.

"I love you."

"I love you too. Bye."

Maggie folds up her phone and rubs her cheek.

Purplehead comes by and fills up Maggie's coffee mug.

"Can I get you anything else, ma'am?"

"Sure, I'll have another stack of pancakes." Maggie makes a tight-lipped smile and tears well up in those pretty green eyes.

Now Maggie has really pissed Ryan off. Imagine the nerve of that uppity bitch getting breakfast without asking his permission. Ryan gets out of bed and, despite his hangover, starts his daily two hundred sit-ups.

"One," Ryan growls.

His overly worked-out body folds up and down.

"Two."

His mind is flooded with black and blue images of knocking Maggie around and teaching her that lesson that she is just too dumb to learn.

"Three."

That reminds him of another dumbass: me. And how I refused to learn my lesson.

"Four."

And how good it felt to knock the ever-living shit out of me when I pissed him off.

"Five!" He grunts and starts folding even faster.

Ryan gets a real rush remembering that night, the night just before my initiation.

"Six!"

He had stood above me in this very room, counting out my push-ups.

"Seven!"

I was struggling because I had been force-fed a half-pint of Everclear and my arms felt like spaghetti.

"Eight!"

My racing heart pumped poisoned blood.

"Nine!"

But like a good pledge, I fought my way back up and shook back down.

"Ten!"

Finally, I collapsed on myself and just lay there.

"Get the fuck up!" Ryan raged. He kicked me hard in the ribs. To say the least, that woke my ass back up and I pushed myself back off the ground.

"Eleven!"

I lowered back down, my arms trembling, my head reeling. I fell to the floor and just cried like a little girl. Where was everybody? Why had they left me with Ryan? I was just one night from my initiation, one night away from being an active Gamma Chi, and just one more night away from never being hazed again.

Ryan leaned down in my face.

"You got a long way to go before tomorrow night, boy! Before I call your sorry ass brother."

I just lay there trying hard to suck it up. I didn't want him to see me cry, but I was hurting bad, hurting real bad.

"Get up!" Ryan grabbed me up off the ground. I was crying so hard I was shaking.

You know, the weirdest thing is what was going through my mind at that moment. All I could think about was Sunday school. Yeah, Sunday school when I was a kid, and how my favorite Bible story had always been David and Goliath. And how I played with these Popsicle-stick puppets over and over with David always killing Goliath. But if God favored the Davids of the world, then why the hell was I getting this incredible ass whupping from this frat boy-cum-Goliath? That's when the peace came over me. My crying stopped and so did my pain.

It was like God was telling me to kick his Philistine ass.

So I turned around with all I had and throat-punched Ryan. He gasped for a little bit and then looked up at me in a way that almost seemed sad, like I was the one who was abusing him. I don't know how to describe it, really. But it just wasn't the kind of look a normal person gives when you're in a fight. So I ran out of his room, down the third-floor hallway, and for the stairs. I made it all the way down to the top of the main stairway before he caught me.

I turned around and clocked him in the jaw.

And that's when Ryan's psychotic blue eyes ignited.

Boom!

I was thrown down that grand old stairway. I tumbled hard and fast—first breaking my collarbone and then about halfway down my neck snapped clean in two. Pain—unrighteous, unholy, electric pain—shot clear through from my toes out of my skull. I just lay there at the bottom of the stairs. I couldn't move. I couldn't breathe. It only took a couple of minutes.

And I was dead.

Now dying isn't all it's cracked up to be. For me at least, I didn't meet any angels or loved ones from the great beyond. There was no white light shining bright or any of that crap. Just a jolt, a shift really, out of the real world and into nothing. Next to my pledgeship, being dead is about the most disappointing thing to ever happen to me. Without a body, a spirit is pretty useless. To most people, you're just a bunch of whispers and creepy feelings in the air. And speaking of whispers, I hear someone calling my name right now, wheezing like some kind of asthma attack.

"Con-rad (wheeze), Con-rad (wheeze), Con-rad!"

Four

"Con-rad (wheeze), Con-rad (wheeze), Con-rad! I need to talk to you, boy!" Miss Etta sits in her kitchen, in front of a box fan. She's rubbing her tiny gold cross and nursing a mason jar half full of what looks like whiskey.

"Boo!"

"Oh! Sweet Jesus!" Miss Etta startles. "You need to learn to announce yourself before you come up in here spooking folks!"

"I thought you didn't talk to the dead."

"Baby, I say that to all the ghosties. The dead always be wanting something: *Help me do this? Help me do that?*" Miss Etta wags her finger at me. "You got to tell them 'No.' They drive me stone crazy asking for favors."

"Just sprinkle some holy water around. I hear we ghosties hate that."

"Don't be telling me my business." Miss Etta takes a gulp from her mason jar. "I been doing this since before you were born."

"You really need to lay off the booze this early in the day."

"What?" Miss Etta holds up her glass. "Lord, you dead *and* stupid! I don't dip in the devil juice, baby. This just a little sweet tea, that's all. The ice done melted down in it." She takes another sip. "Now you listen up and you listen good. You know that new pledge, the big old boy, the redhead, the one you following around? He's gonna help you do whatever it is you suppose to do, and then you can get on back to heaven."

"Tucker Graham?"

"Oh, he a good boy. He just don't know it yet." Etta fans her hands at me.

"I don't want to help him!"

"You suppose to look after the boy. Don't let nothing bad happen to the redhead. He's your ticket out of here."

"How am I supposed to help anybody? Nobody but you can even see me."

"You just going to have to work a little harder, that's all, baby."

"Let me get this straight. I died so that I can baby-sit that redheaded fuck. Is that what you're telling me?"

"Don't you cuss me, boy! I'm doing the Lord's work here!"

"Tucker Graham made his choice. Let him live with it. I didn't have any special agents from God looking after me, that's for sure."

She turns her milky blue-brown eyes to heaven and then back at me. "Listen, you got to rise to the occasion, Conrad. Something evil be all up in that house."

"*Ryan* is all up in that house. And I couldn't stop him when I was alive."

"You going to figure it out, baby." Miss Etta stands up and walks over to the fan. "Lord, it's hot up in here. Hey, you think you could run over to the Super Fresh and fetch me some lemons?"

"Lemons?"

"Yeah, lemons. Be a good ghosty and go fetch me some." Miss Etta cocks her head to the side. She's so frail, and her skin is so thin and old that she looks like a skeleton dipped in chocolate. She actually looks more like a ghost than I do.

"I don't know how to do that," I tell her.

"Well, then you need to learn! Damn lazy-ass ghost ain't good for nothing. I get my own damn lemons! Ghosties always coming up in here asking me for favors!" Etta grabs her keys, stomps her old bones out of the house, slamming the screen door behind her.

I drift back to the Gamma Chi house and look for Tucker Graham like Miss Etta said. I'm pissed. If I had had half a brain when I was alive, I would have pledged Sigma Chi or Lambda Chi or some other milk and cookies club that doesn't allow hazing. Sure as hell wouldn't be dead, stuck in a frat house for the rest of eternity.

Back at the Gamma Chi house, Tucker has cleaned himself up. And aside from the fact that the whites of his eyes are now a few shades redder than his hair, he's really no worse for the wear. In fact, how Tucker got those red eyes is everybody's favorite bid night story.

"Yeah, that hooker rode Tucker Graham so hard, the blood vessels in his eyes popped." Alex Trudeaux, a new pledge, points to his own wide eyes.

Jay Kimbrough, Gamma Chi's social chairman, shakes his hair out of his face and smirks at Alex.

"I shit you not, bruh, go check out Tucker's eyes. They're blood red."

"Hey Tucker, come over here!" Kimbrough motions Tucker over.

Tucker walks over, looking down at the ground.

"What's up?" Tucker sort of whispers.

"Trudeaux tells me that Cherie-Elise nearly fucked you blind."

Tucker laughs and shakes his head, "Well . . ." Tucker looks up and his eyes glow red.

"Whoa!" Kimbrough jumps a little out of his skin. "What's the matter with you? Ebola or something? Shit."

They all laugh and rib Tucker Graham. And then there's an awkward silence and a few sighs left over from the laughing.

"Well, come on, Ebola, let's go get some lunch." Kimbrough points to the front door and the three file out of the house with that odd sense of brotherhood that shared hangovers often bring.

Now let me tell you a little something about Jay Kimbrough. He's not a bad guy—even though he tries to be all crunchy and shit with his pucca shells and worn-out flip-flops. In fact, for a neo-crunch-hippie-wannabe he's funnier than hell. I used to get stoned with him on a regular basis. Being the social chairman and all, he always had the best ganja—it's all hydroponic and Hawaiian—and he didn't mind sharing it with me, even if I was just a pledge.

You should see him when he's dropped some acid, he's funnier than shit—tripping out, thinking he's a piece of bacon sizzling on the floor, popping and snapping and screaming, "Move over, bacon, for something meatier!" He's a weird dude sometimes, but I have to admit I liked the hell out of him. So I follow Tucker, Alex, and Kimbrough.

The three pile into this old Explorer that's got dancing skeletons and roses all over the back window. Kimbrough put these decals on his Explorer last summer, and then he actually started listening to the Grateful Dead because you can't have all their stickers on your car unless you're something of a fan. It was just too embarrassing when hot little hippie chicks would ask Kimbrough about his favorite songs, and Kimbrough would just sort of stutter. So now he's got all the Dead's CDs, even if he doesn't really like their music so much.

"So Tucker, I hear you're from North Louisiana?" Kimbrough starts the engine.

"Vidalia," Tucker mumbles.

"So what do y'all do up there besides stump-break the cattle?"

"Stump-what?" Alex asks.

"Stump-break. The cattle. You know." Kimbrough plunges his finger into his fist.

Alex turns to Tucker and frowns. "You do that to cows?"

"Gross. No."

"One in four rural male residents have had sex with a farm animal. That Kinsey guy did research and shit. I read his book."

"I can't believe we're even talking about this." Alex cringes.

"Alex, dude, I was just kidding."

"You're a sickwad." Alex looks out the window.

Now there's something you need to know about Alex Trudeaux. His brain is sort of broken. He fell off his bike when he was nine, causing him to confuse odors with colors. His sense of smell and color perception returned to normal by age ten, but his brain never fully recovered. I mean, he looks normal and he makes decent grades and some girls even think he's cute, but there's something just slightly askew with him. I'm not sure what you would call it, but he's almost pathologically naive. He's completely unable to read the subtext of a conversation or situation. For example: When other guys make off-the-cuff boasts about whacking off, Alex will add to the conversation by going into overly detailed accounts of his own whacking off. As you can imagine, no girl has ever spun a bottle his way. He's still a virgin.

Alex's dad, who owns a big Baton Rouge air-conditioning company, donated a bunch of high-end air units to the Gamma Chis right before rush. Alex's mom and dad were ecstatic when Alex called them and told him he got bid. And now, Kimbrough for whatever reason has taken the little diarrhea-of-the-mouth virgin under his wing and will hopefully look out for him.

College is a weird time in life. People are wildly inconsistent. I guess they're just trying to find themselves. But now that I am dead, all this inconsistency just gets on my nerves. Like when Kimbrough pulls into the Burger King parking lot today. Here's a guy who, at the same time he's looking out for socially retarded Alex, double-parks his SUV in two handicapped spots.

"Hey, Kimbrough, you're parked in handicapped, bruh." Tucker gets out of the Explorer.

Kimbrough, the invincible, Kimbrough, the hook-up, Kimbrough, the eternally twenty-one and funny, flips his hair out of his eyes. "Screw the handicapped, they always get the best parking spaces."

He slaps Alex on the back and they both go inside yucking it up. Tucker just shakes his big head. See, I like Tucker. Maybe he's not the brightest guy but at least he's consistent.

Inside the Burger King, the three approach the counter and are greeted by this zit-faced manager wearing a Burger King crown and a name tag that says "Dick."

"Wuddup, Dick?" Kimbrough raises an eyebrow.

"What can I get you gentlemen today?"

"I'll have the number three value meal with cheese and super size it. Okay, *Dick*?" Kimbrough stifles a laugh.

"I'll have the same thing." Alex looks at Kimbrough and then smiles back at the manager. "Okay, *Dick*?"

The two bulletproof jackasses laugh while Tucker stands there taller and quieter than a pine tree.

Dick just rubs his greasy forehead and sighs as he looks at Tucker.

"I'll also have the same thing." Tucker pulls out his wallet and pays the manager for all three orders.

"Hey, you didn't have to do that." Kimbrough's smirk widens into a smile.

"Wow, thanks a lot, Tucker!" Alex grabs a fry off the tray and shoves it in his mouth.

Now, when you're eighteen, picking up the tab is one of the surest ways to win life-long, or at least semester-long, loyalty from your fraternity brothers. The opposite holds true if you're late paying your dues. Woe be it to whoever is late. That's the surest way to get blackballed if you're a pledge, or deactivated if you're an active. At Gamma Chi, you got to have paper, or at least your parents do. You can't buy kegs and reefer on warm fuzzy brotherhood. It takes lots of cash money. All the God-Damn Independents on campus gripe and moan that the Gamma Chis just buy their friends, but I'd have to disagree with them. It's really more like renting them.

"Hey, y'all want to go for a round of golf this afternoon?"

Alex dumps a pile of pepper into his ketchup.

"Sure, what course?" Kimbrough pulls the pickles out of his burger.

"LSU. I can get us in for free." Alex talks with his mouth full of meat and bread.

"Free! That's my favorite word. I'm in." Kimbrough looks at Tucker. "What about you, Ebola?"

"Sounds good to me." Tucker shrugs.

Five

ow there's something real nice about a pledge's grace period, the first two weeks of the semester before the line-ups and the yelling start. It's sort of like an extended Rush. The new pledges are pretty much treated like actives. There are lots of brothers tossing the football in the front yard, and everybody goes out and gets drunk a lot.

Tucker Graham is loving Gamma Chi. Hell, he has it made with Ryan wanting to be his big brother and all. And with Kimbrough and Alex by his side, life is just one big beer-chugging, backslapping moment.

The only thing that seems to get in the way is class. Calculus is dropped for dairy science and computer science is dropped altogether, bringing Tucker's schedule to just twelve hours. But hell, that's a heavy enough load to carry freshman year. After all, Gamma Chi's pledgeship is hard enough without having to worry about integers and crap. Besides, in dairy science, they've got this special cow with a lid surgically attached to its side and you get to stick your hand inside one of its stomachs. Now if that doesn't beat the hell out of calculus, I don't know what does.

The only hard class that Tucker couldn't get out of is geology. Everybody used to call it "rocks for jocks" because it was so damn easy, but now there's this new prick of a professor from Harvard or something and he's got the nerve to take attendance. When I took his class, that rat bastard gave us a test the Monday following the Ole Miss football game.

It is now the week after drop/add registration and Tucker is pretty much locked into his classes. He makes his way through the quad to Howe-Russell Building, for geology class. The sweat is dripping off Tucker and when he goes inside to find his class, he shudders from the draft of the air conditioner.

In this crowded hallway full of ironic T-shirts, flip-flops, and plaid, Tucker focuses on the prettiest girl he has ever seen. She's all tan and smooth and blond and cartoon flowers spring from under her pretty feet. It's Maggie Meadows, and like half the campus, Tucker has just fallen madly in love. But then Tucker sees Ryan come up and kiss her, and all Tucker can do is look away.

"Hey Tucker! My boy!" Ryan hollers at him from across the way. "Come over here! I want Maggie to meet you."

He shoulders his backpack from left to right and walks over to the couple.

"Maggie, this is Tucker. Tucker, this is Maggie." Ryan grins.

"Nice to meet you, Tucker." Maggie gives a girly handshake. "You're all Ryan talked about during Rush. He just had to get that Tucker boy from Vidalia."

Tucker sort of smiles and looks down.

"Ryan is just dead set on getting you for his little brother. Aren't you, Ryan?" She looks up at Ryan.

"What do you mean? Tucker is my little brother! I'm not waiting around for Big Brother night. I'm taking him out tonight after the exchange."

"See, Tucker, how lucky you are? Ryan has already staked his claim." Maggie looks at Tucker straight on. "Oh my God, Tucker. What happened to your eyes? They're so red."

"Um, bid night, some mud got in them and you know, I was pretty wasted and . . ." He looks away from her.

"Hey, that's enough, Tucker," Ryan laughs. "We don't want to give away any secrets now, do we?"

"Secrets? Tucker Graham, you've already got secrets?" Maggie lowers her gaze and shakes her head. "My, my, my. You bad old Gamma Chis and your secrets. What am I going to do with you boys?"

"Love us." Ryan pecks Maggie on the cheek and grins.

Tucker takes a deep breath and tries smiling again.

"So are y'all both in this geology class?" he asks.

"Sorta." Ryan raises an eyebrow. "I'll be here on test days, but Magpie's going to take notes for me."

"Looks like you're my study buddy, Tucker." Maggie flashes her pretty green eyes.

"What about you, Ryan?"

"I don't need to study, Tucker. I got it covered." Ryan squeezes Maggie close to him. "Ain't that right, babe?" He kisses Maggie on the lips, trying to slip her a little tongue this time.

"Ryan Hutchins, no PDA! You're going to get me in trouble with my sorority."

"Hey, woman, don't make me tame you." Ryan swats Maggie's little butt as they walk inside the classroom.

Tucker drops back a little in hopes that there won't be three open seats together.

The wind blows from the north tonight, carrying one hell of a thunderstorm with it. But that doesn't seem to kill anybody's buzz around the Gamma Chi house. Tonight is the first mixer of the semester. The chosen tribe for the evening is Alpha Alpha Gamma. I'd have to say that they're just about my favorite sorority. They love to get drunk and loud, and most of them are real pretty—with the exception of a few fat legacies. Maybe I just like them because my ex, Ashley Sonnier, is one, and every time I see AAG stretched across some girl's chest, I think of her.

Ryan likes the Alphas too, but for other reasons—mainly because Maggie's a Tri-Phi, and she won't be anywhere around tonight. As a matter of fact, Ryan has gotten all pumped up at the gym today and now he's upstairs in his room getting ready for some Alpha pussy.

After a short pose down in his mirror, Ryan puts in this mouthpiece thing. The asshole's bleaching his teeth. He walks over to his closet and pulls out his ski parka. He unzips the inside pocket and pulls out an empty bag dusted with white powder. Ryan works real hard getting the cocaine off the bag and onto his desktop, but there's hardly enough coke for even a tiny bump.

Ryan sniffs up the little dust-bunny of coke; it doesn't even make his nose tingle. So he pulls out his wallet and opens it. There's only two one-dollar bills and four maxed-out credit cards, and Ryan's daddy won't be sending him another check for about a week.

Something outside hits Ryan's window and he jerks around to see what it is. It's just a tree branch from the storm. His hands shake as he puts the baggy back in his parka and rips open another hidden pocket. He pulls out a bag that's half full of a clumpier white powder. Looks like Ryan is slumming tonight with crystal meth. He snorts about three lines and makes this big-ass grin. With that mouthpiece pushing his lips out, he looks like an orangutan foaming and drooling.

By the time Ryan has primped and preened and snorted to his peculiar satisfaction, the exchange is already in full swing. The sound system in the chapter room is blaring some Granddaddy song and one keg is already floating.

Drunken Alphas abound.

Alex and Kimbrough are in my library with Tucker and a bottle of Jägermeister. They've decided since Tucker's eyes are still so repulsive that he will never score tonight and that he should just get snot-slinging drunk.

"Have y'all ever had a buttery nipple?" Alex asks.

"That's a chick shot, you puss." Kimbrough ashes his cigarette and exhales out his nose.

"No, it's not! It's a really good shot." Alex nods his head. "Tastes like butterscotch. I got real drunk on them on my senior trip. I did like five buttery nipples and I was so gone." Alex's eyes are wide with self-amazement.

"Listen, Alex, I hope you don't go around talking this shit to girls. You'll never get laid." Kimbrough puts his cigarette out in his empty beer cup.

"Buttery nipples, huh?" Tucker raises his shot glass to Alex.

"Here's to all the buttery nipples in the next room." Tucker slams the deep brown syrup.

And then Tucker's toast is answered by a sharp knock against the heavy library doors.

"What are you boys up to in there?" a sweet, raspy voice calls out.

Kimbrough opens the door, and damned if it isn't the most beautiful, brown-eyed girl to ever wear an Alpha key. Damned if it isn't Ashley Sonnier.

"Ashley!" Kimbrough almost lunges at her.

"Hey, Jay." She pecks him on the cheek.

"I thought you transferred to Ole Miss. You know, after last semester and all." Jay offers a weak smile.

Ashley looks down and her long brown hair falls in her face, "No, I decided that I should stay. That's how Conrad would have wanted it."

"That's how Conrad would have wanted it? You dumped me for a Sigma Chi two weeks before I died. And I can guaran-damn-tee you that's not what I wanted."

"Yeah, well I'm glad you stayed. You know?" This is really killing Kimbrough's buzz; memories of how he found my twisted body are racing through his head. It's really making him jones for a drink or some hooch to quiet his mind.

"So this is it, huh?" Ashley looks around at all the expensive books and wood paneling and brass fixtures my daddy bought.

Tucker and Alex look at each other trying to figure out why this Gamma and Kimbrough are so bummed out all of a sudden.

"Pretty impressive, isn't it? Ole man Sutton dropped a wad for this place." Kimbrough looks at the Jäger and wonders if it would be rude to take a shot right now.

"Yeah, I think Conrad would have really liked this." Ashley wipes a tear away.

"No, Ashley. I don't really like this. What I'd really like is to be alive and holding you and wiping that tear from your cheek. What I'd really like is to yell at your ass for dumping me and then make up and kiss you real hard and soft. That's what I'd really like."

"Hey, how about a shot of Jäger? That always makes me feel better." Kimbrough holds up the green bottle.

"No, thanks." Ashley glances over at Alex and Tucker. "Do you mind if I just take a second to . . . you know?" Ashley starts to choke up.

"Sure." Kimbrough pats her arm. "Come on, guys, let's take this party out of here."

Alex and Tucker pick up the big green bottle and the shot glasses and follow Kimbrough out into the hall.

Ashley looks around my library and starts to cry.

"I'm sorry, Conrad. I'm so sorry." She puts her hand over her mouth and sobs. The lightning flashes and the lights flicker in my library.

"Come on, Ash. It's okay. Don't cry. I'm still here."

It's no use. She can't hear me over her own crying. She always was a bit overemotional, but I guess now she really has something to cry about. You know, this is the hardest part about being dead— watching shit like this and not being able to make anyone hear you.

"Is everything okay in here?" Ryan walks in like he has an S on his chest.

"Uh, yeah." Ashley nods her head and sniffles. "Just give me a few minutes to pull myself together." Ashley takes a couple of hic-cuppy breaths.

"That means go away."

"You're . . . you're Ashley Sonnier, Conrad's girlfriend." Ryan puts on his best church face and walks over.

"Yeah, I am," she sniffles. "Are there any Kleenexes around here?"

"Uh, you know, I don't think there are." Ryan shuts the door behind him and looks around for something to substitute for a Kleenex. "Hey, just use this." Ryan unbuttons his shirt and takes it off. He wipes the tears from her face with it.

"Wait a second! What are you doing?" Ashley starts to giggle and cry at the same time.

"You got to have something to wipe the tears away from those pretty eyes."

"You're very nice, thank you." She takes his shirt and blots her face with it. "What's your name?"

"Ryan. Ryan Hutchins." He stands there with no shirt on looking all sheepish and shit.

"Oh. I thought I recognized you. Conrad hated you." She hands him back his shirt. "I'm through with it. Thanks."

"Oh-kay . . . I guess you're welcome." Ryan shakes his head and puts his mascara and tear-stained shirt back on. Ashley folds her arms and looks out the window.

"You know, I don't know what Conrad told you about me, but I really did like him." Ryan touches Ashley's shoulder and she turns around. "I mean, I know I gave him some shit, but that was just part of pledgeship. He was a great guy. I never would have pledged him if I didn't want him to be my brother." Ryan's voice shakes. "I miss him just like you do. I mean, he was a real Gamma Chi, you know?"

Ashley touches Ryan's hand. "Thanks."

She points to the stains on Ryan's shirt and sort of laughs through her tears, "Sorry about your shirt."

"What are you doing, Ashley? He killed me."

"I'm really sorry. I think I should be going." Ashley gets up and pulls her hair back at the nape of her neck.

"No, stay. You shouldn't be alone right now." Ryan gives her this charming look of compassion. "Talk to me about Conrad if that will make you feel better."

"No, I can't. I've really embarrassed myself. I just need to go." Ashley walks to the door. "But thanks for the shirt, you're very nice." She wipes the black crap from under her eyes and reaches for the doorknob.

I can hear Ryan's heart beating fast from all the crystal meth and Ashley's perfume.

"Hey, wait a sec—please!"

"What?"

"I have something. Something of Conrad's that I think you should have. It's upstairs." Ryan points to the ceiling.

"Really?" Ashley tilts her head. "What is it?"

"Just come with me. You'll see."

Ashley pauses and takes a deep breath.

"Okay."

Ryan opens the door for her and they enter the hallway that's now crowded with drunken Gamma Chis and Alphas scamming all over each other.

Ryan takes Ashley's hand and guides her through the crowd. He turns around and Ashley gives him this little wink like "thanks, you're such a great guy."

"How about a beer?" Ryan asks. "I sure could use one,"

"You just read my mind." She squeezes his hand.

Ryan makes a detour by the keg and fills up two cups. Sipping their beers, the two of them sneak up the back stairs to Ryan's room.

"I could get into so much trouble for doing this, Ryan."

"Trust me. It will be worth it."

Once upstairs, Ryan puts his key in his door and turns it open. "After you."

Ashley walks in. Ryan's room is a study in anal retention—everything's all calculated and perfect. The bed is made and the room smells like Carpet Fresh and Lysol.

"Nice room. It's so clean." Ashley walks over to the pictures hanging on the wall. "Is this your girlfriend? She's very pretty."

"She's my ex. Broke up with me about a week ago. I guess I should take those down."

"Oh-kay." Ashley rolls her eyes. "So where is it? Where's this thing that I'm risking life and limb for?"

"Oh yeah, shut your eyes."

"I don't think so." Ashley places her beer on his desk and her hands on her hips.

"You can't see where I'm getting this from. I've got ritual stuff in here."

"Oh, whatever. Just get it so I can get out of here."

"Then shut your eyes and put out your hand."

She blows her bangs off her forehead. "Okay."

Ashley closes her eyes and thrusts her hand out.

"Turn around, you're peeking."

"Listen, I don't have time to do the hokey pokey, Ryan. Just get me the damn thing and I'll be out of your hair. God."

"Turn around," he says.

She turns around and taps her foot.

Ryan opens his closet and pulls out a small lockbox. In it are neatly arranged packages of Trojans, a gold Tag Heuer, a bag full of Gamma Chi pledge pins, and a few small vials of GHB.

He grabs a pledge pin and a Georgia Home Boy.

"Are you peeking? You better not be looking." Ryan glances over his shoulder.

"Just hurry up, Ryan," Ashley groans.

That son of a bitch walks over to Ashley's beer, pours the GHB into it, and stirs it with his finger. He carries the beer to her.

"Okay, you can turn around, but don't open your eyes and keep your hand out." He puts the beer in her hand. "First, you have to finish this."

She opens her eyes. "I'm not one of your little pledges."

Ryan smiles. "Finish it and you get a prize."

Ashley glares at Ryan and downs that beer in one gulp.

She burps in his face.

"Why, excuse me. How very unladylike of me," she laughs. "Now give me whatever it is you've got of Conrad's or I'm so out of here."

"Whoa, whoa, champion, take it down a thousand. Just put your hand out."

She slings her hand out in front of her, and Ryan drops a pledge pin in it.

"It's Conrad's. I took it off him and put an active badge on him just before his funeral started."

Ashley looks at the tiny gold shield shining in her hand and she weeps, "Oh my God. Thank you."

She hugs him.

I rage and I scream. I yell and I cry. I will windows and mirrors to break all around them, the TV to explode. I try to open the floodgates of hell on Ryan.

But nothing happens because I am dead.

Ryan just holds Ashley and rubs her neck. She can't stop cry-ing and after a few minutes, her sobs get softer and she smiles with her eyes closed.

"I feel really weird." Her head wobbles and her knees buckle.

"Really? Does it feel good?" Ryan whispers hot in her ear.

"No, I feel like a cotton candy machine," she slurs, and then falls limp in his arms.

Ryan takes her over to his bed. He kisses her on the neck and rips open her blouse. He then pulls her pants down and runs his fingers over her crotch. She just lies there with her eyes shut, smil-ing like a corpse in a casket.

I'm sorry, but I've got to run the red light on this one. I can't let this happen to Ashley. So I fly out of Ryan's room and I find Tucker Graham. He's on the second floor, in Kimbrough's room, passing a bong. He's drunk and stoned. So I rush into him and slide right in, no problem. I beat what's left of his consciousness back and take over; I possess his ass. I throw the bong down and rush out of the room.

"Hey Tucker, where are you going?" Kimbrough chases after me while Alex laughs at the spilt bong water.

I take the stairs two at a time and I tear down the hall with all the piss and rage of a tornado. I throw Tucker's body against Ryan's locked door and it falls away as if it was made of balsam wood, revealing Ryan on top of Ashley's half-naked body. Light-ning crashes and I can taste the hate in my mouth as I chew on Tucker's bottom lip.

"What the—?" Ryan looks up.

I clobber him upside the head with Tucker's bowling ball of a fist, throwing him off Ashley and hard onto the floor.

"Uhhh," he groans and touches his head. He stares at the dark blood on his hand.

And that's exactly when Kimbrough and about six or so ac-tives make it up to Ryan's room, but I couldn't care less. I grab Ryan by the throat and smack his pretty face with the back of Tucker's hand. However, before I can really tear his head off, I am tackled by this pack of Gamma Chis. They beat me down to the floor. Through the fists and elbows, I see Kimbrough cover up Ashley and carry her out of here.

It takes seven actives to hold me while Ryan punches me in the stomach. Damn, I had forgotten how bad fists and bones can hurt. But just seeing Ryan's face puts the rage back in me. So I use that blood anger to throw everyone off of me and run out of the room, down the hall, and down that grand old stairway.

I mean Tucker Graham is strong and all, but eight against one is only a fair match in a Bruce Lee movie. I don't press my luck. I learned the hard way, it's much better to live to fight another day.

Six

The brothers are busy tending to Ryan's busted face, so I get out of the house without any real problem. I run through the pouring rain and puddles as fast as Tucker's big bones can carry me. I make it all the way down Dalrymple, near the Deke house, before it dawns on me:

I'm alive. I'm in a body again. I mean it's real nasty, sort of like wearing somebody else's dirty underwear, but at least I can make things happen.

I want to go home, home to Shreveport. I want to see my mamma and daddy and tell them what really happened. And when they know the truth, they can send Ryan's ass to jail. You know—like they do on all those made-for-TV movies, the ones where the son is killed by a drunk driver or some other politically incorrect vice and the parents avenge their kid's death by starting an action group or something like that.

I fish around in Tucker's pockets and find his keys. Now I bet you Tucker parked behind the Gamma Chi house. So I carry them back to the house. I look at the keys: They're Ford. I spot a red Mustang parked right up to the curb of the house. I guarantee you that's Tucker's car.

I run over and try to open it and the car alarm goes off.

Everybody in the house looks out the window and sure enough, they see me. I drop the keys. Before I can even think, I swoop down and pick them up, but by the time I look up, there's about a hundred of the Worthy running out of the house ready to beat my un-Worthy ass.

I get it together and get the car unlocked. I slam the door and lock it, just as this active throws himself against the window. All

these wet and pissed off Gamma Chis surround me, blocking me in
my space. I start the engine and rev all eight cylinders to let them
know I'm not playing. This buzz-cut active, Jeff Couvillion, pounds
the hood of the car to let me know he's not playing either.

I put it in reverse and slowly idle backward. The crowd beats
and pushes on my car. I blow the horn and push down hard on the
gas, peeling out of my space and knocking a few of those jackasses
on the ground. Before I can throw it into drive, Couvillion jumps
up on my hood and tries to put his fist through my windshield. I
shift into first, then second, and Couvillion makes a real pretty
hood ornament for about a block.

I've never laughed so hard in all my life. Couvillion is just a-
cussing and a-screaming.

"I'm going to ball your sorry ass! Stop the fucking car! Stop!"

I'm only going about twenty. I slam on the brakes and he goes
flying off the side of my car. Couvillion has watched one too many
action flicks, getting up on a moving car like that. Dumbass.

I drive down Dalrymple and out of the campus gates. Even
with the seat pushed all the way back, I feel really cramped in this
car. Why would someone as ginormous as Tucker Graham buy a
sports car? Just stupid, I guess.

Anyway. I cross the bridge over into Port Allen and I look at
all the white lights from the Exxon refinery in my rearview mirror.
I make a wish, since those are the only stars out on this rainy night,
and try not to think about what Ryan did to Ashley.

The lightning flashes left and right as I get on Highway 190. I
put in a White Stripes CD, turn on the heater, and cruise on home
to Shreveport. You know, I just love a good thunderstorm.

It's not long before I drive out of the rain and I'm flying north on I-
49. If I keep the pedal to the metal, I could be home in about two
or three hours. But as my luck would have it, blue and red lights
flash me from behind. That cop doesn't mean me; I was only going
seventy.

The cop bleeps his siren. He means me.

I fumble through the ashtray for pennies to shove in my mouth before I pull over. I heard that screws up breath tests and Lord knows, Tucker's breath tonight could send a Breathalyzer to Mars. I can only scrounge up two pennies. One of them has this sticky pink funk on it, but I go ahead and put both under my tongue.

The cop shines his light in my face and I roll down the window.

"Get your license, registration, and insurance together."

I grab Tucker's wallet out of his pocket and I hand his license to the officer along with the registration and insurance from the glove compartment.

"You been drinking, boy?" He shines his flashlight in my back-seat and then back at me.

"Uh, no sir. Just trying to get to a rest room. I got a little diar-rhea, you know." I stare at his badge and not his face. I don't want him to see Tucker's blood-red eyes.

"No, I don't know, boy." His face turns from slightly dull to slightly pissed. "Why don't you step out of the car."

"Sure." I get out of the car and an empty beer can falls out. The officer picks it up and holds it to my face.

"Are you familiar with this parish's open container laws, son?"

"Uh, yes sir. Like I said, I wasn't—I was just taking those cans to be recycled."

"I bet." He pulls out this red penlight and waves it in my face. "Follow this without moving your head, only use your eyes."

I pass all of his stupid tests: the ABCs backward, walking the straight line, touching my nose, and standing on one leg with my arms out. So he pulls out the big guns, the Breathalyzer.

I put the tube into my mouth and I blow real soft-like.

"Come on, boy, blow like you're blowing out your birthday candles." The cop snarls at me. "Blow harder or you'll have to do it again."

I just ignore that stupid cop. Like I care if I get arrested. I'm dead. I'm just trying to help out Tucker.

"You're done." The cop jerks the Breathalyzer out of my mouth and moves the digital display closer to me. It begins to flash, and images of jail cots, and rats, and tough guys named RoRo—prison-type tough guys who want to make you their bitch—flash with each pulse of that display. Suddenly, I start to regret being such a smartass to the good officer.

The display goes blank and a lump rises up in my throat. My numbers pop up all red and happy: 0.00

"Do it again." The officer hands me the pipe thingy. I blow on it, but the results are the same—not one trace of alcohol. Obviously, there's more to this possession thing than I thought, because by all laws of chemistry, physics, and criminal justice, Tucker's Breathalyzer should be off the charts. Go figure. Maybe that penny thing really does work.

I get back in the Mustang and keep it under sixty-five because that asshole cop follows me all the way to Natchitoches. I swear to God, I-49 is the darkest, loneliest stretch of highway I've ever driven on. A drive like this just reminds me of how alone I am in this cold blue world. It's like my daddy always used to say, "The only person you can count on being at your funeral is yourself." But I have a feeling that after my funeral, Daddy doesn't say that much anymore.

All that obeying the speed limit has given me some serious narcolepsy. Now that I've lost the police escort, I floor it and that big old V-8 growls at me and I feel my stomach drop just a little. I mean this Mustang's a piece of crap compared to my 911, but it can go fast, and we like fast.

It's not long before I'm in Shreveport. It's funny how doing a hundred and ten will do that for you. As I drive into town, I get that tug of a feeling you get when you're someplace that's home. I mean, you can say what you want about Shreveport with all its glittery casino boats, but I still love it. It's my home. And I'm not talking about all that neon gambling shit. I'm talking about my home on Fairfield Avenue with all its big trees and old houses and nice, clean-living folk—doctors and lawyers and oilmen's families who go to the Baptist church and play golf and deer hunt. That's where I came from and I got to say, I'm proud of it. I had it real good growing up. My daddy had just taken over my granddaddy's company, Royal Oil, and my life was all fried chicken and Rolexes. If I could throw this Mustang in reverse and go·back to those times, I would.

Before I know it, I'm pulling into my driveway. My parents' house is a big white job with mighty columns and tall pine trees all over the front yard. I park on the circular driveway. The lights are still on, which is weird because it's three in the morning, and Mamma and Daddy have never been ones for staying up late. I sit in the car for a second and look for a cigarette. All I can find is a can of Copenhagen. I'm nervous, so I go ahead and put that worm dirt under my lip. I mean, how do you explain to your folks that you've come back from the dead and possessed somebody's ass like the goddamn *Exorcist*? How do you tell your parents that you weren't some drunk screw-up who broke his own damn neck, but were really killed by a guy who everybody thinks is Jesus H. Christ in a Gamma Chi jersey?

This is going to shock the shit out of them. Hell, Mamma's so religious, she'll probably have a breakdown. This kind of carrying on is definitely against the Baptist religion. Besides, it makes me nervous when people lose it—especially my parents.

I spit out the Copenhagen and walk to the front door. I ring the doorbell and knock. The folks have gotten hard of hearing in their old age. I look through the window right next to the door; there's nobody stirring inside. I bet you they're out of town. Daddy's got this thing from the Radio Shack that turns the lights on and off, and it would make sense for him to have programmed it to have the downstairs lights on at three in the morning, even though this is just screaming to all the burglars that they're out of town.

I get the key out from under this cement toad in the flowerbed, and I let myself in. The alarm starts beeping to let you know it's about to go off. I punch our dead dog Flip's birthday into the keypad—Zero-nine-fourteen—and the beeping stops.

"Hello? Anybody home?"

I don't know why I'm asking this because if Daddy is here and he sees this overgrown farm boy in his house, he'll blow him, or rather me, away for sure. I go back to Mamma and Daddy's bedroom and their big old sleigh bed is empty. When I was a kid, my sister, Shannon, and I would play like that bed was Santa Claus's sled and we'd fly all around the world in it. Speaking of, I bet my parents are in Europe or some shit like that. Since I died, Mamma has made Daddy take her traveling all over the place.

Tucker's body is getting sort of hungry so I go into the kitchen to feed it. This is the kitchen where I spent my adolescence drinking Kool-Aid, eating Doritos and Oreos. My sister used to sit over there at the island and talk to Althea, our maid, about someday going to Hollywood and being a movie star. Althea always called Shannon "Moving Star" because she was always running around, cooking up half-baked schemes to be on *The Real World* or *The Bachelor*. Althea would encourage all of Shannon's stupid ideas about being famous. Daddy finally got Shannon to get her MBA, and now she's married and has two kids here in Shreveport. I bet she still wants to be a movie star. She was always a little crazy like that.

I fix myself a BLT. That was my favorite, especially when I was drunk. I think all that bacon grease and bread soaked up the alcohol and the next day I wasn't hung over as bad. Besides, they taste good. After my sandwich, I'm actually feeling sleepy. Which is weird because I haven't felt sleepy since I was killed.

I leave the dishes out. I can clean them later. I yawn and go upstairs to my room. I pass all these family portraits and baby pictures and wonder what Mamma and Daddy and Shannon think when they pass them. It makes me too sad to even think about it. I start to tear up. So I try not to look at them anymore. It's just too painful. Plus, I'm tired. I just need to go to bed and I'm sure I'll feel better when I wake up. Or maybe not. After all, I am dead and this rent-a-body isn't going to really fix that.

The door to my room is locked. I'm fading fast and really don't have the patience for this. I go to the hall closet, find the key, and open my door. Not one thing has been touched since I died. My dirty clothes are still on the floor from my last Christmas break. Once I turned fifteen, Althea wasn't allowed to clean up my room anymore. "If you don't clean it, you have to live in it," is what Daddy always used to say. My bed is still unmade with the same sheets I left on it the day I went back to school. All my stuff is still here: my Wilco movie poster, my tennis trophies, my worn-out copy of *Fight Club,* my old iMac, and the stupid Blue Dog painting Mamma got me in New Orleans.

I take off my clothes, shut off the light, and fall fast asleep. I have the craziest dreams about Shannon, Althea, Mamma, and Daddy and this Hollywood premiere which is really my funeral, and Shannon's crying because she lost her dream and Althea is holding her.

I don't wake up until way after noon, and damn if I don't find myself outside of Tucker Graham. This is not good. I try to force myself back into Tucker's body, but for whatever reason it's not working this time. He must have sobered up overnight. You'd think I could get in while he's still sleeping, but I can't, no matter how hard I try. This really is not good.

Tucker is snoring away in my bed. He's got to get up. What if my sister Shannon drives by and sees his Mustang parked out front? What if my parents are coming home today and they find his fat ass sleeping in their dead son's bed?

"Come on, Tucker. Get up. Get up!"

He twitches and shakes.

"Tucker, get your ass up! Get up!"

Tucker pops up, all bleary-eyed and mouth open. He looks around my room, rubs his red eyes, and tries to figure out where the hell he is. His breath stinks so bad even I can smell it. I always hated the morning after; waking up with ass-breath, trying to figure out whose bed you're in and what happened to get you there always made me feel out of sorts.

Tucker obviously doesn't recognize any of this. The people in my prom pictures are complete strangers to him. None of the stuff in my room rings a bell. He's completely confused. The only thing that he can identify are his soggy clothes that are scattered on the floor.

Tucker gets dressed and with keys in hand, he slowly sneaks

out of my room. I guess he doesn't want to wake whoever was kind enough to bring his drunk ass here. He studies all the pictures in the hall and then I think it dawns on him that he's in some family's house and not some rental where college kids live. Tucker hightails it down the stairs, out the front door to his Mustang.

While Tucker is racing down Fairfield, driving to no particular destination other than away from my house, he realizes that he's nowhere near Baton Rouge and he has no idea how he got here. He calls Kimbrough on his cell phone. It rings and rings.

"Come on, man, pick up." Tucker pinches some Copenhagen and puts it in his bottom lip.

"Hullo," Kimbrough answers.

"Kimbrough?"

"Tucker, where are you?"

"I don't know."

"What do you mean you don't know?"

"I mean I don't know!" Tucker spits into an empty Icee Cup. Just then, Tucker passes a billboard that says:

Shreveport-Bossier City On The Red River.
We're Making It Happen!

"I'm in Shreveport."

"Shreveport? What are you doing in Shreveport?"

"I don't know."

"Just get back to Baton Rouge. You've got some explaining to do."

"Explain what?"

Tucker's phone cuts out, and his call to Kimbrough is dropped. Tucker gets back on I-49 headed south to Baton Rouge and he tries repeatedly to call Kimbrough back, but he can't seem to get through. I make the trip back to Baton Rouge in ghost time, which is just a matter of seconds.

Seven

I t's late Saturday before Tucker makes it back to Baton Rouge. He goes straight to his room in Power Dorm, locks the door, and lies low all weekend. His roommate, this GDI with hearing aids named Maxwell Bonecaze, went home to Ville Platte. So Tucker keeps to himself. I think he can remember me busting Ryan upside the head and I think Tucker's pretty messed up about it. He stays in bed for most of the weekend and watches ESPN and MTV. I think he's all bummed because he figures Gamma Chi will blackball him and he'll be a GDI loser just like his roommate.

His pledge brother, Alex Trudeaux, comes by to see him and Kimbrough calls nonstop, but Tucker Graham stays holed up in his room, not answering the phone or door. In fact, he even pisses in his dorm room sink instead of leaving to go to the bathroom.

Tucker's solitude is broken up when Maxwell comes back from Ville Platte late Sunday night, all happy and a-smiling.

"Whaddup, bee-atch?" Maxwell lugs in his clean laundry and duffel bag, grinning ear to ear.

"What's so funny?" Tucker sits up in his bed and stares at Maxwell.

"I got liquid twice this weekend with this high school chick," Maxwell shines. "What about you? You didn't come home Friday night."

"Maxwell, just shut up," Tucker pulls the covers over his red head.

"Okay. My boy obviously didn't get any this weekend." Maxwell grabs the remote control and starts flipping channels.

* * *

Monday night is chapter meeting for Gamma Chi. That means all the pledges have to have the meal served and cleaned up by six o'clock sharp.

This is the first chapter meal where pledges are actually treated like pledges. It's their first taste of the humiliation they will be force-fed the rest of the semester. Tucker Graham is conspicuously absent, but Alex Trudeaux, the loyal pledge brother that he is, is working this meal in his place along with three of their pledge brothers, Charlie Simon, Tony Audoin, and Clay Weaver.

The actives have got them running all over the place for more "scabs" (chicken fried steak), milk, tea, gravy, and spoons. Alex forgot to put those down when he set the tables.

Ryan's hand goes up and Alex runs over to his table.

"What can I get for you?" Alex looks like some kind of black Lab puppy just drooling to go fetch something.

"Name the table." Ryan doesn't look up; he just keeps shoving food into his cake hole.

"Sure." Alex squints his eyes, but he holds his smile. "You're Ryan Hutchins, and this is Trey Cordova, right?"

Ryan drops his fork and stares at Alex.

"Are you asking me or are you telling me?"

Alex freezes.

"Are you deaf? Answer me. Are you asking me if this is Trey Cordova or are you telling me?"

"I-I-I'm telling you."

"Continue." Ryan folds his arms and taps his biceps with his fingers.

"Um, Jason, Jason Cefalu, and this is Michael, I mean Matthew McCallahan." Alex points to this really tall and skinny active who always reminded me of a stork or some kind of crane.

"Which is it, Matthew or Michael?" Ryan's eyes narrow.

"Hey, Ryan, lighten up. It's his first meal, man," the stork-dude chimes in.

"This puke should know this." Ryan holds his fork in his fist and slams it on the table. "And McCallahan, if I want any shit out of you, I'll squeeze your head."

"You're just pissed because that Tucker pledge kicked your ass. Nice stitches, by the way." McCallahan takes a bite of mashed potatoes and holds up his empty tea glass. "More tea, Alex."

"Alex isn't finished naming the table!" Ryan explodes.

"Sure he is; I'm Matthew McCallahan, that's Brad Domingue, Corey Cascio, and Sam LaCroix. Now go get me some tea before I blackball you." McCallahan grins as he hands Alex his glass. "Go!"

The guys at the table all laugh. Ryan smiles like he thinks McCallahan is funny too, but you and I both know Ryan is just dreaming about ways to knock the crap out of him.

Back in the kitchen, Miss Etta is sitting in her folding chair, smoking her no-name brand cigarettes and sipping on a glass of iced tea. Alex dashes into the kitchen with McCallahan's empty glass.

"Where's the tea?"

"We out, baby." Miss Etta exhales and recrosses her ankles.

"We need to make some more, then." Alex panics.

"Not we. *You,* baby. You need to make some more tea. All this cooking done worn me out, and I'm going to sit here and rest myself. Thank you."

"Come on, Miss Etta, help the boy," I say to her as I hang over Alex's left shoulder.

"Oh baby, I got a bone to pick with you." Etta shakes her cigarette at me.

"What are you talking about?" Alex steps back a little.

"I ain't talking to you, boy. Go make yourself some tea and leave me alone. I got the Lord's work to do." She points at me. "Damn ghostyheaded fool, come here!"

"You're nuts, lady," Alex sort of laughs.

"Boy, get out my kitchen calling me crazy." Etta grabs a nearby bottle of ketchup and holds it ready to throw at Alex's head.

"What about the tea?" Alex whines.

"Tell them fools we out of tea. If they want tea, tell them go to McDonald's. Now get out my kitchen calling me crazy!" Miss Etta

fakes tossing the bottle. Alex flinches and hurries out of the
kitchen.

"Now, you." She stares me down as she rubs the gold cross
around her neck. "Conrad, you in big trouble. I told you to look
after that Tucker boy and look at what you done."

"I had to save Ashley."

"Don't be giving me no excuses. Taking over people against
their will be evildoing!" Miss Etta stands up and walks over to me.

"Ryan was going to rape her!"

"Fighting evil with evil ain't the way to go. The Lord, He got a
plan and you be interrupting it, left and right."

"So it was God's will for Ryan to rape Ashley?"

"No, but it sure ain't His will for you to be taking over Tucker
Graham. Sad as it be, maybe Ashley be the one strong enough to
send Ryan to jail. I don't know. It ain't for you to say."

"Whatever."

"I know you mad, baby. But don't stray now. You can't do this
on your own, child. Just follow the Lord. He got a plan." Her scary
blue-brown eyes don't blink. She just stares at me.

"Forget it. If God wants to stop me, let Him."

"Child, it don't work like that!" Miss Etta beats her fist into
her hand and I disappear.

I don't need her harshing on me for what I did. I mean, I know
Miss Etta means well and all, but who is she to tell me I shouldn't
have saved Ashley the other night? All her turn-the-other-cheek
bullshit really pisses me off sometimes. Let's see Ryan break her
neck and see how well she turns the other cheek.

Alex Trudeaux, Charlie LaPrairie, Tony Audoin, and Clay Weaver
bust their pledge asses to get the meal cleaned up in time for the
actives' Monday night meeting. Behind all the steam and Clorox of
the big old dishwasher, Alex and Charlie scramble to get all the
dishes washed up while Tony and Clay bus the tables and mop the
floor.

Jeff Couvillion comes into the chapter room and yells at Tony and Clay.

"Okay, you pukes, you have exactly five seconds to get out of this house before we ball you!"

"But we haven't gotten our food for working the meal yet, man." Clay pushes his greasy blond hair back into his baseball hat and leans on his mop.

"Too bad, ladies, you should have thought about that before you decided to screw off after dinner."

"We've been busting our asses, man." Clay holds his mop up a little.

"Are you popping off to me?" Couvillion clenches his teeth and gets all up in Clay's face.

"No, I was just saying that—"

"Saying what? That I'm a liar?" Two squiggly veins pop out on Couvillion's temples and his blond spiky hair stands on end like a buzz saw.

Alex and Charlie step out of the kitchen with their rubber gloves still on to see what all the commotion is about.

"No, I mean. I don't know what I was saying," Clay stammers.

"I didn't think so!" Couvillion backhands Clay across the face, knocking the mop out of his hand. "Now get the hell out here! All of you!"

Clay is stunned; he just stares at Couvillion as a handprint welts up on his face. Tony grabs Clay by the arm, and the four pledges run out of the house via the chapter room's back door. Couvillion stands there and watches them get in their cars and leave. He locks the door behind him, and walks over to the far back wall of the chapter room. A huge metal Gamma Chi crest, a black onyx shield with a huge gold cross the size of a door, is mounted in the middle of the wall. In the very heart of the gold cross is an emblem of a skull and crossbones. Couvillion pulls out this funny-shaped key from his pocket and puts it in the skull's mouth. The skull pops out like a doorknob, and Couvillion turns it to open the crest. He enters the dark vault and descends the narrow steps to the hidden room below.

After a few minutes, Couvillion comes up the stairs wearing a black-hooded druid robe, lugging stacks of similar robes in his arms. He dumps the robes on one of the dining tables and goes back down the stairs. By the time he comes up again with a second pile of robes, active Gamma Chis are filing into the room, moving tables and chairs around while some are putting on their robes.

"You left the front door unlocked." Ryan taps Couvillion on the back of the head.

"Hey, I was busy running off the pledges." Couvillion helps Ryan into his robe.

"Hurry up and get the candles. I want to get this show on the road so we can get out on time to watch the Saints' game." Ryan adjusts his robe.

Couvillion runs down the stairs while Kimbrough and Mc-Callahan move a table in front of the vault. Ryan and Kimbrough cover the table with a black velvet cloth embroidered with a golden ladder, a pointing finger, a skull, and a flying serpent.

Couvillion comes out of the vault with a gold candelabrum in one hand and a heavy gold Celtic cross in the other. He places the candles on the right and the cross on the left of the table; Ryan takes a seat between the icons at the center of the table. McCallahan shuts the vault and the Gamma Chi crest shines behind them.

"Where's my gavel?" Ryan puts his hand out and Couvillion pulls the gavel from under his robe and hands it to him. Couvillion covers his head with his hood, lights the candles, and takes a seat at Ryan's right hand. Matthew McCallahan covers his head and sits to Ryan's left.

About a hundred or so active brothers also pull their hoods up as they form a semicircle with their chairs around the sacred table. Someone shuts off the lights, and only the candlelight flickers over the room.

Ryan raps his mighty gavel. "Hear ye! Hear ye! Are only the Worthy assembled?"

From the feral darkness, the Gamma Chis yell back, "Worthy-worthyworthy!"

"Holy knights, please join me in the invocation!" McCallahan shouts.

Click click click click.

The room is filled with the finger snapping and then there is silence.

"Please bow your head in prayer." McCallahan's head drops, and the rest of the heads of the brethren fall one after the other like dance line chicks at a halftime show.

"Our Father"—McCallahan clears his throat—"we humbly beseech thee to watch over these proceedings. May your wisdom fill us with honor, valor, and courage. May the Golden Cross and the Bloody Chalice teach us to be true and noble to You and to the Worthy. We are Knights in Your Son's service. In His name for whom the fiery Golden Cross of Gamma Chi blazes, we pray. Amen."

Ryan raps his gavel.

"Let the meeting of the Worthy Brothers of Gamma Chi begin." Ryan raps the gavel again. "Let's keep this short so we can get out of here to watch the game."

Couvillion hands Ryan a crumpled piece of paper and Ryan reads from it. "The first order of business is to remind everyone about the blood drive this week. It's at the house all day Wednesday. So make sure you all come by and bleed for Gamma Chi. Second order of business is, as I'm sure you all know, grace period is over for the pledges. Make sure they know how far they are from initiation and that they will have to work for it just like we all did. That's all I've got. Does anyone have anything else?"

"Yes, Worthy Chalice Keeper, I do." Jeff Couvillion stands up. "I would like to bring Tucker Graham up for depledging."

The room clicks like it's full of a bunch of locusts and someone hollers, "Ball him!" Derrick Stone, one of the actives who held me down the night I saved Ashley, comes forward.

"I second that motion, Worthy."

The Gamma Chis go wild. I guess Tucker, or better yet, I, have really pissed everybody off.

Ryan hits the table hard with his gavel.

"Order! Order!" Ryan turns to Couvillion. "Sit down, Jeff, I've got something to say."

Ryan stands. "Okay, guys, I know you all think Tucker Graham should be blackballed, but hear me out, okay? I think he deserves a second chance."

"What?" Couvillion pops up out of his chair.

Ryan pushes him back down. "Shut up, Couvillion, and let me finish."

The room is silent. Nobody can believe this.

"Tucker Graham smoked some bad shit the night of the mixer. He didn't know what he was doing and I think we should keep him. He's a good guy and that's all I'm going to say, and if this chapter has any respect for me or my position, that's all I need to say."

Ryan takes his seat and a lone snap can be heard from a brother and then a few more join in and then the whole room crescendos in support of Ryan and Tucker.

Couvillion just shakes his head.

"I still want a show of hands. I only need eight."

"Okay, dick." Ryan glares at Couvillion and then looks back out at the brothers. "All those in favor of depledging Tucker Graham please raise your hand."

No hands are raised except for Couvillion.

"Are you happy, Couvillion? Tucker Graham is still a pledge."

Ryan strikes his gavel hard on the table. "Is there anything else to be addressed?"

The room sits silent and then a brother comes forward.

"I move we adjourn this meeting."

"I second it!" yells another anxious Saints fan.

"Okay, this meeting is adjourned." Ryan bangs the gavel again and the lights come on. Lanky McCallahan blows out the candles.

Eight

The Saints are down by ten against the Dallas Cowboys, and everybody is sitting around Gamma Chi's big-screen TV, cussing those sorry bastards. Ryan, however, is watching the game in his room, sitting on the floor around a bunch of newspapers, cleaning his revolver, catching a buzz off the gun oil fumes and beer. He takes a sip from a can of Foster's and continues polishing his gun with all the verve and concentration of a monkey at the zoo jacking off. He smiles at his reflection on the side of the barrel.

I have to admit, it's a damn nice piece—a Smith & Wesson thirty-eight special. It's a pretty little killing machine with its silver barrel and pearly handle. With a flick of his wrist, he opens the cylinder and crams a bullet into the chamber, spins it, and then claps it shut. He braces his wrist and aims the pistol at football players on the TV. He pretends to knock them off one by one.

"Yeah, baby!" Ryan talks to himself in this stupid Austin Powers accent.

He puts the gun down on the newspaper and picks up the pledge phone list off his bedside table. He takes a deep breath and calls Tucker Graham.

The phone rings a couple of times. An answering machine picks up. It's a dragging message of Maxwell Bonecaze doing this rapper bullshit:

"Yo all you bizsnitches and all you hos, you reached the macdaddy Masta Max and his main geeeeee, Tucka, the frat boy mutha-fucka. Word up and leave a shout!" Beeeeeep.

Ryan shakes his head and clears his throat.

"Tucker, I don't know what that message is about, but this is Ryan. Just calling to let you know you've been assigned a special line-up for what happened at the exchange. You need to be at the house tomorrow night at eight in a coat and tie. When you get there, wait outside with your head down and eyes shut. And one more thing—if you and your butt-pirate roommate don't change that message, you can count on tomorrow being a lot worse. Catch you later, little bro."

Tucker sits up in his bed and looks at the answering machine and then glares at Maxwell.

"Yo, homey's not down with the Masta Max and his flo like a mofo." Maxwell throws gang signs like he's Eminem or something.

"Just change the message."

Tucker Graham gets out of bed all pissed off, leaving Masta Max and his flo alone in their dorm room.

Now, Sarah Jane Bradford really isn't the self-righteous bitch that everyone thinks she is. She was Ashley's freshman-year roommate, back when I was alive and still dating Ashley. Sarah Jane and I never saw eye-to-eye much. She was all hellfire and brimstone, thumping her Bible for the Christian Collegians, and I was, well, you know how I was: The only use I had for those Christian Collegians was for my "Big Mac attacks." Me and my buddies would drive around in my Porsche with a bag full of Big Macs. We'd take the top bun off and toss the Big Macs at the religious nuts who were barking about the end of the world in front of Murphy's Bar and Grill. It was funnier than shit. I mean, all that nasty-ass special sauce and lettuce hanging off their pious faces was pretty hilarious. But now that I'm dead and unable to find heaven, maybe that wasn't such a bright idea.

Sarah Jane—even though she's a Xi Omega—had been all caught up with the Collegians for about a year. She's always outside of Murphy's Bar with her goofy buckteeth yelling with the best of them. But Ashley and Sarah Jane have been friends since kindergarten and no matter how freaky for Jesus Sarah Jane gets, Ashley always stands by her.

So it's really no wonder that Ashley has been staying with Sarah Jane ever since the whole Ryan thing. This morning, they're sitting in Sarah Jane's kitchen with their ponytails piled on their pretty heads. Her kitchen looks like that crazy Martha Stewart lady hijacked it. It's all wicker baskets and flowers and stripes and pink and green cutesy shit. Anyway, Ashley is drowning her sorrows in a bag of microwave popcorn while Sarah Jane sips on a Diet Coke and quotes from her Bible.

"The righteous shall rejoice when he seeth the vengeance: he shall wash his feet in the blood of the wicked! Psalm 58:10." Sarah Jane shuts the good book and grabs a handful of popcorn.

"That was beautiful, Sarah Jane, thanks." Ashley reattaches her hair clip to her pony tail. "That was just what I needed." Ashley rolls her eyes and gets up to grab herself a bottled water.

"Stop being so bitchy, I'm just trying to help." Sarah Jane wipes her greasy hands on the tablecloth and takes a gulp of Diet Coke. "You know you have like every right to press charges against that Ryan guy."

"I know that, Sarah Jane!" Ashley slams down her water. "I just want to forget about it. Okay?"

"Okay. Sorry." Sarah Jane grabs the popcorn and leaves Ashley alone in the kitchen. Ashley slides down onto the floor, curls up into a ball, and cries. I hover around her like a smoke ring trying to keep its shape. I try to hold her, but she can't feel me for all the pain she's got inside.

Tuesday night gets here a lot sooner than Tucker Graham would have liked. And come eight, he stands outside the Gamma Chi house wearing a coat and tie. His navy blue blazer is way too small; his long gorilla arms hang out of the sleeves, exposing his thick, orange-haired, and freckled wrists. Tucker keeps his head down and eyes closed just like Ryan told him and he waits under the snaky shadows of the oak trees.

I always hated this part. The waiting, that is. You know you're going to get your shit jumped and the whole time you've got to tell yourself just to be a man and take it. But your good sense kicks in and you have to strong-arm it with whatever made you pledge in the first place. That way, you don't do something like kick someone's ass or, better yet, just leave.

However, from the looks of it, Tucker's good sense is in no danger of kicking in anytime soon. He stands there not even peeking to see what's going on. He doesn't even lift his neck to stretch it. Either he's a big chickenshit, or he's got more willpower than I ever did. Maybe it's a little bit of both.

It's nine o'clock before Couvillion comes out, smoking a cigar.

"So, Mr. Big and Bad is back." Couvillion blows smoke in Tucker's face and whispers all tight-lipped and heavy in Tucker's ear, "You ready for this, big boy?"

Tucker squints his eyes tighter and coughs a little.

"Wus a matta? Mamma's little fatty don't like smoke?" Couvillion pushes Tucker, but Tucker keeps his head down and his eyes shut.

"I asked you a question, boy!" Couvillion thumps Tucker's big red ear. "What's the matter? You deaf and dumb?" Couvillion chews on that turd of a cigar and tries to stand face to face with Tucker, but Tucker's too tall for that.

"Now let's try this again. Does Mamma's little fatty not like um smokies?"

Tucker's breath is shallow and fast. "No-uh-I mean, no sir, I don't like smoke."

"Ah, now. I so sorry. Mamma's little fatty don't like um stinky old cigaws?" Couvillion blows a stream of smoke in Tucker's face. "Can you say that, Tucker? Mamma's little fatty don't like um stinky old cigaws."

Tucker responds like a robot. "Mamma's little fatty doesn't like stinky old cigars."

Couvillion runs his hand through his spiky blond hair and smirks.

"So Tucker doesn't like cigars, huh? Well, let's see what we can do about this. Put your hand out, Tucker."

Tucker's enormous left hand trembles as he raises it. Couvillion takes a couple of fast puffs off the cigar and gets the cherry glowing bright orange. Couvillion puts the cigar out in Tucker's palm. Tucker yells and drops to his knees

"So you like standing on your knees, Tucker?"

Couvillion grabs Tucker's tie and drags him into the darkened house. Tucker sucks the burn on his hand as he bumps along on his knees. Couvillion pulls Tucker into the pitch-black chapter room. The smell of spilt beer is everywhere. Couvillion then leads him over to a bunch of broken beer bottles. The glass snaps and crackles under Tucker's weight.

Tucker screams and bolts up from his knees. Couvillion tries to push him back down into the glass, but Tucker isn't going to play that game.

"Keep your pledge ass down, you puke!"

Tucker holds his ground, all three-hundred-plus pounds of him. And no matter how hard Couvillion tries to push him back down, Tucker's not moving.

"Get your ass back down!" Couvillion rages.

Tucker just stands there, not knowing whether to knock the shit out of Couvillion or to leave. But the fear of being depledged holds Tucker tight, so he sort of checks out and stares off into the darkness.

A match scratches and explodes from the shadows.

"What's the matter, Tucker? Can't you take orders?" Ryan appears from out of the darkness and lights a candle with the match.

Ryan leans over to Couvillion and whispers, "Give me a few seconds alone with him."

"But I thought we were going to do the Tabasco enema." Couvillion pulls a bottle of the Tabasco from his back pocket and holds it up.

"Maybe later, Couvillion, I need to talk to him."

"Damn it, Ryan. He almost ran my ass over."

"Don't argue with me." Ryan grits his teeth and whispers, "Now go take it in the other room while I have a word with Tucker. Okay?"

"Whatever, man." Couvillion jerks away and walks out of the chapter room. He throws the bottle at Tucker, barely missing his head and breaking it all over the floor, "Tucker, don't think it's over between you and me!"

"Tucker, my boy, it looks like you've pissed a few people off." Ryan puts his hand on Tucker's shoulder and halfway laughs, "You can open your eyes, bruh."

Tucker opens his eyes and squints at the bright candle.

"You okay?" Ryan flashes one of his 100-percent-cotton smiles.

"Yeah. I think so."

"Good. I'm real sorry you had to go through this. Couvillion can be a real bastard, you know."

"Yeah, I know." Tucker cracks a weak smile.

"Ah, there we go." Ryan tousles Tucker's red hair like he's some kid in Little League.

"So tell me Tucker, do you still want to be a Gamma Chi?"

"Uh, yes sir."

"You don't have to call me sir. We're friends. Or at least we were until this." Ryan holds the candle to the stitches on his scalp.

"I'm real sorry, Ryan."

"Are you, Tucker?" Ryan narrows his eyes and packs his cigarettes against his leg.

Tucker just stands there, with his head bowed, breathing through his mouth.

"So what are you going to tell your pledge brothers about what happened tonight?" Ryan lights a cigarette with the candle.

"Uh, nothing?"

"Good answer."

"Do you know how close you were to being balled, Tucker?" Ryan takes a long drag and smiles. "And do you know who saved you?"

"You did." Tucker looks at the floor.

"That's right. The same guy who brought you into his house. The same guy who called you brother. And how did you thank me, Tucker?" Ryan points to his stitches. "Is this how you thanked me?"

' "No."

"Sure it is!" Ryan's face turns wooden and mean. "What is Gamma Chi to you? Just some place where you can drink all my beer and then screw me over? Is that what you think this is all about?"

"No," Tucker whispers, looking down at his feet.

"Do you see that shield over there?" Ryan points to the Gamma Chi crest over on the far wall. "What is that in the middle of it?"

"A cross."

"It's a gold cross." Ryan takes another drag. "And do you know what that cross stands for?" He turns his head and blows his smoke away from Tucker.

"Uh, no."

"Of course you don't. Because if you knew what this place was really about, you wouldn't have cast a stain of dishonor upon that cross." Ryan moves closer to Tucker and Tucker flinches.

"Do you think I'm going to hit you, Tucker?"

"Yeah."

"Do you think I have the right to hit you?"

"Yeah."

"Well, it's not going to be that easy. The Golden Cross of Gamma Chi isn't about an eye for an eye, Tucker." Ryan lowers his head and then looks up at him. "Every pledge has a cross to bear. What's your cross? That's what I want you to figure out. How will you earn my forgiveness?"

"I don't know."

"You will."

Ryan just stands there staring at him. The silence is as painful as a rotten tooth—all full of pressure, bad breath, and abscessed shit.

"What's your cross, Tucker? Remember that."

Ryan snuffs out his candle and the room is black. And in the blackness, fingers snap and voices chant, "Worthyworthyworthyworthy."

Out of the blackness, active brothers swarm around Tucker like flies to a turd. Their fists pummel his face. There's a blow to his stomach and then his kidneys and then one to his nose. He falls to the ground and the shadows kick and stomp on him. But Tucker takes it like a good pledge and doesn't fight back.

The blows are swift and hard and cruel.

As quickly as it all began, it stops. Couvillion's voice calls out from the darkness, "Go home, you puke!"

Tucker gets up, fat lipped and eyes swollen. He hobbles out of the dark house, all broken and bleeding. Outside on the sidewalk, he passes Sarah Jane Bradford; they both look away from each other and walk a little faster.

Tucker staggers his Quasimodo-looking ass to his Mustang. Once inside, he turns on the dome light, rolls his pants up, and starts picking out the brown glass from his bloody knees.

The next morning is all sunshiny and beautiful. It's one of those September mornings in Baton Rouge when the air is heavy and little fog clouds lurk under the big oak trees and dance on the lakes, but the sky is blue and clear.

Ryan gets up, does his compulsory sit-ups, then puts on his running shorts and straps an iPod to his bicep. He double-times it down the back stairway and out of the house. He runs through the parking lot behind the Gamma Chi house, past his hunter green Jeep.

Ryan jerks the headphones out of his ears and stands there, slackjawed. Under the glistening morning dew, neon orange graffiti screams from the hood of his Jeep. Two angry words glow in big sorority girl letters:

GOD KNOWS

I laugh so hard even thickheaded Ryan can hear me this time. He looks around slinging sweat everywhere to see where the laughter's coming from.

Boy, I got to hand it to crazy Sarah Jane. She got his sorry ass pretty damn good.

Nine

aggie. Maggie. Maggie. I just like saying her name. If I really concentrate on these feelings, I drift toward her and in her presence, my lost soul finds a place that is warm and beautiful. I may not have heaven, but at least I get to see Maggie Meadows naked. Today, she's putting on her jog bra and her running shorts, getting ready to go for a run. She's perfect. In fact, she's so fine, I would drink her spit, a big cup full of it like Mother Teresa used to do with the lepers in India. Just drink it on down and smile.

I float above Maggie as she runs along the Campus Lakes and something bizarre starts to happen. I can see parts of her life trailing behind her—little movies of her past. I see her dad teaching her how to ride a bike without training wheels. I see her first puppy, a little Sheltie, which she housebroke herself. I see her winning first place in a triathlon in high school. I see her busting it every day on the swim team. I see her freezing some girl's panties at a slumber party and giggling. And then the movies turn darker: I see Maggie meeting Ryan. I see her heart floating above her head like a red Mylar balloon. I see Maggie's first time, the clumsy breathlessness of it all and how gentle Ryan was. And then everything just turns ugly. The hitting starts and Ryan's head games spin and swirl. There's all this tenderness and then there's all this pain. These images look like demons chasing her and no matter how hard or fast she runs, she can't get away from them. But the scariest thing trailing behind Maggie doesn't look like a demon at all. It's all beautiful and looks like love, but it's the kind of love that thinks it can fix anybody no matter how broken they are.

After a good hour run, I follow Maggie as she walks back to her apartment to cool down. When she gets to her apartment, she sees that her door is ajar.

Ryan always leaves the door open just a little when she's late. It's one of his games. It means she's going to get a beating.

She checks her watch and braces herself and walks into her apartment.

There are hundreds of tiny white candles flickering all over her apartment and the warm smell of grilled chicken and primavera sauce coming from the kitchen. Ryan stands up from the couch. He's all spiffed up with his rep tie, starched oxford, and pressed khakis. He's holding eleven long-stem white roses and one red one wrapped in green tissue paper.

"How was your run?" Ryan walks slowly over to her and kisses her on the lips.

"I'm all sweaty," she laughs nervously.

"Just thought I'd surprise you." He hands her the roses.

"They're beautiful."

"I made dinner." He points to the candlelit table.

"Dinner? Ryan Hutchins? What's gotten into you?" Maggie tucks her hair behind her ear and smells her roses.

He looks deep in her eyes. With one smooth move, he puts her roses on the table, pulls her close, thrusting his crotch into hers, and sticks his lying tongue in her mouth.

Maggie's eyes twinkle like they seldom do.

"At least let me go rinse off."

Ryan just grunts and kisses her neck. She kisses him hard and he unzips his pants.

I get out of here before I vomit or do whatever it is ghosts do when we're completely, thoroughly disgusted.

"Are you sure nobody saw you?" Ashley opens her eyes extra wide and puts on her mascara in the bathroom mirror.

"I'm positive." Sarah Jane beams.

"Good. Because the last thing I need is that psycho after me because you vandalized his Jeep." Ashley picks up this pincer-looking pair of scissors and clamps them down on her eyelashes.

"I told you it's okay to strike back at him. He's evil. Here, let me read you this Bible verse about spiritual warfare and the devil." Sarah Jane flips through her Bible, the one she keeps in her quilted Xi Omega carrying case.

"That's okay, Sarah Jane. I've had enough Sunday school lessons about Ryan." Ashley powders her face one last time. "Besides, no telling what he would have done if he caught you."

Ashley picks up a pencil and draws around her eyes.

"Oh Ashley, the Lord is my shepherd. He watches over me. Ryan could never hurt me." Sarah Jane presses her Bible to her chest, puts her left hand in the air, and shouts, "Xi Omega Praise God!"

"What was that?" Ashley puts down her pencil and stares at Sarah Jane.

"That's just my new affirmation. I can't really tell you what it means. It just came to me. Sort of like speaking in tongues." Sarah Jane's buckteeth shine.

"Well, whatever it is, it's weird." Ashley shakes her head and starts messing with her hair. "I don't know what I'm going to do with you, Sarah Jane."

"I pray every day that you'll find the Lord and that you'll eventually understand." Sarah Jane hugs her Bible tight.

Ashley looks so beautiful standing there with her long brown hair and dark eyes. I can't resist; I touch her cheek and remember kissing her.

"Omigod!" Ashley shudders.

"What's the matter?"

"I don't know. I just got the weirdest chill." Ashley touches her face.

"Praise the Lord!" Sarah Jane looks up. "It's the Holy Spirit!"

Sarah Jane's got the spirit part down, but how holy I am is debatable.

"Sarah Jane, you're starting to freak me out. Stop it!" Ashley walks past her to the full-length mirror hanging on the bedroom door.

"Does this outfit look okay?" Ashley turns her mini-skirted butt to the mirror.

"No." Sarah Jane sneers.

"Okay, what's the matter now?"

"I was like totally talking about God, and you change the subject."

"You're always talking about God."

"But he'll do it again! Ryan has got to be stopped." Sarah Jane puts her Bible down and grabs Ashley's hand. "I can't let him get away with what he did to you."

Ashley jerks her hand away, and her makeup runs down her face in little black streams. Like I said, it doesn't take much to make her cry.

"I'm going to bring him down, one peg at a time." Sarah Jane runs into the bathroom. "God is on our side, Ashley. I promise you!" Sarah Jane's voice echoes from the bathroom tile.

"Sarah Jane? What are you doing?"

She runs back to Ashley with a bottle of Nair and a bottle of that high-dollar Aveda conditioner. "See." She hands the bottles to Ashley.

"See what?" Ashley wipes her eyes and looks at the bottles.

"I'm going to fix Ryan. Remember when we were kids at Camp Mystic and that Wendy bitch put Nair in my conditioner? Remember?"

"Yeah."

"Remember how my hair started falling out and I had to go home and then after I left, that Wendy girl told everybody she put Nair in my conditioner?"

"Sarah Jane, are you crazy?" Ashley giggles.

Sarah Jane picks up the conditioner and the Nair and does a little puppet show.

"Mr. Ryan Hutchins"—she holds up the conditioner bottle—"I'd like you to meet Mr. Male Pattern Baldness." She pretends the two bottles are shaking hands. Sarah Jane giggles and snorts.

Ashley laughs so hard she almost pees her pants.

Tucker Graham is lucky in a way. The burn on his hand is only the size of a dime and it's third degree, so he can't really feel it. As for the cuts on his knees, he went to the emergency room of Our Lady of the Lakes, and now he's got more stitches than a baseball. The beating didn't do much to improve Tucker's looks. In fact, his body looks like a piece of rotting steak, all swollen pink, black, and blue.

To remedy his pain, Tucker sits up in his bed, listens to Phish and Widespread Panic CDs, and smokes dope with Kimbrough.

"See, if you hold it for a couple of extra seconds"—Kimbrough tokes on his roach and holds his breath—"You get mo'mellow mo'better." He coughs and laughs snot out of his nose.

Tucker grabs the roach from Kimbrough and takes a hit. His eyes water as he exhales.

"So, dude, you still want to quit?" Kimbrough holds his two fingers out and twitches them for the joint. Tucker takes one more drag and then passes it back to him.

"I'm not sure," Tucker says, choking on the pot smoke.

"Look, Tucker, you'd be stupid to quit now." Kimbrough points at him with the roach clip. "The rest of your pledgeship should be a cakewalk."

"I don't know." Tucker shakes his head. "This just ain't how I thought it was going to be."

"Well, then, quit. And you can hang out with your GDI roommate. I'm sure you'll be pulling all the wool with that action." Kimbrough squashes the burned-out joint in an empty Domino's Pizza box.

Tucker looks down at the ground. He knows Kimbrough's right. Without Gamma Chi, Tucker couldn't even get a sorority girl to piss on him, much less talk to him.

Kimbrough rolls another fatty, lights it in his mouth, and puffs on it.

"Here." He hands the blunt to Tucker. "Things'll get better."

Tucker takes the joint and inhales deep. Thousands of white lights zoom past his head and tiny little cartoon ghosts—little Casper-looking motherfuckers—laugh at him as they waltz around his ceiling fan. Tucker points at them and busts out laughing.

Ten

The afternoon shadows grow longer on the Gamma Chi house, the days grow shorter, and for the first time this fall, the air is crisp and full of static electricity. So most of the Gamma Chi chapter is hanging out at the house, soaking up some brotherhood. In the front yard, in between the two gnarly oak trees, there's a football in the air. Half of the guys are skins and the other half are shirts and the rest are sitting up on the porch nursing their beers while one dude pretends he's Jeff Tweedy and does his best to play Wilco songs on his guitar.

Alex Trudeaux catches a wobbly spiral from Kimbrough, and spins off Couvillion and then bounces off a couple of shirtless actives like a pinball. Alex scores. He spikes the ball and shines in the glory of high school days past as he gets jiggy with it.

Couvillion huffs and puffs and glares at Alex.

"Okay, game over!" Couvillion yells, wiping the sweat from his brow with his hairy wrist, "Pledges start your cleanup!"

"What?" Kimbrough looks at Couvillion like he's high. "The Jif doesn't start for another hour. Let's keep playing."

"The house looks like ass. The pukes need to clean it before the kegs get here."

"Couvillion, who died and made you Chalice Keeper?" Kimbrough smirks.

Couvillion gets up in Kimbrough's face, breathing all heavy and flaring his ugly-ass nostrils. "What are you doing talking ritual in front of the pledges?"

The dude playing the guitar stops and everybody stands up from the porch and watches. Kimbrough pushes Couvillion away.

"Because they didn't know it was ritual, until you just said that, you moron."

It gets real quiet. Everybody's mouths are just watering for a fight. Fights are always fun to watch, especially when it's two actives.

But then Kimbrough does something that surprises us all, because Kimbrough, even though he is a stoner, has something of a reputation as a badass. You should have seen him take this big Cajun dude down one night when we were out at The Caterie. He's a pit bull in a fight, like a white pot-smoking Mike Tyson biting people's ears and shit. But today, for whatever reason, Kimbrough turns his back on Couvillion and walks up the steps of the house.

"Come on, Alex, help me move these couches outside." He throws his hand over his head, motioning for Alex to follow him.

"Pussy." Couvillion grabs his package and shakes it at him.

Kimbrough takes a deep breath and just keeps on walking.

Couvillion picks up his T-shirt off the ground and wipes the sweat off his face. "What the fuck are y'all looking at?"

The active with the guitar starts playing again, the pledges high-tail it into the house to clean it up, and then everybody else sits back down. Just about everybody knows Couvillion can also kick some serious ass, and just about nobody wants a piece of that.

On Friday evenings like this one, all the fraternities pull their couches outside along with their house stereos and everybody sits around getting drunk. They call these little parties TGIFs, but they pronounce it "Jif," like the peanut butter. Don't ask me why they do this. No one has ever questioned it. Just like no one ever really questioned my death. I guess when you're eighteen or twenty or so, that's just how things work; you take whatever answer is ready and available.

Anyway, Gamma Chi's Jif is in full swing. The music is booming. The kegs are flowing. And the sorority girls are orbiting, like little twinkling stars, pulling the brothers outside with their Southern girl gravity. And my boy, Kimbrough, is right there circling the kegs with them. He's all about drunk Southern girls and after that little encounter with Couvillion earlier, he's had a few beers to unwind.

"Hey, don't I know you?" Kimbrough walks up behind this brown-haired girl with a cute little ass and taps her on the shoulder.

"Hey there!" Sarah Jane Bradford turns around and gives him a full-on assault of smiling buckteeth.

"Oh!" Kimbrough jumps back just a little. "Sarah Jane. I thought you were someone else."

"You're drunk."

"And you should be." He winks at her.

"You know I don't do that anymore."

"Here we go with the sermon."

"I can have a good time without liquor." She smiles, tight-lipped and bitchy.

"So who are you here with?"

"See those girls over there?" Sarah Jane points to the other end of the porch.

"The fat ones standing by the column?" Kimbrough scrunches his nose.

She slaps his arm.

"Stop it. Those are my sorority sisters."

"*Sorority sows* is more like it. When did Xi-O become a fat girl sorority?"

"Jay Kimbrough. You are such an effing A-hole!"

Sarah Jane walks off to join her little coven of fat chicks, but Jay chases after her.

"Hey now, Sarah Jane, you know I'm just kidding."

"An A-hole."

"Hey-hey, just a second. I was just messing with you. Look, I really just wanted to ask you about Ashley. How is she?"

"Ashley?"

"Yeah, Ashley. You know, your best friend . . ."

Sarah Jane sort of plays with her earring and smiles.

"She's fine, I guess."

"Oh." Kimbrough looks at his shoes and then back at Sarah Jane.

"Why do you ask?"

"I was just curious. I ran into her about a month ago and I was just wondering how she's doing."

"Well, if and when I see her, I'll be sure to tell her what a complete effing A-hole you are." Sarah Jane swings her hair in his face and walks over to her friends.

Kimbrough shakes his head and feels in his pocket for his dime bag; he goes in the house to smoke out. Sarah Jane stands outside by her chubby little friends and through the porch window watches Kimbrough go up the stairs. She glances at her watch, a Timex Ironman that she synchronized with Ashley's.

"Hey, I'll be right back. I need to get a pad out of my purse and I left it in the car," Sarah Jane whispers to Krista, this Xi-O with long frizzy black hair, brown freckles, and a serious attitude.

"Oh, okay. I'll go with you." Krista scratches at her black pantyhose and wobbles her head.

"No, no. Stay here, sweetie. I'll be right back."

"Oh, okay." Krista turns back around and drinks deep from her lipstick-stained party cup.

Sarah Jane pushes her way through all the preening, smiling girls and loud-talking frat boys. She walks very quickly across the yard and around the side of the house to the parking lot. She stands in the dark by her Blazer and presses the "Indiglo" button on her watch to check the time. And just as she looks up, Ashley's old chewing-gum-gray Volvo rattles into the parking lot. Sarah Jane runs up and taps on Ashley's window.

"Here, give it to me."

"Hold your horses." Ashley reaches over to her passenger side and wrestles with a bunch of ribbons and red helium balloons. She grabs a bath pail all decorated with Gamma Chi letters, crests, and Ryan's name. It's full of bath supplies—shaving cream, shampoo, and razors—and all strung up with the balloons and ribbons.

"Hurry, take it." One of the balloons presses against Ashley's face as she squeezes them out her window to Sarah Jane.

"Okay, okay." Sarah Jane grabs the pail and tries to wrangle the balloons. "Now where is the back stairway again?"

"Over there"—Ashley points to a door on the side of the Gamma Chi house—"right next to the chimney. See it?"

"Okay, say a prayer for me. I'm off."

"Sarah Jane, wait a sec. Where's Ryan?"

"I don't know. I didn't see him at the party."

"What are you going to do if he's upstairs?"

"The Baby Jesus is my co-pilot. Trust me. Now what is Ryan's room number again?"

"I don't remember: it's the room all the way to the end, I think. Three-eleven or something like that. Just leave it by any old door. The bucket's got his name all over it."

"Okay. This is so fun!" Sarah Jane flashes her buckteeth and shrugs her shoulders.

She runs from the parking lot to the back stairs of the Gamma Chi house, with the balloons flapping behind her.

Like all the doors on Gamma Chi house, the back stairs are unlocked twenty-four/seven so she just walks on up the stairs. She covers her nose from the smell of urine and rancid beer.

"Pee-you. Stinky boys." She shakes her head.

Once she gets to the third floor, she tiptoes down the hall, looking at each number on the doors. However, there's no three-eleven; the last door is three-o-nine. So she looks both ways and leaves the bath supplies and the balloons at that door. She can hear the theatrical moans of a girl (Maggie) and the grunts of a guy (Ryan) going at it from behind the door. She covers her mouth and giggles. Then she runs down the hall, back to the stairs.

She trips halfway down them and grabs onto the rail as she starts to tumble. The force of her fall rips the rickety old rail from the wall, but somehow she manages to catch herself.

"Praise God!" She regains her balance and takes the steps one at a time. When she gets to the bottom, she runs out of the stairway and stands in the shadows of the house, trying to catch her breath. She wipes the beads of sweat from her upper lip and whispers one of her crazy-ass prayers.

Then she takes a deep breath and very casually walks across the yard to the front porch and back to her friends who are standing by the keg. Sarah Jane picks up the tap, snags a plastic cup, tilts it and fixes herself a beer.

"Sarah Jane? You're drinking?" Krista stares at her.

"Just this once." Sarah Jane downs it like a frat boy and blows her hair out of her face with a heavy sigh.

Tucker Graham's bruises are turning yellow and they're starting to fade. So he shows up at the Jif with Alex. They move past the crowd into the house. They walk up the stairs to Kimbrough's room. There's a line outside his open door; he's playing dealer man.

Over Kimbrough's unmade bed hangs a black velvet Deadhead poster. He's got his hippie glasses on, the ones with the blue lenses, and there are plastic bags all in a row on his bed. Alex and Tucker take their place in the back of the line.

"Yo Kimbrough, how about another bag? I'll pay you tomorrow. My parents are mailing me a check," McCallahan begs with his lanky stork-ass.

"Is there a sign over my door that says 'Welcome to the fucking Welfare Office'?"

"Come on, Kimbrough. I'll pay you tomorrow."

"Here, you can have the rest of this one. But it will cost you thirty bucks. Tomorrow."

"Hey, I'm good for it."

Kimbrough checks the seal on the bag and throws it at Mc-Callahan.

After McCallahan, all the other guys have their twenty-dollar bills fresh from the cash machine and they pick up their plastic bags one after the other. Tucker and Alex finally make it inside.

"I'm all out." Kimbrough counts his newly minted cash.

"Dude, we just came by to hang." Alex nods a little too much.

"You came by so you can smoke out for free."

Tucker walks in and slaps Kimbrough on the shoulder.

"So did you make a lots of money tonight?" Alex smiles.

"Just shut up and roll me some sticky-icky-icky." Kimbrough tosses a bag to Alex.

"Well, okay, but we really didn't come by to smoke out for free." Alex opens the bag and starts rolling a joint from one of the loose ZigZags strewn all over the bed.

"Alex, you're not shutting up." Kimbrough re-counts his stack of twenties.

Alex lights the joint without a roach clip; it smokes fast as he inhales. Its cherry glows and burns his fingers.

"Ouch!" He tries to shake the joint out, but that only fans the flame. He throws it on the ground and steps on it.

"How old are you? Use a clip next time. Better yet, get Cherry Garcia out of the closet."

Cherry Garcia is the name of Kimbrough's bong. It's a nice little water pipe in the shape of a cherry. He named it Cherry Garcia in honor of Jerry Garcia and the Ben and Jerry's flavor. It's also a nice little code word he uses for getting stupid. Like, "Hey, want to go pick up some Cherry Garcia after dinner?"

They break out Cherry and they get stoned like the sluts in the Bible. Kimbrough puts on a DVD from his extensive porno collection and they sit around and laugh at all the porn stars with their cartoon-size body parts. There's this one part of the tape about a naughty cooking show host, Salad Shooter Sally, who in the middle of her show gets turned on by a greasy cucumber and then through sheer vaginal force shoots the cucumber across the room. Kimbrough keeps rewinding the tape and playing it. They can't stop laughing.

"Man, I need to get me some of that," Alex announces in between hiccups and laughs.

"Alex. Dude. Honestly, have you ever been laid?" Kimbrough takes a hit.

The blood runs out of Alex's face and his eyes bug with terror.

"Uh, yeah. Lots of times."

"Who?"

"I don't want to say." Alex's eyes shift and he inches toward the door.

"You're such a virgin." Kimbrough exhales and coughs a little.

Alex gets up and staggers out of the hazy room.

"He's so weird sometimes." Kimbrough passes the bong to Tucker.

Alex is feeling a tight buzz now from smoking all that purple. The party is an ocean swirl of beer foam and giggles. All the pretty drunk girls and loud music have him thinking that maybe he can cure his virginity, and that maybe he'll do it tonight. So he fills up a plastic cup with beer, and while he's at the tap, he zeroes in on a girl that gives him an immediate woody.

Sarah Jane Bradford.

I guess it's like my mamma always said, "There's a lid to every pot." But it's sort of funny that out of all the ready and able girls crowding the front yard, Alex moves in on the biggest born-again virgin in the world.

"So like, what's your major?" Alex sips his beer and Sarah Jane's eyes kaleidoscope around him.

"Well, I'm in fashion merchandising. I want to be a wedding dress designer like Vera Wang, or maybe a buyer for Neiman Marcus."

"Cool."

"See this miniskirt?" She puts one foot forward like she's some kind of J. Crew model. "I designed it myself."

Alex catches a flash of her white cotton panties as she moves her other leg forward.

"That's nice."

She smiles, batting her eyelashes like Bugs Bunny in drag, but to Alex she looks like she just stepped out of the Victoria's Secrets stashed under his bed.

"What's your major?"

"Pre-law. I'm good at arguing and stuff."

"Oh, that sounds great." She nods her head and twirls her hair on her finger.

And then something wicked comes over me. I have a bad thought. I find myself wanting to move Sarah Jane's mouth, make her say disgusting things with her tongue. So I touch her lips, lips that haven't tasted alcohol for nearly a year now, until tonight, and I dive right in.

But something's not right. I'm in her body, but I'm not controlling things. She is. Sort of.

"Omigod!" Sarah Jane shouts. "I feel like . . . like a vagina!"

"You feel like a what?" Alex's eyes pop.

Krista bounds over and pushes her way in between Sarah Jane and Alex.

"Sarah Jane. Let's go. We're leaving." She flings her hair with her hand and smacks her gum.

Something isn't working right. I can't get all the way inside Sarah Jane. Maybe because she's a girl or maybe there are just some people you shouldn't try to possess. I try to force an exit, but can't. I'm stuck.

Sarah Jane pushes her breasts together and smiles to heaven. "I feel like a birth canal full of life! Like there's someone inside of me trying to get out!"

"Gross, Sarah Jane. Be quiet. Don't say that." Krista grabs Sarah Jane and walks her away from Alex.

"Hey, can I get your number?" dippy Alex calls out.

"Go. A. Way." Krista snarls as she shepherds Sarah Jane and me home.

And just as Krista is about to cast some major attitude, she gets doused with a splash of cold beer from this drunk Couvillion standing next to her.

"Ugh!" She turns around. "Hey, watch it!" She tries to rub the beer off her black outfit.

"Get out of my way, you stupid cow!" Couvillion sloshes his beer everywhere.

Krista's mouth drops open and Sarah Jane and the rest of their girlfriends gather around her so they too can take offense.

"Like what's your problem?" Sarah Jane puts her hands on her hips.

Couvillion tries to muster up the coordination to flip them off.

"Hey Couv, come on, man. Don't do that." Alex sort of smiles and steps forward a little.

This high-energy dance song starts pulsing and booming over the PA. The beat speeds up to a nervous frenzy, so Couvillion starts moving his drunk ass to the electronic beat, ignoring Alex altogether and flipping the girls off as he does this weird-ass chicken dance. The girls stare with disgust.

"You are such a loser," some Xi-O with a headband shrieks.

On that cue, Couvillion drops his pants and boxers, and shakes his fish-belly-white ass in their faces.

The girls scream.

"Put your pants back on, you pervert!" Sarah Jane takes Krista's beer and throws it on Couvillion's gyrating butt. That was a huge mistake. The entire party is now gathered around to watch.

Alex just stands there and whines, "Hey, Couvillion, man, don't do that. That's not cool."

As the bass line speeds up, so does Couvillion's ass. He rushes into the crowd butt-first and shakes it all over Sarah Jane and Krista, rubbing his naked buttocks all over their legs. They turn their heads and frantically claw and try to push him away.

"Omigod, get off us!" Sarah Jane cries out.

I try to rally. I try to flood Sarah Jane's brain with all my hate and anger so that she can kick Couvillion's ass, but all I can do is watch this happen through her eyes.

The girls try to get away, but they're trapped by the crowd that's now circled tightly around and laughing. Krista trips and falls backward.

Couvillion and his butt go down with her.

"Get him! Get him off! His butt! Omigod! His butt is touching me! Stop it!"

Sarah Jane takes off her shoe and hits Couvillion with it.

Krista crawls away from him, crying hysterically. The crowd just stands there and watches as Sarah Jane beats Couvillion with her shoe.

Then Ryan runs out of the crowd and pulls Sarah Jane off Couvillion.

"Let me go!" Sarah Jane squirms, but Ryan bear-hugs her, picking her up off the ground with her legs kicking. "In the name of Jesus Christ, I demand that you let me go!" Sarah Jane screams, and Ryan puts her down.

"Couvillion, put your pants back on, cuz." Ryan helps Couvillion up off the ground.

Sarah Jane is all out of breath and crying. Her drunken sister is wailing as their little coven paws and huddles around her.

"You! You!" Sarah Jane points her shoe at Couvillion.

Ryan turns around to Sarah Jane and gets all up in her face.

"Listen, little girl, you need to settle your crazy ass down."

"What are you going to do? Hit a girl?"

Ryan just stares and breathes his beer breath all over her.

"The power of Jesus in me is stronger than the power of Satan in you," Sarah Jane intones.

"You're crazy."

"The power of Jesus in me is stronger than the power of Satan in you." Sarah Jane lowers her head and stares through Ryan.

He starts to back up a little.

"The power of Jesus in me is stronger than the power of Satan in you!"

The music from the stereo system just shuts off for no reason. Everybody shuts up and watches.

"The power of Jesus in me is stronger than the power of Satan in you!" Sarah Jane shakes and sweats.

"The power of Jesus in me is stronger than the power of Satan in you." Sarah Jane says it faster and faster. "The power of Jesus in me is stronger than the power of Satan in you. The-power-of-Jesus-in-me-is-stronger-than-the-power-of-Satan-in-you."

Everyone is frozen. Time feels thick and slow, like life is happening under water. Ryan just shakes his head and keeps stepping away from Sarah Jane. Then this pressure builds up in Sarah Jane's ears, sort of like it does when you fly on an airplane.

Sarah Jane whispers her chant and closes her eyes tight like she's in terrible pain. Blood starts dripping from her forehead and her palms. I mean, lots of blood, blood so thick and dark it almost looks like ink. And freaky Sarah Jane holds her hands up to heaven and the blood just rolls out of her hands and down her arms. It runs down her head, covering her face. She just laughs. "Praise ya, Jesus! Praise ya!"

And then, boom!

I pop like a zit, her body completely rejects my soul, throwing me into the air and crashing me down into the beer kegs, causing the taps to shoot up into the air like bottle rockets. The beer sprays out the top, drenching everybody on the porch. Everyone runs into the yard and away from the showering beer.

Sarah Jane wipes the blood from her head and smiles. Ryan passes out and Alex, who is right behind him, catches him.

A beer-soaked Couvillion walks up to Sarah Jane, who has her bloody palms out to catch the beer rain.

"Get the hell out of here," he growls.

"You know, I think I just did that. Thank you." Sarah Jane's buckteeth shine, and she turns on her heel and walks off the porch. The crowd parts for her like the Red Sea.

"Sarah Jane, you're bleeding. Are you okay? Did you hit your head?" A beer-soaked Xi Omega puts her arm around Sarah Jane. All the Xi-Os huddle around Sarah Jane and Krista as they all hurry away from the Gamma Chi house.

Despite his drunken stupor, Couvillion has the wherewithal to try to get things back to normal. So he gets the music blaring again, and everybody just kind of nods their head and goes back to talking and drinking—just like nothing happened.

Amazing.

I guess it's just one of those things where people have two realities. The one they can live with and the one that they're living but don't want to admit is happening. And it looks like everyone here is going to opt for the reality they can live with. Which is:

What just happened with Sarah Jane didn't really just happen. It was just some kegs exploding and a drunk Christian Collegian chick that got cut and bumped on the head.

I would reckon this same double vision is why nobody can see me or would care even if they could.

Eleven

Now I know I'm the proverbial pot calling the kettle black here, but whatever Sarah Jane just did isn't right. And what's with her bleeding from her head?

So I swallow my pride and I go to Miss Etta's house. She's bound to know what's going on.

"Miss Etta?"

Her crappy little TV with its aluminum foil and rabbit ears is full of static. Behind all that snow and fuzz, Pat Sajak is going on and on about how pretty Vanna is. Aside from Pat and Vanna, Miss Etta's den is empty, and the blue-green light of the TV shines and reflects off of the plastic furniture protectors covering her old red velvet sofa.

"Miss Etta?"

I go into her kitchen, but all I find in there is a homegrown rose in a mason jar and a rosary on her breakfast table.

"Miss Etta, where are you?"

I go into her bedroom. It's empty and still, with this sad little bed bowing in the middle. There's a brown bed sheet hung over the window.

"Miss Etta?"

There's a closed door with white paint peeling off of it. I try to go through it, but can't.

Miss Etta yells out from behind the door.

"I'm in the bathroom taking care of my business! Let me alone now!"

"I need to talk to you."

"I said I'm on the toilet!"

"Okay. Sorry."

"I know you sorry. Busting all up in here while I'm taking care of my business. Now get out my house."

"Please, Miss Etta."

"I thought you don't need nobody. You Conrad the big bad ghost and you going set the world straight. That's what you told me."

"Look. I'm sorry. I lost it. Please."

"Yeah, you sure did lost it. Possessing that poor girl."

"Maybe you can help me."

"Stop your moaning now. Go to the front of the house and let me do my business. Watch the *Wheel* or something."

I do as she says and I try to watch TV. Just as Vanna is about to turn the third vowel, the toilet flushes and I can hear the water running in the sink. Miss Etta finally comes out. She's wearing striped tube socks and this ratty pink housecoat that she's got fastened with a diaper pin. She slumps across the house with her terrycloth slippers slapping the wood floor.

"The Lord, He got a plan." Miss Etta sits herself on her red couch. "And if you ain't going to follow it, maybe somebody else will."

"Then Sarah Jane is the one who's supposed to bring Ryan down."

"Now you don't listen, now do you? I ain't never said nothing about Sarah Jane or that boy. I'm talking about you. You supposed to be watching after that big-boned, red-headed boy."

"What about Ryan?"

"What about him?"

"Is there a plan?"

"The plan be for you to stop crawling up inside people and taking them over. That's the plan."

"Look, I won't go near Sarah Jane again. Promise."

"That girl got a good heart. That's why God blessed her with the bleeding, but she ain't got good sense."

"Wait a second. I'm little confused. Is that why I couldn't take her over?"

"Ain't nothing to confuse yourself with, baby. You watch after that Tucker boy. You leave Ryan and Sarah Jane alone. God, He gonna take care of everything."

"Like He took care of me?"

"I don't talk to no blaspheming spirits. You keep your sassing about the Lord to yourself." Her eyes get all fiery and liquid. "You got a much longer row to hoe, baby, with all that hate you be carrying around with you."

"Look, I just want to do whatever it is I'm supposed to do so I can get out of here. Okay?"

"And you expect me to tell you exactly what that is, don't you?"

"Yeah, what's wrong with that?"

"Don't work like that," she laughs. "Shoo, wish it did, but it don't."

"Why are you doing this to me?"

"All I can say is forgive, baby, you got to forgive."

At about nine o'clock Sunday morning, a pimply high school kid pulls up in a white Ford Festiva and parks in front of the mighty red brick Xi Omega house. The magnetic sign on the Festiva's door says DAYLIGHT DONUTS in big pink letters. The pimply dude puts on a name tag that reads "Ricky," checks his look in his rearview, and then does a couple of blasts of Binaca.

Ricky steps out of the little egg of a car and walks around to open the hatchback. He pulls out white and pink boxes, one after the other. He stacks them high in his arms and staggers up the walkway to the Xi-Os' front door.

At the big green door, he bends to ring the doorbell with his elbow. The boxes sway and the top one slides off and falls open to the ground. A couple of chocolate doughnuts hit the pavement. Ricky sets the leaning tower of doughnuts down and picks up the fallen ones. He shrugs his shoulders,

He carefully lines the dirty chocolate ones back in the box, closes the lid, and replaces it on the top of the stack.

Ricky rings again and before he can ring a third time, the door swings open.

"Hi, can I help you?" Krista peeks her face from behind the door. She's hiding because she's still wearing her nightshirt with no bra.

"Oh yeah, sure, I am Ricky and I have doughnuts for, for . . ."

He puts the boxes down on the ground.

"Just one second."

He holds the top of the boxes with one hand and pulls a wadded piece of paper out of his pocket with the other.

"These are for Sarah Jane Bradford."

"Ah, how nice. Bring them in." Krista opens the door wider and steps out of the way.

"Just put them right there." She points to this antique-looking cherrywood thing in the foyer.

Ricky smiles and his eyes immediately dart to Krista's hard nipples. She looks down and crosses her arms. Ricky carries the boxes in two at a time so he that he can maximize his nipple staring.

"Who are they from?" Krista asks.

"Uh, they're from, uh, wait, I got a card here somewhere." Ricky pulls an envelope out of his back pocket and hands it to her.

She opens it and reads. The letter is written in this very controlled, happy—almost architectural—handwriting and it says:

Dear Sarah Jane and the Sisters of Xi Omega,

Please accept these donuts as a token of our sincerest apologies. What occurred this past Friday night was not typical of the conduct that Gamma Chi promotes or condones. The offending members have been disciplined. One in particular was even deactivated. We are sorry if you experienced anything less than a good time at our mixer.

Again, sorry for any misunderstandings. Please enjoy this breakfast on us.

Xi Omega is one of the best, if not the best sorority, on the LSU campus and we hope to continue our good relationship with your organization. The men of Gamma Chi stand for the honor of the Golden Cross & Chalice and its highest ideals. We are perpetually at your service.

Sincerely,
Ryan Hutchins
Gamma Chi President

"How nice. That Ryan Hutchins is such a sweetie." Krista slips her hand into a box, pulls out a glazed donut and takes a bite. "Mmm, they're still warm."

"Tee-up?" Ricky holds out his hand and smiles.

"What?"

"Do I get a tee-up?"

"Omigod, are you like asking me for a tip?"

Ricky pulls back his hand.

"I am so sure. You don't ask for a tip." Krista lowers her bedhead and her ponytail falls forward.

"But what about my tee-up?"

She pushes a confused Ricky out the door, slams it, and fastens all four dead bolts.

"I am so sure. Asking me for a tip. Whatever." She chomps on the doughnut and wipes the white crusty icing from her face.

Ryan is back from his morning run around the Campus Lakes and he's getting ready to take a shower. He grabs the decorated bucket full of bath shit that Sarah Jane and Ashley left on his doorstep the other night.

He examines the shampoo and nods his head. "Pretty good shit."

The brand meets Ryan's stringent approval. It's that expensive shit girls buy from their hairdressers. He takes the toothpaste, razors, shaving cream, and deodorant out of the bucket and puts it in his medicine cabinet. He takes the shampoo and conditioner with him to the shower and dumps the hand-painted bucket in the hallway garbage can.

Who he thinks left that little gift for him, I don't know. As conceited as Ryan is, he probably thinks it's some secret admirer. For whatever vain-ass reason, he's falling for Sarah Jane's little Trojan horse.

After about fifteen minutes in the shower, Ryan emerges from the steam with his towel around his waist and his hair still intact. He drips back to his room and starts getting dressed. He takes his towel and dries his hair. As he rubs it all over his head, his hair goes flying like someone's tossing a salad.

"Huh?"

Clumps of Ryan's brown-gold hair are everywhere—on his shoulders, stuck to his back, and on the floor. He pulls at his hair and a few more strands come out. He looks at them in his hand.

He runs to the mirror; he sees his hair missing in big patches with pink chemical burns on his scalp. I think he's about to cry.

"Sarah-fucking-Jane."

"Sarah Jane, are you sure you don't want one?" This little hotty with blond hair pulls a doughnut out of the box and holds it up.

"No thank you. I'm not hungry." Sarah Jane replies.

"Well, I think it is so sweet that Ryan Hutchins sent us these yummy doughnuts. He is so cute." Krista takes a bite of her fifth chocolate doughnut.

"He just sent these doughnuts because he had to." Sarah Jane sighs.

"He's probably scared you're going to sue them after that guy mooned you and made you hit your head." The good-looking blonde pats Sarah Jane on the shoulder.

"I didn't hit my head."

"Whatever. You were bleeding all over the place," Krista scoffs.

"I didn't hit my head."

"I told you we should have taken you to the emergency room." Krista gets up to get another doughnut. "You probably have like a concussion or something. But you were so hilarious last night, yelling at that guy about Jesus and stuff. He like totally backed off. And then that bump on your head started bleeding and that like freaked everybody out. Like Carrie or something."

Krista opens the last full doughnut box and pulls out an envelope taped to the inside.

"Hey, what's this?" Krista opens the grease-stained envelope and pulls out a Polaroid. "Oh. My. God!" she screams.

"What is it?" This black-headed chick grabs the picture from Krista's shaking hands.

"Omigod! Stop eating! Stop eating the doughnuts!" The black-headed girl yells.

Then she and Krista run around the room grabbing the doughnuts out of everyone's hands.

"Spit it out! Spit it out!"

"Why? What's the matter with them?" the good-looking blonde asks.

The black-headed chick hands her the Polaroid.

"Omigod! They're wearing them on their thingies! Awww!" She covers her mouth. "I'm going to be sick!"

The entire room clears in a panic; all the girls race for the upstairs bathrooms. You can hear them all gagging and choking as they make themselves puke.

Sarah Jane just sits on the couch and prays for her sisters. She rewraps the Ace bandage around her hand and prays that she will quit bleeding soon and that Ryan will somehow be stopped.

Twelve

ucker makes his way through all the folks yucking it up in the middle of the quad. The quadrangle is the heart of the campus, the center of LSU's Italian Renaissance buildings. It's full of arched walkways, crawling oaks, palm trees, and azalea bushes. Everybody stands around with their backpacks slung over their shoulders, talking and cutting up. When I was alive, I used to call this kind of bullshitting "quadrilizing."

The big talk in the quad today is Gamma Chi's doughnut-on-the-dicks story. And to top it off, the Gamma Chis are all wearing new party shirts emblazoned with two doughnut holes at the bottom of a longjohn. This is the stuff that campus legends are made of. All the sorority girls—that is, all the sorority girls except the Xi-Os—are pointing and laughing. Despite any retribution Xi Omega or the university might try to seek, Gamma Chi has just gone down in LSU Greek history as being one of the ballsiest fraternities ever. Pun intended.

Tucker cuts through all the commotion to his geology class, just outside the quad to Howe-Russell. Maggie walks up behind him and tugs on his backpack.

"Hey, Tucker."

He turns around.

"Uh, hey, Maggie."

"Nice shirt, Tucker."

"Thanks."

"Did you help out with all that?" Maggie toys with him like a kitten boxing a ball of yarn.

"Yeah, just about everybody did."

"You boys are so bad. I keep telling Ryan, y'all are going to get kicked off of campus."

"Ah, that'll never happen." He grins.

"Well, just do me a favor." Maggie wets her lips and looks away.

"What?"

"Just let me know when you send doughnuts to the Tri-Phi house."

She pats Tucker on the shoulder and laughs. Tucker's red head bounces up and down as he tries to laugh without looking like a goose.

"So Tucker, are you heading over to geology?"

"Yeah, we've got a test in two days."

"Omigod, I know, and I've only been twice all semester. Ryan is going to kill me. He was counting on my notes."

"You can borrow mine."

"Really? That is so sweet of you, Tucker."

"Yeah, I can just go to Kinko's and make you copies."

"Oh Tucker, you are just the sweetest. Do you want to maybe come over tomorrow and study? I'll order pizza or something since you're helping me."

"Sure. Yeah. Great." Tucker bobs his head.

"Super. Let's shoot for around five-ish?"

"Is Ryan going to be there?" Tucker wrinkles up his forehead.

"Oh, don't worry about Ryan. He's not mad at you anymore." Maggie gives Tucker quick little pats on the back.

"I was, uh, just wondering if I should make him a copy or something."

"Are you kidding? Ryan isn't studying. He's going to look off me during the test." Maggie winks at Tucker and smiles. "Call me. I'm in the Greek Directory." Maggie walks off in the other direction.

"Hey, where are you going? What about class?"

"Got a nail appointment, silly boy. Take good notes for me!" She blows him a kiss and waves.

Tucker smiles and tries to keep the butterflies from flying out of his mouth.

Now, due to Ryan's little hair-loss problem, he's not in the quad to shine in all his doughnut glory. Nope, instead he's sitting up in the Student Union barber shop. He's got on a ratty old LSU baseball cap and he's hiding behind the sports page of the Baton Rouge *Advocate.*

"Ryan," the old black barber croaks.

Ryan tosses the paper on the cracked vinyl seat next to him and walks up to the barber chair. He plops down in it, all pissed off like. The barber spins him around pumps the chair up higher.

The old man shakes the red barber cape. He looks like some kind of arthritic bullfighter the way he waves that cape around. His knotted black hands shake a little, but he manages to fasten the cape around Ryan's thick neck.

"Now, what can I do for you today?" The barber smiles.

"I need you to shave it all off." Ryan doesn't smile.

"So?" The wrinkles rise and then fall around the old man's yellow eyes.

"So what? I want you to shave my head. Is that too hard for you to understand?"

"Well, some folk say I'm a pretty decent barber. But I can't cut your hair through that hat."

Ryan pulls the hat off his head, revealing these blond wisps and a patchy, red scalp.

"Sweet Jesus." The barber sucks on his dentures and shakes his head. "Boy, you got the impetigo or fungus or something. I ain't touching your head."

"What?" Ryan looks up at the old man and tries not to snarl. "Look, it's a joke. They did this joke on me and . . ."

"Now, you look—joke or no joke—you need to take it to a doctor or shave your head yourself. Me and the health department, we don't do jokes." The barber snatches the red cape off of Ryan and points his finger at the door.

Ryan, like he always does in public, holds in his acid and bile, letting it boil inside him while he smiles the whitest of smiles. He puts on his dirty baseball cap and politely walks from the barber-shop back to the Gamma Chi house.

I follow Ryan like one of those plastic black kites with blood-shot cartoon eyes, dive-bombing his head. It's like there's this string that attaches me to him and the more I hate him, the stronger and shorter that string gets. I think drifting around in limbo-land is driving me crazy. Or maybe it's just Ryan driving me crazy. Whatever it is, there's something mean, something horrible stirring up inside of me. And I'll tell you what—I'm starting to wel-come it. And that scares me. So I try to think about Jesus or Vaca-tion Bible School or the Easter Bunny, something happy and nice so that string will lengthen and let me away from Ryan.

I keep thinking happy thoughts and I float one way while Ryan walks the other. It's real hard not to hate him, especially when my body's buried up in Shreveport along with my future, but I just keep thinking my happy thoughts. I think about the time I was five or six, and Shannon and I were looking for those plastic Easter eggs in my parents' backyard. We started fighting over jellybeans and malted milk balls. It's a good memory. Innocent. And it's good enough that I float far away up into the sky, but I can't seem to go too far; my anger tethers me to Baton Rouge.

You'd be pissed off too if all you had were memories of some half-ass life. I miss being alive. I especially miss the physical part of it—a beating heart, a blinking eye, a hard-on. Having a body felt in a way you never know after you're dead. I know a lot of religious folk talk about how it's all about the soul and that the flesh doesn't really matter. But you know what? The grass is always greener when you're on the other side. I'd do anything right now for the chance to eat a big, thick, juicy steak or make sweet love to a pretty girl. Hell, at this stage in the game, I'd settle for a Happy Meal and a hand job.

Up here in the sky, it's peaceful. It's how I thought heaven would be when I was a little kid. Everything down below looks like a train set with little broccoli-looking trees and Matchbox cars. And as the sun sets, the clouds up here look like giant swirls of cotton candy. The only difference is that I thought I would be an angel when I died. I thought I would be all blissed-out and shit, playing a harp like Yosemite Sam after he gets blown to kingdom come.

Instead I feel all fucked up and all I'm carrying is this blood-soaked grudge; it makes me feel heavy and sick. But after all I've seen, I think forgiveness is beyond me. Ryan has got to be taken out. I'm not saying I'm not going to take care of Tucker like Miss Etta said, but who says you can't kill two birds with one stone. And if God's got a problem with that, I'll have to remind Him that He's the one who started this whole eye-for-an-eye-tooth-for-a-tooth bullshit in the first place. I believe that there is a time to kill, and Ryan's alarm clock has been going off in my head since I died. It's time to stop hitting the snooze button. It's time to take a stand and put his evil ass away. No more pussying around. I aim to kill Ryan Hutchins and I aim to make it good.

And just as I say this, that invisible string tugs at my very core. It starts to pull me down, but instead of fighting it, I descend. I rocket back to the earth like a meteor. I burn bright like a falling star. I crash back into the Gamma Chi house. Back to Ryan's room where he's doing a line of coke with Couvillion. They're both as bald as cue balls. Those two assholes have shaved their heads.

"Now that's what I call some brotherhood." Couvillion looks at himself in one of Ryan's mirrors and runs his hand over his shiny head. Ryan is busy sucking the rest of the coke up his nose.

"See, Ryan, we look tough."

Ryan looks at himself in the mirror, shakes his head, and snarls.

"Hey bruh, I'm telling you, it will freak that Bible-bitch's shit when she sees the whole chapter like this."

Ryan tightens his lips and scratches his palms hard like they're itching something terrible; he tears into them.

"Look, man. I'm really booming. I've got to go do something.

Talk to somebody. Fuck something. I don't know." Couvillion's face is all red and splotchy. His eyes tick. "We can set up a time for the chapter to shave their heads after I come down a little." Couvillion gives Ryan the secret handshake. He jerks his hand back with Ryan's sticky blood all over his hand.

Ryan has scratched through the skin on his own palm.

"A little too much coke, dude."

Couvillion pats Ryan on the head like one of the Three Stooges. "Nuck, nuck, nuck, nuck."

Ryan rears back and slugs him hard and fast on the arm.

"Ouch."

Ryan just stands there breathing hard.

"Come on, bee-atch." Couvillion smiles and puts up his dukes. "Come on. You want a piece of me, huh, you want a piece? Come on."

Couvillion thumb-scratches his nose while keeping his fists over his mouth and chin.

"I'm not playing." Ryan lowers his eyes.

Couvillion dances around and shadowboxes Ryan.

"I said I'm not playing!" Ryan lunges at Couvillion's neck with his bloody hand and pins him to the wall, choking him.

"Hey!" Couvillion gasps, "Can't breathe!"

Ryan's eyes get big, blue, and murderous—and he squeezes Couvillion's neck. Couvillion pushes hard with his forearms against Ryan, but can't break his coked-up grip. Ryan looks Couvillion dead in the eyes and right when Couvillion turns purple and his veins are about to pop, he lets go. Couvillion slides down the wall sucking in as much air as he can choke into his lungs. Ryan's bloody fingerprints are smeared all over his neck, and Couvillion crawls out of Ryan's room.

"You asshole, man. I was just messing around."

"Well, I wasn't." Ryan slams the door as Couvillion sits in the hall and tries to catch his breath.

Ryan goes to his closet, pulls out his gun, and starts to rub his bloody hand all over it.

"Psycho!"

* * *

It's been almost two weeks since Sarah Jane started her stigmata. She hasn't eaten or slept since. She stays in bed and reads the Bible and prays constantly. Over in the corner of Sarah Jane's room, I witness the most bizarre thing. There are two angels, a man angel and woman angel—real angels, the big kind you see in Catholic churches with white wings. They're arguing in some language that I don't understand, sounds like Spanish or something. I walk over to them, but they're so busy bitching at each other, they don't pay any attention to me.

"Hey, excuse me." I touch the wing of the girl angel.

They both look at me with big godly eyes. And then the lady angel knocks the guy angel upside the head and starts yelling some more. He grabs her angry ass and they fly off into nowhere. It was beautiful. The most beautiful thing I've seen since I've been dead.

"What do you want?" Sarah Jane rolls her eyes.

"What? You can see me?"

"Obviously . . . Now would you please leave? Disincarnate souls are not allowed in my room. That deviltry is best left up to that voodoo cook of yours."

"How do you know I talk to her?"

"I'm chosen. God has chosen me." She shows me her bandaged palms.

"For what?"

"To spread His Gospel. To convict the wicked and free the meek." She looks up to heaven and smiles like she's stoned.

"Of course. What was I thinking?"

"That's why you're still here." Sarah Jane sighs.

"Huh?"

"You're a smart-ass unto the Lord, basically. You have no reverence. No repentance."

"Saints aren't supposed to cuss."

"Ass? It's in the Bible. You should read it sometime. Oh, that's right, you can't. You're dead." Sarah Jane cocks her head and glares at me.

"I didn't come here to argue. I came to make sure you're okay. You and Ashley. Ryan's got your number. You know that, don't you?"

"Ryan can't hurt me. I've been sent to humble him before Jesus and then save his soul."

"You're kidding me."

"That's how God works. We're all sinners. He loves us all." She hugs herself and twists side to side.

"I so don't need this right now." I jump up and out of her room onto the Xi Omega house's rooftop.

The night sky is everywhere. Stars are shaking while the crickets and locusts buzz. Looking up at that black perfection of a sky, I wonder what the angels told Sarah Jane. You know, it's just my luck. I haven't talked to anyone except Miss Etta for going on a year now and the first person I get to talk to is kooky-ass Sarah Jane. She probably won't even tell Ashley I stopped by to see her. She was always pulling stuff like that when I was alive. She never gave Ashley my messages when they roomed together.

And what's with her trying to save Ryan's soul? Why didn't somebody do that before he saw fit to kill me? I mean, I finally get up the gumption to off Ryan and Sarah Jane's setting about to save him. And it looks like she's got God on her side to boot. But I don't care. I'll be damned if Sarah Jane is going to save Ryan's soul before I get ahold of him. I want him good and unforgiven when I take him out.

Hell, it's only fair.

Thirteen

A lex sits in Tucker's dorm room, just inches away from the TV, with Maxwell Bonecaze and they play *Grand Theft Auto* on the PlayStation. Meanwhile, Big Tucker crouches over his tiny desk and puts together the copies of his geology notes for Maggie.

Alex holds his game pad over his head with his fist.

"Haaaaawwwwh!" He makes that fake crowd-roar noise by cupping his hands over his mouth.

"That's enough for me. I hate this game anywuh." Being hearing impaired, sometimes Maxwell gets lazy with his speech.

"Whatever, dolphin-boy. I just schooled you." Alex smirks.

"What did you just say?"

"I said I just schooled your deaf ass. What'sa matter? You hard of hearing?" Alex cracks himself up and elbows Maxwell in the ribs.

Maxwell doesn't budge or laugh.

"You're real funny, fwat boy. Real funny." Maxwell throws down his game pad, walks out of the room, and slams the door. "Your fwiend is real funny, Gwaham!"

"Jeez, some people are jus' so thensitive." Alex flings his hands around.

Tucker staples Maggie's notes together.

"That was a real dick thing to do, Alex."

"Hey, I was just kidding with him. I mean it's not like nobody knows he's deaf. I'm just trying to help him so he doesn't talk like that in front of girls."

"That was cruel." Tucker shakes his head.

"I was just joking."

"Jokes are funny. That wasn't."

"What's your problem?" Alex starts up the solo game.

"You being a dick is my problem."

"Whatever, dude. He's just a GDI." Alex keeps pretending he's some car thief, pushing those thumb buttons like his sorry life depends on it.

"When Maxwell gets back, you're going to apologize."

"So are you nervous about tonight?" Alex taps on that game pad faster and faster.

"I'm serious. When he comes back to the room, you're going to say you're sorry."

"Or what?"

"Or, I'll have to hurt you."

Alex and Tucker drive up to the Gamma Chi house in Tucker's Mustang. Like the rest of their pledge brothers, they have each brought with them a two-by-four wooden beam and a burlap sack full of stuff that the active chapter has demanded: a four-pack of sixty-watt light bulbs, a brand-new buck knife, matches, Ivory soap carved into a cross, rubbing alcohol, shaving cream, a new Bic razor, Daisy air gun pellets and BBs, three red bricks, and a Gideon Bible. They lug their heavy sacks over their shoulders and wrestle their two-by-fours up to the house. McCallahan is standing at the front door and pushes them inside.

"Come on. You're late. Hurry up."

The curtains are drawn throughout the Gamma Chi house and all the lights are shut off too. As the pledges arrive, the actives hold candles and lead them into my library. The actives seat them at the big shiny tables my mamma picked out. At each table, a single white candle flickers.

"Keep your heads down, eyes shut!" McCallahan shouts.

The house is still and quiet. The only noise besides the occasional whisper of an active is the faintest hint of a song coming from the chapter room. It's Guns N' Roses' "Welcome to the Jungle," playing again and again, very softly. It's not long before the air in my library stinks, smelling like bad breath and farts from all the scared pledges who are all worried about what the burlap sack is for. I remember being particularly nervous about the light bulbs.

Time just hangs in the room. All the pledges' necks and heads are sore from being bowed. Each flicker of the candle seems like an hour. They're sitting in there for almost two hours before McCallahan comes into the library.

"Okay, you can stand in place. Keep your shit in hand. Don't let go of it. No matter what."

The thirty pledges stand. Alex opens his eyes and stretches his neck.

"Alex! Did I tell you to open your eyes?" McCallahan barks.

"Uh, no. I mean sorry." Alex immediately drops his head back down and shuts his eyes.

Couvillion walks in carrying a candle; the light shines and dances on his shiny bald head.

"Okay, you pukes can look up and open your eyes."

Alex tries not to notice Couvillion, but his eyes are drawn to the active's shaved head.

Couvillion catches Alex looking at him and walks over. "You staring at my head?" Couvillion pushes Alex. "Huh, you little bitch? You trying to make fun of me?"

"No, sir." Alex looks straight ahead. He's trembling and about to cry.

"Sit down!"

Alex drops back into his chair. Couvillion pulls out this big-ass pair of scissors from his back pocket and holds the open blades to Alex's neck.

"Didn't your mamma and daddy teach you not to make fun of folks, Alex?"

A tear runs down Alex's cheek, and he keeps his head turned so that Couvillion's sharp blades won't slice his neck. Couvillion pulls a handful of Alex's dark hair and yanks his head around. Couvillion then grabs another chunk of Alex's hair and chops away. Alex just goes limp, letting that bastard hack away at his hair. When Couvillion is through, there are little black haystacks all over the place. Alex is totally scalped with long hairs in the front and bald patches all over. He tries his hardest not to cry, but he's not having much luck.

Couvillion reaches down into Alex's burlap sack and pulls out the Bic razor.

"Get Tucker to shave the rest of it for you." Couvillion swats Tucker upside the head.

"Okay, you pukes! Your pledge brother is just about to get his head shaved. I think it's only fair for the rest of y'all to do the same. Get your Bics out and get to work. And when you can't get laid because you ain't got no hair, you can blame your titty baby pledge brother." Couvillion stabs the table with the scissors, leaving them stuck standing in the wood. He grabs a candle, and slams the door behind him.

"I'll go get y'all some water," McCallahan whispers almost apologetically as he slips out of the room.

Since they only have one pair of scissors, Clay Weaver, the pledge class president, cuts everybody's hair as close as he can get it. Then they all take turns shaving each other's heads. Tucker refuses to shave Alex's head, so Clay Weaver does it instead. A few real suck-up pledges try to get started before McCallahan even comes back with the shaving cream and bowls of hot water. They get horrible razor burn and cuts, but for the most part the entire pledge class's heads turn out all shiny and white—like hard-boiled eggs. That is, except for Tucker Graham and Tony Audoin.

"I ain't shaving my head." Tony runs his fingers through his long and wavy hair. Alex walks toward Tucker with the scissors and a razor. Tucker shakes his head and lowers his eyes at him.

"Come on, Tucker. You have to shave it off," Alex pleads. "It's not that bad if we all do it."

"Nope." Tucker sits there bigger than Buddha and just as quiet.

"You have to. Couvillion said!" Clay pops off like he's an active or something.

"Look, ain't nobody shaving my head, bruh. They can ball me. They can do whateva. I don't go that way. Okay?" Tony smacks his gum like the New Orleans West Banker that he is. "Ain't that right, Tucker?"

"Fine. Tell that to Couvillion, then. You're just screwing yourself, dude." Clay throws the plastic razor at Tony and sits back down. The rest of the pledges roll their eyes and sneer at the two.

"Tucker, shave your head, you fat bastard. You're going to get us all in trouble!" Roger Moody, this suck-ass pledge from Shreveport, yells out.

"Yeah, Tony, stop being such a stupid yat, and shave your goddamn head!" another pledge brother shouts.

Tucker doesn't care what they say, and neither does Tony, really. For one, Tucker's got this big purple birthmark all over his scalp and he figures he's ugly enough as it is. Tony's got just the opposite problem. He's thinks he's far too much of a stallion to shave his head. The boy gets laid more than concrete and he's not about to screw that up by being some bald-ass freaker. So like real men often do, Tucker and Tony take a stand.

"Why aren't they shaving their heads? They're going to get us all in trouble," some little coward whispers.

Well, of course, the actives are pissed that Tucker and Tony won't shave their heads. They rant and rave like the world's going to come to an end. But the only actives at the house are Kimbrough, who's really too stoned to care; McCallahan, who's probably scared of Tucker anyway; and Sam Blanco, who's only five-six and far too little to do anything about it. The rest of the chapter is already out in the woods getting ready for the evening's festivities. So they decide to let Ryan take care of Tucker and Tony once they get there.

"All right, you pukes! Drop your pants and take off your underwear!" Blanco yells at all the pledges. They look at each other in disbelief.

"Now! Ladies! Now!" Blanco shouts so hard his tiny face turns red and the veins in his little neck squirm like worms.

They do as the little Napoleon says. They remove their underwear and stand there, praying to God that the little power-hungry bastard doesn't make them do the elephant walk or something.

"Okay, dump everything out of your bags. And put your buck knives on the table."

Alex goes pale. Hell, they're all nervous. Even Tucker. Especially Tucker, because he's already had a taste of the Gamma Chi wrath. Besides, standing there with your dick hanging out and playing with buck knives is bound to make anybody a little uptight.

"Now, give your underwear to your pledge brother next to you. Then take your knife and cut holes in your bag for your legs so you can put it on."

They all tug and pull at the burlap with their knives, but they manage to get those scratchy bags cut into makeshift underwear.

"Go ahead, pull your pants up! That's right, button'um up, boys!" Blanco shouts.

While a few guys struggle with the zippers on their jeans, Mc-Callahan walks around and collects all the buck knives. Kimbrough takes a garbage bag and picks up everything else. That is, everything except for the underwear. Then Blanco and McCallahan take black blindfolds and tie them around all the pledges' heads.

"Okay, say 'ah.'" Blanco takes Clay Weaver's boxers, wads them up, and shoves them in Alex's mouth. "Clay, I hope you were wearing clean undies. Or should I say Alex hopes you were."

McCallahan follows Blanco around with a roll of duct tape and wraps it around the pledges' mouths and heads to keep everyone from spitting out their brother's underwear.

After the blindfolds are in place, the three actives walk the pledges out back to three flatbed pickup trucks and make them all cram in. Used to be they'd tie you up. That's what they did with me and my pledge class, but I think they found it was way more humiliating to gag you with ass-dirty underwear and let you walk to the trucks.

It's not long before the truckloads of pledges are out in the middle of nowhere in the woods. They run the blindfolded pledges through the forest in a single-file line with their arms on each other's shoulders. The actives yell and cuss them and kick their legs out from under them every few feet. Hell, it's hard enough running like that with a blindfold—imagine choking on somebody's skid-marked grippies while you do it. They should all just quit. I know they're all thinking about it, but none of them has the courage to do it. Not even big Tucker.

Once the actives have the pledges choking and gagging and totally disoriented, they line them up into neat little rows and they rip the duct-taped gags off their faces. The pledges spit the butt-nasty underwear out of their mouths and gasp for air. They're sputtering and spitting. Most are hyperventilating; a few even vomit.

The actives scramble to get the fifteen-foot wooden cross lit. Sam Blanco douses the rag-covered cross with gasoline one last time, then lights a match, throws it, and carries his Tiny Tim ass away from it. Once it gets going good and mean, Ryan gives the command and an active stands behind each pledge and jerks the blindfolds from their eyes.

"Behold! The Fiery Cross of Gamma Chi!" Ryan reads from this palm-size book as he stands behind a velvet altar. McCallahan holds a flashlight over his shoulder. "The omen revealed first to the mighty Emperor of Rome before battle is now revealed to only the Worthy." Ryan's got his cult leader hood on—the black one that he wears for special occasions just like this.

"Neophytes! The men of Gamma Chi ask if you are worthy. Are you worthy?"

"Worthyworthyworthyworthyworthy!" the actives chant, clicking their fingers as loud as a plague of locusts.

"I, the Worthy Chalice Keeper, charge you, the pledges of Gamma Chi, to take a solemn blood oath before our Father, the Lord Almighty, and the Holy Brotherhood of Gamma Chi, that from this moment forward you will never speak or transcribe the sacred rites that you are about to witness."

An arm of the fiery cross breaks off and falls to the ground. It's popping and burning something fierce. Little bitty cinders fly all over the place in a swarm of lightning bugs and smoke.

"Respond nay if you are willing to betray the sacred, or if you are worthy, repeat after me: This blood that I spill is my own."

Everyone repeats like robots and they all wince at the sting of a cold blade. The actives stand behind each pledge with buck knives, cutting a small cross into the base of their skulls. Blood drips all down their necks; it goes everywhere.

"And with this blood, I am washed free of my sins and will sin no more. I will seek to be Worthy, and I pledge before God never to betray the favor of the Worthy, and if I do break this covenant, may I walk in the Valley of the Shadow of Death with no one to call me brother."

"Worthy! Worthy! Worthy! Amen!" the actives and Ryan shout together.

Now this is the pledges' first glimpse into the secret world. Tonight is all about becoming a real pledge. It's about making a promise, a blood promise, and allowing the initiated to break you down and build you back up as their brother. Tonight, the uninitiated make a pledge to be worthy, and that means keeping your mouth shut when the hoods go on and the lights go out. And this lesson is taught the only way it can be—with knives, bruises, and fire. Tonight's oath means doing what you're told and not questioning it. It means having the faith of a blind man and trusting your brother, even if he's Cain and you're Abel.

The actives separate the pledges into groups according to how well the pledges have done thus far. The pledges who the actives like, the ones who are cool but not too cool, are taken away and their hazing will be minimal, a few push-ups and a shot or two of Everclear. They'll be back home within the hour. However, the farther you get down the list, the less popular the pledges get, and the worse the night gets. Tucker and Tony are at the bottom. Dead last. Tucker for being so big and dumb and beating up Ryan, and now Tony for not shaving his head.

You know, Tony's just stupid for not shaving his head. He was at the top of the pledge list tonight. The actives really liked him a lot, but by refusing to shave his head, he's fallen to Tucker Graham's level. And that's a dangerous thing. And what's with Tucker? He knows how bad things can get. I can't believe he has the balls to call more attention to himself. I think the problem with him is that he's brave enough to face whatever they can dish out, but he's too stupid to realize that he doesn't have to. But then again, who am I to be casting stones; I stuck around long enough for Ryan to kill me.

Tucker and Tony are the last two to be taken away from the burning cross. Couvillion and Ryan are the actives in charge of whipping them into shape tonight. Ryan's got a pellet gun crammed down the front of his pants, and Couvillion's holding a sack full of fireworks in a brown paper bag. He's also French kissing a bottle of Jack Daniel's like it's his girlfriend, or in Couvillion's case, his sister.

Ryan has put his robe up and is now outfitted in camouflage. Couvillion is dressed in black and has on this Eminem-looking black ski hat.

"Put your blindfold back on!" Couvillion hands both of them their black blindfolds.

Ryan takes the bottle of whiskey from Couvillion and takes a couple of nips. He breathes all in Tucker's face while checking to make sure the blindfold is in place.

"Hey Tucker. You hanging in there?"

"Yeah."

"Maggie told me you took some real good notes for geology. Thanks."

"Uh, sure, no problem."

"Look." Ryan puts his hand on Tucker's shoulder and sort of rubs it. "I'll do what I can so you don't get it too bad. I mean, you've already paid your dues with me. But you not shaving your head, man. I don't know what I can do about that . . . I mean you got some balls, man. I'm telling you. I personally respect the shit out of you for it, but you might get some shit for it. Just be ready. Okay?" Ryan pats Tucker on the shoulder. "Here, take a little sip. You're going to need it. Trust me."

Tucker takes a chug or two of the Jack Daniel's and then holds it out to where he thinks Ryan is standing.

"Go ahead, take another one." Ryan pushes the bottle back at him; Tucker takes another swig.

"What was that? That wasn't even a sip. Drink up, Tucker. Trust me, you don't want to be sober tonight."

Tucker takes the bottle and puts it full tilt to his mouth.

"Now that's more like it!" Ryan slaps Tucker on the back. "Take one more like that for good measure." Tucker takes another swig from the bottle and Ryan takes one right after him.

"Tucker." Ryan holds the bottle close to his heart and puts his arm around Tucker. "After tonight, we're going to let bygones be bygones. So hang in there. Okay, bruh?" Ryan holds the whiskey up to Tucker's mouth. "Here, take another."

Tucker reluctantly takes another sip.

"That's my boy." Ryan tousles Tucker's hair. "Here, hold this." He hands Tucker the bottle and walks over to Couvillion.

A blindfolded Tony Audoin keeps scratching his crotch and pulling his pants away from himself.

"What'sa matter, Tony? Burlap getting to you?" Ryan asks while he lights his cigarette off of Couvillion's.

"Yeah, man. This shit hurts." Tony reaches into his pants and scratches.

"Are you complaining?" Couvillion rushes Tony and throws him down in the wet dirt.

Tony crawls around, and Couvillion kicks him in the side, not real hard, but hard enough to knock Tony off his balance and face first into the pine needles and mud.

"Come on, complain some more. Come on! I want you to tell

me how much it hurts. Complain some more, you greasy yat!" Couvillion yells.

Tony rustles around in the leaves and dirt trying to get away from Couvillion's combat boot. But every time he starts to get himself back up, Couvillion kicks him back down.

After a few well-placed punts to Tony's stomach and ribs, Couvillion finally gets tired of kicking him around and walks over to Tucker. He snatches the whiskey out of his hand.

"Give me that."

Ryan hands Couvillion his lit cigarette. Tony turns his head trying to hear what's going on as he feels for the blood on his skinned elbows. He pushes his long hair out of his face and tries to act like nothing happened.

Tucker stands by Ryan, shifting his weight from one leg to the other as the alcohol makes his head swim.

"Do you have the razors?" Ryan asks Couvillion as he walks over to Tony. He grabs Tony's long hair and puts his cigarette out behind Tony's right ear lobe.

Tony screams, but Ryan puts his hand over his mouth.

"Sh-sh-sh-sh-sh. What did Couvillion just tell you about complaining?" Ryan presses his hand tight over Tony's mouth. Couvillion hands Ryan his cigarette.

"Now let's try it one more time without all the whining." Ryan turns the left side of Tony's head to Couvillion. Ryan presses the cherry of the cigarette behind Tony's other earlobe.

Tony fights it, but Ryan has got his head in some kind of judo-looking hold and his hand over his mouth. Tears burst out of Tony's eyes, and he lets out a deep sob when Ryan lets go. He does his best to catch his breath and to suck it up.

"Okay, boys, it's shaving time." Couvillion shakes up a bottle of shaving cream and puts the tip into Tony's nostril. Couvillion presses the button and shaving cream and aerosol start coming out of Tony's nose. Tony starts spitting and coughing up the white foam. Tucker stands there blindfolded and chews on the inside of his cheek.

"You know what I think we should do?"

"What, worthy Chalice Keeper?"

"I think we should shave them like we shave actives if they get engaged." Ryan smirks.

"You mean shave them all over?" Couvillion asks.

"You got it."

Now that's about all I need to hear. So I try to push my way into Tucker Graham's mind, but he's not really drunk enough for me to take over. I get stuck halfway in and halfway out of his consciousness like I did that time with Sarah Jane.

So instead of taking over, Tucker and I become this zombie, unable to speak or move. I can't see anything now because Tucker's blindfolded, but try as I might I can't make him even twitch his pinky. I can, however, in the darkness, smell the dirty sweet smell of pot, and I can hear Ryan and Couvillion laughing.

I feel the cold barrel of a gun at my temple and Couvillion grumbles in my ear, "Take your pants off, farmer boy."

Tucker's body just stands still. The smell of pot is real strong now. Couvillion must be smoking a joint.

"Here, take a toke on this. This'll relax you." Ryan puts a doobie up to Tucker's lips. I inhale deep, hoping that the pot will help me take Tucker over better. And it does, except I feel light-headed and sluggish all at the same time. Like I'm moving around in Jell-O. Which is weird because when Tucker was stoned or drunk last time, I never really felt it.

I hear Tony fight and yell, "Please, man! Stop! I don't want to!"

Then a bright light flashes and Tucker's body starts floating off the ground with me inside it. I slowly drift up and over their heads. I take off my blindfold. I float up and hover over them like a Thanksgiving Day Parade balloon, but they don't even notice. I start laughing for no good reason, and that's when they turn around.

"Hole. Lee. Shit!" Couvillion shouts and points.

"No," Ryan whispers to himself.

I'm just hanging there in the air about six feet off the ground, and Tucker's body is glowing this weird Gatorade-green-colored light.

Tony is in the dirt with his pants around his ankles, his hands tied behind his back and half his head shaved off. Couvillion has a razor in his hand and Ryan has a pellet gun to Tony's head.

I can't speak; I can only smile and shine like a fat-ass glow worm.

"What the hell are you?" Couvillion stands there staring at me and then he begins screaming like a cheerleader.

"It's just some bad pot, man." Ryan tries to pull him away.

"Then why are we seeing the same thing?" Couvillion drops the scissors and runs into the woods.

Ryan aims the pellet gun at me and shoots. But the pellets don't come anywhere close to me. Which is weird because Ryan is a lot of things, but a lousy shot he's not. So I just float here, feeling sort of stoned. Laughter bubbles up in this body, and it echoes and shakes the forest like thunder and lightning.

Ryan follows Couvillion's trail, firing his pellet gun at me as he runs away. Tony just lies there with his head half bald and bleeding and his blindfold still on. I hang in the air for a while. I try to will myself back to the ground, but Tucker's body just sort of floats there in the air. Eventually, the green glow flickers on and off, and then just fades away. I drop from the air, landing hard on Tucker's hands and scarred-up knees. I think I might have sprained his wrist.

I stand up and brush myself. I'm in the driver's seat now. I twitch my fingers and wiggle his toes just to be sure.

Where Tucker goes when I take him over, I don't know. I am, however, sure he's in here somewhere. I'm also pretty sure this doesn't really hurt him or anything. He seems to have fared okay the last time I possessed him. And besides, I have to borrow his body to do what must be done.

I untie Tony's blindfold and hands. He doesn't say anything, not even a thank you. He just sort of stares through me. I think he checked out the moment they started talking about shaving his pubes and kicking him in the stomach. That's what I used to do when I was hazed. You just fall into yourself and hide. And then later you start to wake up and realize you got the ever-living shit beat out of you.

If I could figure out how I shimmered and floated in the air like that, I would pick up Tony and fly back to the dorm like Superman, but for all intents and purposes, I'm a normal guy again. Albeit a normal dead guy possessing a seven-foot farm boy, but I don't know how to work any special bells and whistles to make this body fly. It was probably the pot that helped me float. Who knows? At least I scared off Ryan and Couvillion.

Fourteen

T ucker's roommate Maxwell is d'man. I called him from a pay phone at this closed-down old Stuckey's on I-10 after Tony and I walked out of the woods. Maxwell picked us up and took us back to the dorm. I've got to say that if I was alive, I would have hung up the phone and gone back to sleep. Especially considering it was almost four o'clock in the morning. But Maxwell's the kind of guy who you can count on, mainly because he wants you to like him, and mainly because he's just good that way.

Back at the dorm, I start to get all anxious and shit about having Tucker's body again. I especially don't want to slip out of it by going to sleep. So as everybody else nods off, I lie awake in Tucker's bed and try to figure things out. It's going to be hard being Tucker Graham. I keep wondering if people will be able to tell. Plus, having to figure out who Tucker knows and who he doesn't is going to be tough. And then there's the whole question of school. I sure as hell don't want to study. I hated that shit when I was alive, and Tucker's got a geology test day after tomorrow. Besides, I don't have access to any of his memories. Not that that would help. The boy's dumber than dirt. But I don't think it would be right to take Tucker over and then make him flunk out of college.

I go through all of Tucker's school stuff and find his class schedule, and I resolve that while I've got custody of this big boy, I'm going to do the best I can for Tucker. It's only right. And then maybe God won't be so pissed off at me.

It's all hypothetical. I don't know why I'm even worrying about it. I've got to kill Ryan first. Then I'll deal with the wrath of God.

As soon as the morning comes, I take Tucker's body to the quad. I'm the only Gamma Chi who doesn't have his head shaved. After what Tony went through last night, he shaved the rest of his hair off himself. Guess he figured his dignity wasn't worth that much shit. All the actives shaved their heads too. It was as much an act of solidarity for Ryan as it was a legal issue. Shaving the pledges' heads is physical evidence of hazing. However, if the whole chapter did it and not just the pledges, nobody could say it was hazing. It was just something the Gamma Chis decided to do, pledges and all.

Whatever.

Ryan has always been good about staying right under the law when it comes to destroying people. He's smart that way. In fact, I could learn a thing or two from him. I mean, if I'm going to kill his sorry ass and I'm going to use Tucker's body to do it, I've got to make sure Tucker doesn't take the rap.

I meet Alex in the quad this morning. He looks like a big idiot. His scalp is white and shiny like a boiled egg, and he's got a Band-Aid over the cut on the back of his head. He's smiling. The goose is actually enjoying all the people staring at him.

"Man, Tucker, you sure are stupid." Alex points and makes this bang-bang motion with his pointer fingers at some sorority girls walking by. "Patchew! Patchew! Catchya later, ladies!"

The girls cover their mouths and whisper and laugh at his Humpty-Dumpty-looking ass.

"How so?" I ask.

"What?" He turns back to me.

"How stupid am I, Alex?"

"Tucker, do you know how many girls have rubbed my head today? Do you?"

"Fifteen."

"Yeah! How'd you know?"

"Lucky guess."

"I'm telling you, this shaved head bit is going to get me laid. Uh, I mean, laid a lot more than I have been. I'm just going to get laid more now." He folds his arms and puffs up his little pigeon boy chest.

"Hey look, you've got a big red mark on your head, man." I point at the top of his head.

"No, I don't."

I slap his shaved head.

"Well, you do now!" I bust up laughing and walk off while Alex holds his head and cusses Tucker Graham.

Alex is so easy he makes me laugh, which feels so good that I can't even begin to tell you. That tickled feeling a body gets when something strikes you funny is a feeling you never get to fully experience when you're floating around dead. I am really glad I have this body for a while. So instead of going to class, I walk around the campus, remembering what the leaves on all the plants felt like and fingering the stucco walls. And as flaky as this sounds, I like this moment—this sort of rush of being alive that just takes me over.

I'm telling you, when you've been dead it feels good just to be able to touch something. It's like Christmas morning for a dead soul. And then there's hearing words, not just people's thoughts and intentions, which is all you hear when you're dead, but to actually feel the sound, the wave in the air causing the tiny anvil inside your head to collide over and over with your eardrum. It's beautiful. Having a body is a blessing you never realize until you lose it. It feeds you in a way that you will never know until you die.

It's all too much. The tanned legs of sorority girls passing by. The mockingbirds fighting. The cell phones exploding and the cicadas screaming. I breathe in deep and smell the sweet olive. I close my eyes and feel the thick Baton Rouge air all around me. I open my eyes and all the students are slowing down and staring at me like I'm some kind of wing nut. So I flip them off.

"I'm alive! I'm so fucking alive!"

I am happy right now. I mean, Tucker Graham may be big and dumb, but he's alive and that is something to be so overjoyed about that I can't even tell you. I drop to the ground with a feeling so good that I might bust open like a some kind of supernova. I roll around in the lawn and feel its itchy cold blades and smell its green grass sweetness.

The people begin to crowd around me. I'm totally freaking everyone out.

"He's probably dropped some acid."

"Hey, isn't he a Gamma Chi?"

"Nah, he's got hair."

Life is funny. Having this body again is hilarious. It's like being stoned. Hell, possessing a real live body full of pumping blood and guts is better than being stoned.

Anyway, after I make a complete ass out of Tucker Graham, I go out to the parade grounds, this wide-open lawn with a giant flagpole in the middle. LSU used to fly this giant-ass American flag the size of a circus tent from it, but one day this doofus grabbed onto the tip of the flag, and the wind was blowing real good and it flipped his stupid ass halfway across the parade grounds and liked to break his neck. So now they just fly a regular old flag from the pole.

The parade grounds are where all the dreadlocked white girls hang out barefooted while their peace-dog boyfriends play hacky-sack and wear Rasta hats. These hippie-wannabes bring their dogs out here and play Frisbee and sit on blankets. Occasionally, you'll see a touch football game going on. It's a great place to waste the day. So I do just that. I play Frisbee with this art-freak girl named Mae for about an hour or so. I keep missing the damn Frisbee because I can't stop thinking about kissing her. I have to leave because I'm starting to catch some major wood. We're talking a pup-tent of embarrassing proportions. I'm hornier than a New Orleans funeral and, unfortunately, being Tucker Graham isn't going to help me take care of that. So I grab my backpack and hold it over my crotch as I walk to the bathroom over in the Student Union. Once inside, I splash some cold water on my face, take some deep breaths, and decide that getting some food might get my mind off of getting laid.

It's about lunchtime so I go to the Gamma Chi house to go get some of Miss Etta's fine dining. There's a steady flow of shaved heads walking down fraternity row to the Gamma Chi house. They all look at me like I kill babies. But I keep on walking. I'm hungry.

As I walk across the lawn, under the monster oak trees, Kimbrough motions to me. "Hey, Tucker, come here!"

I almost don't respond. It's hard getting used to people calling me Tucker, especially when I knew them when I was alive. I walk over to Kimbrough. He's wearing a baseball cap to cover his newly shaved head.

"What's up?" I mumble, not sure how my accent will sound coming from Tucker's farm boy mouth.

"Check it out! Do you have some balls or what?"

I just kind of grin and look down. Kimbrough leans in and smirks.

"You know what Ryan told everybody about you not shaving your head?"

"What?"

"He told them that you had 'religious reasons.' Now what's that all about?"

"I dunno. I just didn't want to shave my head, that's all."

"Yeah, I figured that, which was a real stupid thing to pull. But why is Ryan backing you up?"

"I dunno." I look around at all the pledges and actives who are glaring at me as they walk up to the house. Tucker's stomach growls at me. "What's for lunch?"

"Fried chicken, mashed potatoes." Kimbrough sort of laughs. "You really don't care, do you?"

"Care about what?"

"That they all hate you now. I mean it's not real fair, Tucker."

I look Kimbrough square in the eyes.

"Life's not fair, Kimbrough."

"I'm an active, Tucker. You need to show a little respect."

"Grow a backbone and maybe I will."

I walk off and Kimbrough stands there yelling at me, "Tucker, I don't know what gotten into you!"

I go inside and everybody stops what they're doing and stares at me.

"Asshole," one of Tucker's pledge brothers whispers behind my back.

"We should have balled him," an active mutters.

I stand in line and ignore all their posturing and sneering. I couldn't care less. My goose was cooked a long time ago. I follow the line into the dining room and walk up to the kitchen window where Miss Etta is slinging plates full of yardbird and buttery mashed potatoes.

"Praise Jesus! What have you done, boy?"

"Settle down. Just fix me a plate. I'm hungry."

She grabs the tiny gold cross around her neck, puts her left hand in the air, and she starts speaking in tongues.

"Shuma lama duma lama shuma lama duma lama."

Two tiny angels—pint-size versions of the girl and the guy angels I saw arguing up in Sarah Jane's room—appear in the service window. I grab a drumstick off my plate and take off through the back door of the chapter room. The little angels come barreling after me like a couple of fierce sparrows, but they more or less evaporate as soon as I get out of Miss Etta's sight.

I munch on the drumstick and kick pebbles all the way back to Tucker's dorm room. So much for Miss Etta. She doesn't play around when it comes to taking her advice seriously. I was expecting maybe a lecture or two about taking people over, not a full onslaught of heavenly hosts.

I stay in Tucker's dorm room studying for the geology test that he's got tomorrow. He takes real good notes, and I always liked studying about rocks and shit. My daddy always talked about geology because that's how my family found oil. So I guess I might have some aptitude for this after all.

Tucker's got Maggie's phone number and "five o'clock" scribbled down on his calendar. Tonight's the night that they set to study together. And I have to admit, I'm a little nervous. Not about Ryan being there or anything, because he won't be. You see, Wednesdays are religious for Ryan. He and Couvillion go to this titty bar just across the river in Port Alex called the Kitty Kitty Klub. It's a classy joint, dollar call brands and fifty-dollar blowjobs. Ryan hasn't missed a Wednesday afternoon at the "KKK" since he first discovered it as a freshman three years ago.

While Ryan is busy gnashing his teeth at some stripper, Maggie will have her geology book out with a handful of No-Doze washed down with a cup full of Community Coffee and that nondairy powder stuff.

I decide against calling Maggie. I don't know why. She just makes me too nervous. So at five, I just show up at her door with books and her photocopied notes in hand. I tap her doorknocker and accidentally knock off her Halloween wreath. I pick it up and look at it. It's got fake orange leaves and happy little wooden ghosts and witches all over it. Maggie answers the door just as I'm trying to hang it back up.

"Why, Tucker Graham. What are you doing?" Her hair's up in a ponytail and she's in a long white nightshirt.

"Uh, sorry. It fell."

"Oh, that's okay. Here, let me." She takes the wreath from my clumsy hands and hangs it on the nail.

She smells so good it hurts. I think I'm starting to catch a semi.

"I, uh, got you copies of my notes," I say.

"Well, you are just too sweet."

"Do you still want to study?"

"Well, Tucker, you didn't call. I wasn't really expecting company. But thanks for the notes." She gives me this pitying little smile.

"But I thought you said . . ."

"Why didn't you call?" Maggie sings to me. "I'm not really ready for company, Tucker. Look at me, I'm in my pj's."

I'm definitely catching a semi. I lower my backpack down to my crotch.

"But I thought you said five o'clock?"

"Well, I did, but that doesn't mean you're just supposed to show up unannounced."

"Oh."

"Look at you. I've hurt your feelings." Maggie tilts her head and play-frowns.

"No, you haven't. I just need to go. Here're your notes." I hand her the stack of paper and turn around all hangdog and sad as I walk away.

"Tucker. Wait."

I turn around, and Maggie's got her hand on her hip and she tucks her hair behind her ear.

"You can come in. I guess I could use some help, but next time, you call." She pulls me into her apartment and locks the door behind me.

"Put your stuff over there." She points to the dining room table. "Hold on. Let me get a tablecloth first. My roommate would kill me if you scratched that up. Pottery Barn just delivered that yesterday." Maggie disappears into the kitchen and pulls out this blue-checkered tablecloth. She shakes it out and spreads it over the shiny, butterscotch wood.

"Now, make yourself at home while I go put on some clothes."

She returns wearing a T-shirt and shorts; she sits across the table from me. We order a pizza and start to study. After about fifteen minutes or so, she reaches across the table for a book and I notice a big purple bruise on her upper arm.

"What's that?" I point to her arm.

"It's a bruise." She winks. "Ryan beats me, you know, but don't tell anybody."

"Truth comes out in jokes."

"I bruise real easy. Please."

I look her in the eyes and shake my head.

"Why are you looking at me like that?"

"Look, I know the truth about you and Ryan." I reach over and hold her hand. "You don't have to lie to me."

"What's your deal? I told you I was joking, Tucker."

"I know." I just rub her hand and give her the gentlest smile I can muster.

The silence is heavy. I want to say something else, but don't.

"Why are you doing this to me?" She starts to cry.

I stand up and walk over to her. I put my arm around her and the floodgates open.

I rub and pat her back; she cries all over me.

"He hits me, Tucker."

She collapses into a ball of shaking bones and tears. She looks so small and broken against Tucker's big shoulders. I feel pitiful for not having protected her from Ryan. I feel ashamed as she cries in my arms, like I let her down in the worst way, like for whatever reason it's my responsibility to save her, like she somehow depends on me to do something. It's like deep down she knows that someone sees what's going on and they're not stopping it. It makes me feel like shit. I mean she's getting the life beat out of her and all I can do is apologize.

"I'm sorry, Maggie." Hot tears swell up these eyes and sting as they run down Tucker's face. Maggie just curls up in my arms and sort of whimpers. My tears drop on her forehead and she looks up at me. Her eyes are swollen—pink and bright green. Her face is all wet and dewy, and she smiles at me. She sniffles and kind of wipes the snot from her upper lip.

And then out of nowhere, she gives me the softest kiss.

Where the hell did that come from? She might as well have just punched me in the nose. I'm totally stunned. She just kissed me. And before I can get Tucker's mouth to stutter out a question, she kisses me again and then again. So I kiss her back and she pulls me close and kisses me with her tongue now. We kiss for a real long time and then I kiss the tears off her face and neck and she runs her fingers through my hair.

And then before I know it, we're kissing and groping each other in her bedroom. It's pitch black. I feel a tug at my zipper and her hands fumble in my boxers. It makes my stomach feel all tight and electric. I swallow the lump in my throat and help her pull off her shirt. I suck on her tits and she slides off my boxers. I think I'm officially about to get laid.

I reach inside her panties and touch her. She smells nice, sort of like rain. I feel like a toaster oven about ready to spring, all jittery and hot. I'd almost forgotten what feeling like this was all about. Damn, Tucker has no idea how lucky he is. I hope some part of him remembers this. Because I'm sure whatever lies between Maggie's thighs is going to be sweeter than sunshine.

I kiss her all over and she pulls me with her as she lies down on her bed. She slides off her panties and we get busy. We do it real slow. She's still sort of crying. I do my best not to be rough or fast. You can't very well just tear it up and slap ass when a girl's crying. So I try to move the way I think she would want me to. With Tucker's big ass, I try to show her what love is.

And in return, though she doesn't know it, Maggie is showing me what being alive really is. With all its sorrow and pain, there's this incredible thing. It's all about being a human and taking life for what it is. And at this particular moment, it's all about enjoying the finest thing that God ever gave a man and woman. It's all about a good slow fuck in the afternoon.

After we get completely liquid, a warm, irresistible wave of sleepiness washes over me. I can't fight it. Sleep just feels too good after that kind of sex. And before I know it, I've slept my way out of Tucker's body and I'm floating over him and Maggie. It's the oddest pairing I've ever seen. Maggie is so incredibly beautiful and perfect, and, well, Tucker's not. He's overgrown and freckled like a redheaded stepchild. But there they are all curled up under her down comforters. Maggie's smiling up at Tucker's sleeping face and then she rests her head on his giant shoulders. Now I must say, I'm pretty impressed with myself. Just the fact that I can get someone like Tucker laid by a girl as hot as Maggie Meadows is nothing short of a miracle.

However, if Tucker wakes up, this miracle could turn into a disaster real fast. So I dive into him, but I bounce back. It's always like this when he's sober. I can't seem to find a crack in him to slip back into. But I try again. I push real hard this time and I feel something shatter like plates breaking and I pop up inside Tucker once again. I wake up looking through his eyes all startled and shit.

"What's the matter?" Maggie jumps up off my shoulder.

"Uh, nothing." I wipe the sweat off my forehead. "I just, uh, got that feeling you get sometimes when you feel like you're falling."

"Oh, I hate it when that happens." Maggie smoothes her fingers over my face. "But I guess we should get up anyway. We've got to study for that test tomorrow."

"No, stay here in bed with me." I cuddle up next to her.

"We have to study." Maggie pushes me away and wraps the bedsheet around herself as she gets up.

"Just blow it off and get back in bed." I pat where she was lying.

"I can't afford to blow it off and neither can you. Come on." She stands there with that white sheet on like some goddess in a toga. "Besides, Ryan is counting on me for tomorrow."

"What?"

"Ryan is counting on us for his answers tomorrow. You know that."

"You're kidding me."

"Look, I've got to study. Okay?" She walks into her bathroom and shuts the door.

I get up, grab my boxers off the floor, and walk over to the bathroom door. I can hear the water running, but I knock anyway.

"Tucker, I'm in the shower!" Maggie shouts over the rushing water.

"We need to talk! Get out!" I pound on the door.

"What?"

"I need to talk to you!"

"I'm taking a bath," she sings.

I bust into the steamy bathroom and I throw open the shower curtain.

"We need to talk. Now."

"Omigod! Get out!" Maggie tries to cover herself with her hands as I shut off the water.

"Stop it!" She slaps and slaps my hand. "What are you doing?"

"We're talking. That's what we're doing." I hand her her bathrobe. "Here."

She puts on the robe and steps out of the tub.

"Tucker, what's your problem?"

"We need to talk."

"Don't do this to me." Maggie brushes past me out of the bathroom. I follow her. She checks her face in her bedroom mirror and then looks at my reflection standing behind her. She doesn't turn around to face me, she just keeps inspecting her neck and cheeks.

"What just happened here? Why won't you talk to me about this?"

Maggie looks at a red mark on her neck and then one on her cheek.

"I'll tell you what happened. Your stubble just left red marks on my face and neck. That's what just happened."

"So?"

Maggie turns around all pissed off, pointing at the blotch on her cheek.

"Look at me. What do you think Ryan is going to say when he sees this?"

"I'll kill him if he hurts you."

"You need to get your clothes on and leave."

"What are you talking about?"

"I have to study."

"You're not going back to him."

"Tucker, stop it!"

"I don't understand you."

"You just need to go home. Okay?"

There is something so sweet about Maggie, but it's like once you get past that beautiful candy coating there's something deformed inside. It's nothing mean or evil. It's just broken and sick; and no amount of logic or reasoning is going to talk her out of being this way.

So I leave just like she asks me.

Fifteen

A s sure as the sun comes up this morning, Maggie is back with Ryan and they take the geology test together. I sneak in late to class and end up sitting in the back. Watching them together makes me ache. She's flashing her pretty green eyes at him and he smiles back at her. You know, the kind of smile that says he knows what she looks like naked, the kind of smile that I should be smiling right now.

I can't concentrate on the test. I can barely breathe, much less write an essay explaining the difference between the fossil records of the Mesozoic and Jurassic eras. What does it matter anyway? It's all history and so am I. I get up and turn in the test mostly blank. Maggie looks up at me as I leave the room, but I act like I'm too busy to notice.

I need a beer.

I go back to Tucker's dorm room and I take a six-pack of beer out of the dorm refrigerator and I kick back a cold one. Nothing like beer for breakfast. I flip on the TV and watch *The Price Is Right*. I down the whole six-pack, and I lie on Tucker's bed and try to forget that I fucked Maggie less than twenty-four hours ago and that she just fucked me over in less than two. I sit here and have a real big pity party for myself and wish that life was like *The Price Is Right*, where you get up and guess and win, and the studio audience cheers. And if you do lose, you at least get some Turtle Wax and not a kick in the nuts. And just when I get myself real sad and shit, there's a loud-ass banging at my door. Maxwell must have forgotten his key. I sweep all the empty beer cans under the bed and I stagger to the door. Standing up kind of makes me feel my drunk, and it feels good and fuzzy.

The asshole at the door beats on it harder and louder. I hope it's Ryan. I could go for beating his bald ass this ugly morning.

"Hold your horses!" I unlock the deadbolt and open the door.

It's crazy Sarah Jane Bradford and she's sweating blood something fierce.

"I need to talk to you, Conrad." She pushes me aside and walks in like she owns the place.

"What?"

"Shut the door." The door slams without me or her anywhere near it.

"Bind ye Satan in the name of Jesus Christ." The blood pours from her temples and I feel stuck. It's weird. I can't really move, but I don't want to move either.

"What do you want?"

"I want you to leave this body, Conrad Sutton. You have no right to be doing this." She's shaking. I think she's scared. Probably thinks I'm the devil or something.

"Sarah Jane, this is none of your business. I'm taking care of Tucker."

"I bet. God has lost track of your soul and I'm here to help Him find it again."

"You'd be better off if you found a good orthodontist for those buck-ass teeth of yours."

"You've fallen, Conrad. And every second you stay in Tucker's body, you fall even harder." She wipes some of the dripping blood away from her eyes.

"Who says?"

"Get out of Tucker."

"No."

Sarah Jane looks at her fingernails and scratches the dried blood from around her cuticles. "Are you getting out of that body or do I have to jerk you out?"

"You don't scare me."

Sarah Jane smiles with her front teeth hanging over her bottom lip. She shuts her eyes and a golden light shines around her head and she sings. She looks all extra-virgin. But you can ask anybody at the Deke house and they'll all tell you she's not.

"A-uh-ma-zing grace. How-ow sweet the sound . . ." She touches her thumb and pointer finger together like she's holding an invisible needle and thread. Dark streams of blood flow from her palms down her wrists. She sews with her make-believe needle in and out and around in circles like a belly dancer. Her voice is loud and sweet, and I find myself shutting my eyes to listen to her. I can't help but hum along. And before I know it, things start to sparkle and fade, blur and shake, and all of a sudden, I'm outside of Tucker Graham.

That sneaky bitch.

"Praise the Lord!" Sarah Jane looks up and opens her bloody palms to heaven. "Thank ya Jesus! Thank ya Jesus!"

"Huh?" Tucker Graham wakes up. "Where am I? Who are you? What's with the . . ." He points at the blood on Sarah Jane's head.

"Oh, praise the Lord, Tucker. You're back!" Sarah Jane glows.

Tucker takes a couple of steps back. It's only natural; Sarah Jane's teeth are a little unsettling and the blood dripping down her face isn't doing much for her either.

"What's going on?"

"Tucker, everything's going to be all right. Just have a seat and rest. You've been through a lot." She rubs Tucker's shoulder, smearing her blood on his sleeve.

"Who are you? Stop that." Tucker pushes her bloody hand off his shoulder. "Why are you bleeding?"

"Well, of course, I am like so rude. I'm Sarah Jane Bradford. I'm an apostle of our Lord Jesus Christ." She clasps her hands together, tilts her head and smiles sweetly. "I'm also a Xi Omega."

"So what are you doing here and why is there blood all over you?"

"I'm in your room because you have been possessed by an evil spirit. And I'm bleeding because it's a sign from God."

"What are you? A sign of what? From God?"

"Oh, it's just a sign. I asked for a sign and this is what I got."

She widens her eyes all sorority-girl-like and holds her palms out to show the nail wounds bleeding on her hands.

"Ew. Sick."

"Tucker, at this very moment, an evil spirit sits on your left shoulder waiting to possess you again. You must be saved."

"I think I just need to lie down."

"Tucker Graham, you don't know what kind of spiritual warfare has been going on inside your body! You have been lost! And I am your shepherd!"

"I'm sorry. Really." Tucker scrunches up his nose up at Sarah Jane. All that old blood is starting to smell bad like Catfish Blood Bait.

"Your soul is in jeopardy."

"Sure. Whatever. Just leave . . . You're really bleeding." He points at the dark red spots on his floor.

"But you don't understand! You must accept Jesus Christ as your personal savior! You must be saved!"

"I said I'm sorry. I'm not interested. Okay?" Tucker shoves Sarah Jane out of his room. She pushes against him. Sarah Jane's faith might be able to move mountains, but she can't budge Tucker Graham. He's one big mofo.

"Sick! Stop getting your blood on me and leave!" Tucker pushes her out into the hall, shuts the door and looks at the red smears all over his shirt.

Tucker takes off his shirt and washes his hands for a real long time with lots of soap and hot water.

Meanwhile, outside Tucker's dorm room, Sarah Jane stands there praying. I can't resist tweaking her.

"Well, it looks like you made quite an impression on my main man in there."

Sarah Jane opens her eyes and glares at me.

"Oh! I am so mad I could just spit!"

"See, the way I figure it, you forcing Tucker into the Christian Collegians really isn't any different than me taking him over. Either way, he won't be doing what he wants."

"I wasn't trying to force anyone. I was just witnessing to him."

Sarah Jane looks at her palms. They've stopped bleeding for the moment.

"I've got bigger fish to fry." I wave good-bye.

"Wait! You can't leave!" Sarah Jane stomps her foot. "I want you to meet Francis."

"Who the hell is Francis?"

"Francis is my friend from Christian Collegians. He can help you find God. He's got experience with evil spirits like yourself."

"Okay. First off, I'm not an evil spirit. I'm just dead. And secondly, I'll be damned if someone named Francis is going to tell me what to do."

And with that said, I fly out of there before she sics the angels on me or does something biblical.

It's dinnertime at the Gamma Chi house. There's a chapter room full of shiny shaved heads eating mashed potatoes, corn on the cob, and Salisbury steak. The entire pledge class is on their knees, hobbling around instead of walking. By this point in the semester, every time the pledges are at the house, they have to get down on their knees. It hurts and over time it hurts worse, because instead of developing callouses like you would on your feet, you develop bruises. After an hour or so, your knees just go numb and you can sort of handle it. But before you get to that point, it's unbearable. The biggest, toughest guys I've ever seen cry like babies during "knees-down." The worst is trying to balance plates of food while you walk on your knees. Top this all off with an occasional bitch slap or ass-chewing and you've got yourself a real recipe for breaking even the strongest spirit.

Ryan sits at the president's table sipping on a tall glass of iced tea. Tucker and Alex are kneeling, waiting for Ryan's orders.

"More tea. Two Sweet'N Lows and one lemon." Ryan holds out a glass full of ice and tea.

"More tea?" Alex looks at Ryan's full glass.

"What did I just say?"

"But your glass is full."

Ryan dumps his tea on Alex's head.

Everybody just about chokes on their steak from laughing so hard. Alex looks down at the tea puddling up around him.

"Here you go, Tucker. Go get me some more tea." Ryan winks at Tucker as he hands him the empty glass. "And Alex, get your sorry ass in the kitchen and clean up this mess you've made here before you piss me off."

Alex and Tucker bounce as fast as they can on their knees into the kitchen. Once out of sight from the actives, they stand. Tucker rubs on his knees. The stitches in his knees are tearing and really giving the big guy problems. I don't know how he's enduring the pain. Alex pulls a long line of paper towels off the roll and dries himself off.

"I swear to God, the day I get initiated, I'm going to beat the shit out of Ryan Hutchins."

"Take a number, man." Tucker fills up Ryan's glass with ice.

"Here, let me see that." Alex takes the glass from Tucker and spits in it. He fills it up with tea, tears open two pink packets of sweetener, and squeezes a lemon into the glass. Then Alex sticks his finger up his nose and stirs Ryan's tea with it.

Tucker's laughing so hard he's crying.

"Shut up, man." Alex elbows Tucker. "You can't be laughing and shit."

"Okay. Okay. I got it. I'm fine. Really." Tucker's holding his sides as he tries to stop laughing.

"Here, take this to him and I'll go get the mop."

Tucker cringes as he goes back down on his knees. He hobbles across the linoleum and delivers Ryan's iced tea. Ryan grabs the iced tea and takes a long, thirsty gulp.

"Ah." He smacks his lips. "Perfect. Good job, Tucker." Ryan smiles at Tucker and all of Tucker's pledge brothers sneer at him. Ryan knows exactly what he's doing. The nicer he is to Tucker in front of his pledge brothers, the more they grow to hate him and his privilege of not having a shaved head. But despite Ryan's ranting and raving, Tucker can't help but smile on the inside. After all,

Ryan is gulping down Alex's loogey and that's something to be very proud about even if nobody knows what's going on.

After the meal is cleaned up, the pledges line up on their knees in the chapter room and the lights go out. The actives walk in with their hoods on, holding candles. The bleating of a goat can be heard coming from the other room. Alex looks at Tucker with his eyes all big and shit.

"It's a goat."

"No shit," Tucker whispers.

"They're gonna make us—"

"It's just a joke," Tucker whispers a little louder.

"No! I heard a long time ago that's what they make us do," Alex whispers back in a panic. "And then after we have sex with it, we slaughter it and they mount the head on a plaque."

"Do you see any goat heads hanging around here?"

"No."

"They're just trying to scare us."

"Shut up! Show some respect for the Worthy!" Couvillion smacks Alex square in the back with a long wooden paddle.

"Uh!" Alex falls over and doubles up. Couvillion grabs Alex by the arm and pulls him off the ground. "Take it like a man, you little faggot."

Alex gets back on his knees and swallows his tears. And Tucker looks straight ahead.

The room fills up with candles and actives in their ritual cloaks. Couvillion drags a reluctant goat into the chapter room.

The pledges' mouths go dry and they all try to swallow the collective frogs that have jumped up in their throats. It is a goat and it's got on red lingerie.

"Pledges of the Worthy! Behold the sacred goat offered up by Gamma Chi!" Ryan holds his arms up. "A sacrifice was tradition in the times of Abraham and Moses. And today, we will make this same offering, but not before there is communion between pledge and sacrifice."

"Pledge and sacrifice! Pledge and sacrifice! Pledge and sacrifice!" the hooded brothers shout.

"Who will be the first to sacrifice his pride for Gamma Chi?" Ryan walks up and down the row of pledges, looking each of them in the eye.

Couvillion pulls and fights the goat out of the room and up the stairs of the house.

"Tonight, each one of you will prove your worthiness. One by one, we'll be taking you upstairs for your conjugal visit. So kneel here with your heads down and eyes closed until we call you. Let's see, the first on the list is Audoin. Tony Audoin. Mr. Pretty Boy. Let's go!"

Tony is remarkably calm as they stand him up and take him out of the room. But by the time they get up the stairs, he loses it. "No way! No fucking way! I quit! I won't. Sorry."

"Just poke it a couple of times and you can go." Couvillion grabs Tony by the neck and forces him into the room with the goat. Ryan has his video camera out and he's filming the whole thing.

"No!!" Audoin pushes Couvillion off of him. "Get off of me!"

"What'sa matter, you think you're too good? Huh?" Couvillion pushes Tony in the chest and then gets all up in his face. Tony just stands there, all stoic and shit.

"Get over there! Now!"

Couvillion pops Tony upside the head, but he stands there like his feet are super-glued to the floor.

As the actives continue down the list, every pledge has just about the same reaction. Nobody will even touch the goat, no matter how they are threatened. Never before have these pledges shown such a strength of character. It's remarkable, really. Because after they refuse to touch the goat they are taken up to the third floor and they get the shit beaten out of them. Plus, each time a pledge is taken upstairs for his turn he doesn't know that the pledge brother before him didn't do the goat. However, by the time the actives get down to Alex, the pressure is exponential compared to what Tony Audoin experienced.

They call Alex Trudeaux. They pluck him from Tucker Graham's side and he goes upstairs without a fight. Both Ryan and Couvillion are with him.

"Okay, Alex, your pledge brothers have gotten her all good and loosened up." Couvillion makes this thrusting train motion with his hips. "So this shouldn't take very long."

Alex looks at Couvillion and then Ryan. His bottom lip quivers and his eyes get all red and watery. The two actives get on either side of him and walk him up the stairs.

"I don't think I can do this," he hyperventilates.

"Ah, sure you can, Alex. We've all done it. It sucks but you can do it." Ryan puts his arm around him. "Just calm down and take a couple of deep breaths."

"But I don't think I can get it up for a goat. Seriously."

"Just close your eyes and think about a girl. That's what I did." Ryan smiles and kind of shrugs his shoulders.

"Really?" Alex wipes his eyes.

"Really, you can do this, man. Come on!" Ryan pats Alex on the back and smiles all proud-like.

"Stop being such a dildo and just get it over with!" Couvillion shoves Alex into the room and the door slams behind them.

After a couple of minutes, Couvillion pops his head out the door and hollers down the hall, "Hey Brad, Trey, come here! You gotta see this shit!"

Pretty soon, the entire active chapter is pushing and shoving to get a peek.

They're all yelling and pretty soon the whole house shakes with a chant: "Go-Baby-Go! Go-Baby-Go! Go-Baby-Go!"

Sixteen

onight is Halloween and there's a big harvest moon the size of a dinner plate hanging in the sky. There's an excitement in the air, a manic-pop-thrill kind of excitement. That's because tonight is the LSU/Ole Miss game and it's causing a frenzy in this town seldom seen at any other time. It all echoes back to that famous Halloween game of long ago when we beat the shit out of the Ole Miss Rebels. People still talk about it. Billy Cannon and his Chinese Bandits schooled those Mississippi asswipes on the likes of how to play the game of football. That fateful night in 1959, Tiger Stadium was full of a bunch of drunk coon-asses hooting and hollering, all dressed up like devils and monsters and shit. The stories of Billy's Halloween Run abound, and some people will even tell you they saw honest-to-God ghosts blocking for Cannon. But what was written down in the history books is just as incredible. You see, Cannon fielded Jake Gibbs's punt on the bounce at the eleven-yard line. Then Cannon magically careened off seven would-be tacklers and galloped eighty-nine yards. This little Halloween miracle was sure-fire evidence that the LSU Tigers were indeed God's chosen team. Most folks agree that run sealed up the Heisman Trophy for Billy Cannon. I would reckon it also made him the most laid man ever to graduate from LSU.

Cannon's triumph brings real tears to Tiger fans' eyes and they all hope to re-create it every time we play Ole Miss. Folks get all dressed up in their Halloween gear or they paint their faces purple and gold, and instead of yelling, "Trick or treat," everybody hollers, "Go to Hell, Ole Miss! Go to Hell!"

And let me tell you, those Ole Miss fans still haven't gotten over Billy Cannon. Every time we play them in Baton Rouge, Ole

Miss fans drive in by the truckloads. It's an endless caravan of Sub-
urbans and Winnebagos full of those inbred bastards. They're all
waving Rebel flags and throwing beer cans at Tiger fans who are
innocently walking to their own tailgate parties. It's enough to
make you want to go home and get your shotgun. And on occasion
a few Tiger fans have, but as of yet, nobody's killed an Ole Miss
fan. Or at least nobody's found the bodies. And if they did, I do
suspect the Baton Rouge police might even overlook it. They hate
Ole Miss fans worst of all.

The parking lot in front of Tiger Stadium is jam-packed with
campers, minivans, and pickups. Everybody's tailgating before the
game. There's an easy sixty thousand people gathered here. You
got your fat little Cajun grannies all decked out in tiger-striped
jumpsuits, wearing Mardi Gras beads and rhinestone-studded vi-
sors while they cook up big pots of jambalaya. Then you got your
fat-ass white guys sitting in lawn chairs, watching their portable
TVs and drinking Abita Springs beer. Seems like just about every
little girl is dressed in a purple cheerleading uniform while their
brothers toss footballs back and forth. You'll see the occasional
law student or recent alum, but for the most part these tailgaters
are all real freak show Tiger fan material.

On the other side of the parking lot, you've got all your Ole
Miss tailgaters. They're just as fanatical, with their Johnny Reb
hats, playing Dixie on their jam boxes, and kissing their sisters and
mothers full on the lips. And they shout their little Hoddy Toddy
song. Which, if you ask me, is just begging for an ass-whupping.
But when it's a fifty-five-year-old lady, most decent folks can't
bring themselves to open that necessary can of whupass—even if
the white trash old lady is wearing a muumuu made out of the
Confederate flag and cussing God and Billy Cannon.

Right next to all the Ole Miss tailgaters is the Christian Collegians' stage. They've hung up this sparkly purple and gold banner
that proclaims they're tailgating for Jesus. Sarah Jane Bradford is
there with all her wacko friends. They're dressed in "Holy-Ween"
costumes. That means nothing scary or "satanic." Sarah Jane is a
lamb of God with cotton balls spray-glued all over a black leotard.

Then there's this guy and his girlfriend dressed in choir robes, coat hanger halos, and papier mâché wings. There's another dude, all beefy and shit, with a long-haired wig, a bathrobe, and flip-flops. His name tag reads "Hello, my name is Samson."

The Collegians have also put up this big-ass wooden cross and posters everywhere that say "John 3:16" and "He Died for You!" and "Geaux Tigers!" Samson's shouting in a megaphone and passing out WWJD bracelets. Sarah Jane is busy filling cups up with purple Kool-Aid and preaching to all the thirsty little kids. "Remember, tell your mommy that drinking alcohol makes the baby Jesus cry."

It's about ten minutes before kickoff and there's a huge influx of frat boys with their dates. And my favorite frat boy, Ryan, is there with Maggie. He's got a head full of cocaine, and he's dressed up like Indiana Jones, bullwhip and all. Maggie's got on a geisha girl outfit. If that isn't apropos, I don't know what is. Anyway, she's got two flasks of Bacardi taped to her thighs so she's walking like she was just deflowered.

"Ryan, wait up, sweetie."

"Hurry up, Maggie. I'm not missing kickoff." Ryan lights a cigarette while he waits for Maggie to catch up. "Come on. Goddamn it."

She waddles as fast as she can and grabs onto Ryan.

As Maggie and Ryan walk arm in arm to the student gate, there's a huge crowd, an overflow of people from the Christian Collegians blocking the way. Sarah Jane and Samson are causing some kind of commotion.

Samson's standing behind a card table and yelling into his megaphone, "And like it says in Matthew 16:18, 'They shall take up serpents and if they drink any deadly thing, it shall not hurt them!' "

Sarah Jane brings Samson a picnic basket. He puts it up on the table and the rattlesnakes inside it go crazy.

"Omigod, does he have snakes in there?" Maggie pulls Ryan to her as she watches Samson. Ryan tokes on his cigarette and glares at Sarah Jane.

Samson and Sarah Jane lower their heads in prayer. Samson keeps his eyes shut and he opens the basket, real careful and slow-like.

Shake-shake-shake-shake.

The snakes warn him to stop, but he puts his hand in the basket anyway. Samson jerks out a three-foot diamondback rattler. "Thank ya, Jesus! Praise the Lord!" He holds the writhing monster over his head and smiles while Sarah Jane sings, "Yes, Jesus loves me" in that creepy-sweet voice of hers.

People gasp. Women scream. Fathers grab their kids.

"Wait right here." Ryan breaks away from Maggie.

"No, Ryan, don't."

Ryan ignores her and pushes his way to the front of the crowd. Ryan stands right up front, only a couple of feet away from Sarah Jane and the snake-handler. Ryan stares at the cotton balls on Sarah Jane's costume and then looks at his cigarette. He takes a long drag off it and then flicks it at Sarah Jane.

The cherry of the cigarette hits a big glob of cotton balls and glue, and a tiny yellow flame flickers and grows.

Everybody is staring at Samson and the snake coiling up on his arm, so Ryan disappears back into the crowd and nobody gives him a second thought.

That hungry little flicker grows into a quick and silent flame. Sarah Jane's whole left side is a blazing inferno in just a matter of seconds. The heat from the fire blows her hair and she screams.

She tries to run away from the fire, but she bumps into Samson, causing him to drop the snake. The rattler strikes him in the face and Samson knocks over the table. The rest of the diamondbacks go flying into the crowd. People go ape shit, yelling and pushing and running and howling. It's every man for himself and nobody has the good sense to put poor Sarah Jane out. She runs around melting and screaming in a complete ball of fire while Samson holds his bloody face and cries, "Oh God! Oh God! Oh God help us!"

The couple dressed like angels stay back; they just stand there and watch Sarah Jane burn. She eventually falls into the Christian Collegians' banner and rolls on the ground to put herself out.

Safe at the stadium gate, Maggie is crying and Ryan protects her eyes from the terror raging on the stage.

"Don't look, Maggie. You don't want to see this." He holds her tight and safe.

The campus police run past all the screaming people to the stage. They find a charred, bloody body writhing and smoking on the ground. Next to it is a dude in a bloody wig with two diamondbacks coiled up at his feet. Ambulance sirens can be heard in the distance and a news helicopter lowers down from above the stadium, blowing the hats off the cops. A cameraman moves his high-powered light beam all over the scene and he stops it on Sarah Jane's open eyes. She tries to moan for help, but all she can do is wheeze.

Gunshots echo over the campus as the police kill the rattlers, and Sarah Jane Bradford finally gets the help she prayed for just before she died.

Seventeen

Alex Trudeaux is about the only living person in Baton Rouge who didn't go to the game tonight. However, if Alex had his druthers he wouldn't be alive at all. After the goat ordeal, the Gamma Chis blackballed him. It's just their little way of testing integrity. Most of the pledges were tipped off by actives earlier on in the semester about the goat and told not to even touch it. But I guess nobody told Alex.

So Alex sits on his bed in his boxers and T-shirt fashioning a noose out of his neckties while he watches the late-night news. Poor guy figures that offing himself is the only way to go now. They've destroyed him. Broken his spirit clean in two. I actually feel sorry for him. Because like most of the living, Alex doesn't understand one fundamental truth about death: You take your unfinished business with you. Now he'll just be dead and miserable about what he did, and without a life, he'll never be able to make it right. He'll never be able to prove to Gamma Chi that he's better than that. He'll just be a spirit, like me, with all the problems and no way to find the answers. It's a real bitch. I wouldn't recommend death to anyone. That is, unless you've gotten your shit together. But even then, who knows.

As Alex finishes up his noose, a TV news story catches his attention. A pretty blond newscaster reports from a scene of flashing sirens and chaos.

"Tonight at Tiger Stadium, one LSU student was slain and another critically injured in what many are calling a hate crime. One LSU student was pronounced dead on arrival at Our Lady of the Lakes Hospital after being set on fire during a pre-game Christian Collegians' rally. Another student is in critical condition after suffering multiple rattlesnake bites. Police have yet to comment on this bizarre Halloween tragedy at Tiger Stadium . . ."

Alex drops his noose, picks up the remote control, and listens.

"Police are looking for suspects. Eyewitnesses say a young man wearing a Johnny Reb hat was seen throwing a lit cigarette at the student, setting her aflame. Police are still questioning witnesses, but no arrests have been made in the young girl's death . . ."

"That looked like Sarah Jane."

"Ryan did it," I whisper in his ear.

"No. No way." He shakes his head.

"Yeah way."

Alex picks up the phone and dials 911.

"Hello. I need the police. Yeah, it's an emergency. Well, sort of an emergency. It's about that girl who just burned up . . ."

There's nothing like a little revenge to give you a reason to live. Actually, I'm quite proud of Alex. Hell, if I was alive, I would shake his hand. I just hope he's able to convince the police that Ryan is their man. Ryan's family is deep into Louisiana politics, and he's so charming and normal looking he's not a very likely suspect. But I've got to say, Alex at least has half a brain to figure Ryan out. I mean, after I died nobody, not a single goddamn soul, not even my parents, gave it a second thought. That's because Ryan's the kind of guy my mother would have died for my sister Shannon to date, and the mannerly overachiever my father always wanted for a son. I'm here to tell you, watch out for people like Ryan. You know the kind, always flashing you their toothpaste commercial smiles. They do things—bad things—and they always get away with them.

You know, it's the weirdest thing, but Alex's room smells good, like somebody's baking something. In fact, I think I catch a whiff of lemon pies. Sweet, sweet lemon pies baking warm all over Alex's room. Which is weird because I don't usually smell things. But this is definitely a lemon pie smell. I look around, but there aren't any pies in this dirty-ass dorm room. So I follow the scent. Out of the dorm and into the early morning, the odor gets stronger.

Like cartoon hands, the warm smell tickles my ghost nose and beckons me with the best-smelling lemon confection ever. It's magic. And sure enough, it *is* magic. The scent's coming from Miss Etta's house and it's so inviting that I walk right through her kitchen door just so I can stand in the middle of it.

"I thought that might get your attention." Miss Etta holds up a wooden spoon dripping with yellow glop.

"What smells so good?"

"Shoo." Etta licks the wooden spoon and laughs. "Baby, those my translucent lemon pies. Ain't a soul in the world can resist them."

"Why didn't I hear about these when I was alive?"

"I only bake them on special occasions."

"You know I'm going to stop him."

"Conrad, I have told you and I have told you, Ryan is not your business."

"How can you stand here and say that?"

"It ain't the Lord's way. You got to trust me on that. I might be old and crazy, but I talk to the Lord and sometimes He talks back."

"And *He* told you this."

"Well, not exactly to me. But He spoke it in the Bible and that's good enough for me."

"Look, there's got to be more to this. I can't do this shit anymore. I'm sick of it!"

"Baby, calm down now. You be a child of God and that's a mighty inheritance. Yes, sir." Miss Etta smiles and her gold tooth catches the light coming in the kitchen window. "He got a plan for all of us and sometime we don't much like it. You think Jesus like getting up on that cross? You think I like cooking for white folk who just as soon spit on me? Life a test, baby."

"My life was over the moment Ryan broke my neck."

"Watch your mouth, boy! I'd tan your hide if you was still alive!" She stares me down and shakes her skinny little fist at me.

"Okay, sorry. I'm just a little on edge."

"You always on edge, cussing and carrying on. Baby, you got to forgive."

"That's easier said than done."

"Anything worth anything ain't going to be easy, boy." Her kitchen buzzer goes off. "Oh, my pies be ready!"

Miss Etta goes to her old gas oven and pulls out a pie rack with three lemon custard pies on it. The pie in the back of the rack is on fire.

"Oh shoot!" Miss Etta beats the fire out with her oven mitt. "That was Ryan's pie!"

"Ryan's pie?"

"Yeah, I pray for my enemies just like Jesus say, baby." She smiles all proud-like.

"But He didn't say bake them a goddamn pie. I can't believe you."

"Look boy, you can get on out my kitchen carrying on like that."

"I just can't believe you baked Ryan a pie."

"Baby, I bake lemon pies for everyone." She proudly passes her knotted fingers over the brown and yellow pies. "That's how the Lord talks to me." Miss Etta points to the cracks and lines baked into the custard. "See, this pie tell me about Maggie. See that line and that bubble? That mean Maggie be . . . Oh Lord! Maggie be . . . pregnant and you the daddy."

"Shit."

"What have you done, baby? What have you done?" Miss Etta closes her eyes and rubs her tiny gold cross.

Poor Maggie. She has no business with a baby—especially one that looks like Tucker Graham. And what's Ryan going to do when she pops out this redheaded kid? I can tell you this, it isn't going to be pretty.

If I was still alive, this would have never happened. I would have never slept with Maggie Meadows because I would have gotten Ashley back. And we would be dropped or pinned or engaged. Then after graduation we would probably have gotten married and then we'd have a whole slew of our own kids. That's how things should be. Not like this.

I miss my life. I miss dreaming about my future. I miss Ashley and how she'd laugh at all my dumb jokes and forgive me even when I messed around. Dead or alive, I'm not ready to be a father to Maggie's kid. I mean, why couldn't this have been Ashley? I know this sounds sick, but I would do anything right now if I could be alive and Ashley was the one knocked up with my kid. I would straighten up and fly right. No more pot. No more drinking. No more screwing around. If I had to do it, I could have been really good to Ashley. I really could have.

Pining away like this for Ashley and a life that never was, pulls me to her. She's in her bedroom, curled up under a flowery bedspread crying her eyes out over Sarah Jane's death. And then a guy's voice calls out from the other room.

"Ashley. The Chinese food guy just dropped off our food. Come and eat."

It's Jay Kimbrough. What the hell is Jay Kimbrough doing in Ashley's apartment?

"Not hungry." She murmurs and pulls the covers over her head.

Kimbrough gently knocks on her bedroom door.

"Come on. You've got to eat. I'm fixing you a plate. It's good." Kimbrough walks back to the kitchen and goes straight to the plates. He doesn't even have to ask.

"Okay. It's ready!" Kimbrough hollers as he puts the plates and silverware on the kitchen table.

Ashley walks out with her hair hanging in her face and Kleenex in hand. She takes a seat in front of a plate of greasy brown noodles.

"What do you want to drink? A beer?" Kimbrough holds up a bottle of Rolling Rock from Ashley's fridge.

"No, I don't want a beer and you don't either. Remember your promise." Ashley pushes her hair away so that she can glare at Jay.

"Oh yeah." Jay puts the beer back and pulls out two Diet Cokes. "How about this?"

"No thanks, I'll just have water."

Jay pops open the Diet Coke, takes a swig, and then fixes Ashley a glass of ice water. When he brings it to her, Kimbrough kisses her on the lips and she smiles at him.

"Thank you." She looks at Kimbrough all dreamy-like, the way she used to look at me when we first met.

What just happened here? Tell me, when did this happen? When did Kimbrough start screwing my girlfriend? I mean, this really shouldn't surprise me. Most Gamma Chis don't even wait until you're dead before they start trying to do your girl behind your back.

But Kimbrough? I thought we were friends. For chrissakes, he's the guy who found my body the next morning. He's the guy who gave me mouth to mouth even though I was long dead just because he was desperate to save me. And now he goes and does something like this.

Miss Etta has to take three different city buses to deliver her lemon pies to Maggie. Miss Etta may be old, but she's far from frail. She stayed up all night rolling out the crust from scratch, squeezing the lemons, and mixing everything by hand. And now instead of going to bed, she's just as chipper as you please, singing old Baptist hymns to herself, and holding her lemon pies that she wrapped carefully in a brown paper grocery bag. I take the empty seat next to her.

"So what are you going to tell her?" I whisper in her ear.

"What did I tell you about sneaking up on folks?" She swats at me.

"Sorry." I smile at her.

"You always sorry." She shakes her head and the people on the bus begin to stare at her.

"You just going to leave the pie on her doorstep?"

"You must be stupid. I didn't spend all night slaving over these pies so some crazy-ass dog can come along and eat it. I'm going ring the bell and give it to the girl."

"She hates unexpected company."

"Well, baby, she got herself some unexpected company, all right." Miss Etta cracks herself up and then she notices Maggie's apartment complex is passing her by.

"Stop the bus! Stop the bus! Right here, baby! Right here, baby!" Miss Etta yells at the bus driver.

The bus driver grits his teeth and slams on the brakes; the bus jerks and screeches to a halt.

"Next time use the stop cord, lady," the gold-chained bus driver barks at her as she shuffles past him.

"Next time, kiss my ass!" Miss Etta shakes her stuff as the door folds behind her and the bus takes off in a big cloud of blue smoke.

"So which one does she stay in?" Miss Etta asks me.

"I'm not so sure this is a good idea."

"No, baby, let me tell you, this a real good idea. See, a bad idea be possessing people and then getting up inside some girl's panties and getting her pregnant." She smacks her lips. "Now that's a bad idea."

"Okay, okay, okay. Whatever. Just follow me."

I lead her up to Maggie's door and she knocks hard and loud and then she knocks again and again.

"Maggie! Open the door, baby."

Maggie opens the door but leaves the burglar chain on. She's in her robe and has pillow creases all over her pretty face.

"Miss Etta?"

"Is your period late?" Miss Etta smiles with her gold tooth shining.

"What?"

"Your period's late 'cause you pregnant. The Lord told me."

"What!" Maggie opens the door and pulls Miss Etta inside. "Omigod, what did you just say?" Maggie shuts the door and locks it.

"I said the Lord told me you was pregnant and you ain't been eating. That's bad for your baby."

"I'm not pregnant." Maggie wrings her pretty tan hands. "And you can't be coming around here yelling things like that about me. Okay?"

"Is that why you peed all over that plastic stick this morning?"

"How did you know that?"

"The good Lord sent me, child." Miss Etta smiles and hands Maggie the pie. "Here, you need to eat. Let me get you some milk and a plate."

Miss Etta walks past Maggie into the kitchen and then returns with a plate, a fork, and a glass of milk.

"Sit down, baby, and let me explain to you while you eat."

"I'm not hungry."

"Too bad, 'cause your baby is. He's real hungry." Miss Etta takes the pie out of the sack. She cuts a big slice of the lemon pie and slings the plate over to Maggie.

"Do you know how many carbs are in that?"

"Sit down and eat, and I'll tell you what you need to know, girl." Miss Etta takes a seat at the dining room table. Maggie reluctantly takes a bite of the pie.

"Now, don't go telling Ryan you pregnant—'cause it ain't his baby. It's Tucker's."

"Omigod. I'm going to be sick." Maggie covers her mouth. She gets up from the table, runs to the bathroom, and throws up stomach juice and lemon pie.

"Must be morning sickness 'cause I know it ain't my pie." Miss Etta sighs as she grabs the fork and takes a bite off Maggie's plate.

This very same morning some unexpected company also shows up for Ryan: the Baton Rouge police. Two homicide detectives. One white. The other black. Both dressed in cheap blue suits and Men's Warehouse ties.

The white guy's got red zits on his neck and a bushy blond mustache that's got powdered sugar stuck all in it. He's the bloated kind of bastard who looks like he should be a traffic cop. You know, the kind of mirrored-sunglasses-wearing sonavabitch who scares pretty young housewives and college girls into giving him hummers in exchange for tearing up their speeding tickets.

Now the black detective is a different story. He's new to Baton Rouge—from up north in Chicago. Lucien Watkins is his name. He's all bowed up like a *COPS* action figure. I don't reckon he likes his job too much, or, for that matter, his beignet-snacking new partner.

Detective Watkins looks up at the Gamma Chi mansion with its strong white columns and storybook oaks. As he rubs his eyes, I see visions of Southern gentlemen and Southern lynchings go flying out of his head.

"One big cracker house." Watkins smirks.

"Huh?"

"Forget it." Watkins walks in front of him and pounds on the heavy oak door. And before he can beat on the door again, it flies open.

"Yeah, can I help you?" Couvillion stands there all chrome-domed like Mr. Clean.

"Detective Watkins." Lucien pulls out his badge and winks at Couvillion. "Baton Rouge Police. Homicide."

Couvillion's face turns whiter than his granddaddy's Klan robes.

"Uh, yeah. Can I, uh, help you?"

"This is my partner, Detective Boudreaux."

Boudreaux steps forward and flashes his badge. "We're here to see Ryan Hutchins."

Watkins smiles at Couvillion.

"Uh, sure. I'll go get him." Couvillion shuts the door on the detectives and runs up the staircase.

"I guess they don't let niggas in the front door." Watkins grins at his partner.

Boudreaux rolls his eyes and shakes his head. "Give it a frigging rest. All right?"

"Just making a simple observation. That's all."

"Save the civil rights speech for your Black Panther meetings. Down here, things don't work like that."

"All I'm saying is that I don't like having the door slammed in my face."

"Yeah, and I do?" Boudreaux strokes his mustache. "Look, just play it cool until we get a warrant, okay?"

"And whose idea was it not to get one?"

"I don't know how you did it up in Chicago but down here you don't go asking a judge for a warrant on a senator's nephew unless you have something more than a prank call to go on. Okay?"

"Yeah, I see what you're saying. It's a white thing."

"Sure the hell is and your people picked it. Now cut the racial crap and let me handle these boys."

"Ah now, that's dirty." Watkins smirks and shakes his head.

Boudreaux thinks he made a funny. He folds his arms across his marshmallow chest and cracks himself up. Watkins laughs along with him, but he has to muster every ounce of his willpower not to deck his racist partner.

Ryan comes down the old white staircase and opens the door for the detectives.

"Y'all need to talk to me?" Ryan looks at them without the slightest hint of fear or guilt on his face. Instead, he's just overflowing with white-boy innocence and athletic overachievement. And like most people, Detective Boudreaux seems to like Ryan right away.

"Are you Ryan Hutchins?" Boudreaux asks.

"Yes sir, I sure am. Is there something I can help you with?"

Boudreaux offers his sweaty hand to Ryan. "Detective Boudreaux, and this is my partner, Detective Watkins. We'd like to ask you some questions."

"Sure." Ryan holds the door open for the detectives. "Come on in. Let's talk."

Ryan takes them through the wedding-cake-white foyer and into my library. Watkins's eyes are all over the place, checking out the elaborate woods and big brass fixtures of the old house. I don't reckon Watkins has ever been in a frat house before. At least not one this nice.

"Please have a seat." Ryan offers them the leather chairs at a study table, and he takes the seat across from them.

"So what's with the shaved heads around here?" Boudreaux points to Ryan's scalp.

"Oh, it's a little stunt the chapter pulled to kind of shake things up. You know, swallowing goldfish and flagpole sitting's been done."

"Yeah"—Boudreaux sucks on the inside of his cheek—"I remember my college days."

"Really. Were you in a fraternity?"

"Actually, son, I was a Gamma Chi at Louisiana Tech." Boudreaux raises an eyebrow and smiles all proud-like. But if the truth be known, the detective's pride is totally unfounded. Ryan and everybody knows the Gamma Chis at Tech suck.

"No shit, I mean, that's great. Put 'er there." Ryan reaches across the table and gives Detective Boudreaux the Gamma Chi handshake. Detective Watkins rolls his eyes.

"So Ryan"—Watkins clears his throat—"as my partner was saying, we've got a few questions you might be able to help us with."

"Sure. Whaddup?"

Boudreaux glares at Watkins and then looks back at Ryan. "You were at the football game the other night, right?

"Yeah, I was there."

"I'm sure you know what happened." Watkins stares at Ryan.

"Yeah, everybody's saying that some Ole Miss fan torched that girl." Ryan shakes his head like he can barely stomach the thought. "It's sick, man."

"Well, we were wondering if you saw anything. If you maybe saw who did it."

"I wish I did. I mean I was pretty wasted—guess I probably shouldn't say that." Ryan shrugs a little and gives a sheepish grin. "About the only thing I remember was the winning touchdown in the fourth quarter. Man, what a play. Did you guys see that?"

"No, actually we missed it. We were busy looking at the charred remains of a dead girl." Watkins doesn't blink, but instead stares deep into Ryan's skull.

"I'm sorry, Ryan. My partner's a little too involved with this case. You understand." Detective Boudreaux rubs his mustache as he smiles nervously.

"Sorry, didn't know that you—you know. Sorry. I really wasn't trying to be flip."

"Don't worry about it," Watkins mumbles.

"So anyway, Ryan. Did you happen to know the girl?" Boudreaux fumbles with a ballpoint pen.

"No, not directly. I mean I knew she was a Xi-O and all, but I didn't 'know her' know her."

Watkins gets up from the table and begins pacing around the room, touching the fine woods and fingering the leather chairs. Ryan watches him with a measured but friendly eye.

"What about Francis LeBlanc?" Boudreaux presses on one of his neck zits.

"Who's that?"

"The kid who got bit by all the rattlesnakes that night. Maybe you know him from the gym or class?" Boudreaux studies Ryan's face.

"Nope, never heard of the dude."

Watkins quietly strolls over to the bookshelves and acts like he's reading the titles. Ryan can't help but watch the detective out of the corner of his eye.

"Got a lot of books here. A lot of books." Watkins pulls out a hanky and blows his nose.

"So Ryan"—Watkins sniffs and wipes his nose—"what would make someone want to hurt those two Christian Collegian kids?"

"Huh?"

"I'm asking your opinion. Why would someone hurt those two?" Watkins takes a book off the shelf, studies the spine, and then looks back up at Ryan. "What do you think happened that night?"

"You got me. A lot of people get all caught up in that Christian Collegians stuff and just freak out on it. What makes someone pick up a rattlesnake at a football game?"

"So you saw Sarah Jane Bradford and her friend Mr. LeBlanc

handling the snakes before the game?" Watkins clears his throat again and looks up from the book.

"I actually missed all the pre-game stuff. I was busy." Ryan laughs a little.

"Busy?" Watkins's eyes bulge.

"Yeah, I was busy. I didn't get to the game until after kickoff."

"So what were you busy doing? If you don't mind me asking."

"You really want to know?"

"I wouldn't have asked the question if I didn't." Watkins gives a mean smile.

"Well, see, before each game, for good luck and all, I always, you know, do my, my girlfriend."

"Whoa, son, where did that come from?" Boudreaux grins.

"Guess that might have been a little too much info." Ryan shrugs his shoulders and kind of chuckles. "But Maggie, that's my girlfriend, and I always, you know, before the game. For good luck."

"So you do this before every game?" Boudreaux narrows his gaze.

"No, just every home game. It's not as weird as it sounds. See, we did it right before the Ohio State game last year and the Tigers ended a five-game losing streak that night. So it's like our little good luck thing now."

"Okay." Boudreaux is totally flustered. "Didn't mean to get into your personal business, son."

"Wait a second. I thought you just said you were drunk at the game." Watkins closes the library book and holds it close to his chest like he's holding a Bible or something.

"So?" Ryan's face is blank.

"So you were that drunk and still able to have sex?"

"Watkins. They're college kids. That's all they do. Jeez." Boudreaux shakes his head and grins. "That will all change, though. Just wait, son—just wait until you get a job. A few beers and that's all she wrote."

Ryan nods and smiles like he understands what Boudreaux's talking about.

"Anyway, I think we've taken up enough of your time. You probably need to go study or maybe the cross-country team could use a little good luck." Boudreaux looks off in the distance like he's remembering something really sweet and special. "All's I got to say is, enjoy it while it lasts. Anyway, here's my card. If you hear any-thing, anything at all, about what happened to that girl, we expect you to call us, okay?" Boudreaux winks and slips Ryan the secret Gamma Chi handshake.

"We'll be in touch." Watkins looks deep into Ryan's eyes as he hands him the library book he was holding. "Good book. You should read it some time."

Ryan looks down at the title. It's Dostoyevsky's *Crime and Punishment*.

Eighteen

I t's the first of November and the cool fall air has completely disappeared. It's been replaced with a hot Creole sun. Today, it got up to a hundred and two degrees. Seems like everything is out of whack since Sarah Jane burned up. And even the weather wants to tell you about it. In fact, while the sun shines today, casting long shadows everywhere, it starts raining hard, like it usually does in the summer. My mamma used to say it was the devil beating his wife when the sky was blue like this and it rained out of nowhere. That always creeped me out when I was a little kid. Like the end of the world was coming and the Devil was just practicing up on his wife before he got ahold of me.

As the rain hits the asphalt, I can't help but think of Maggie. And as usual, thinking about Maggie pulls me to her. I find myself in her bedroom. Her gold hair is up in a ponytail and she's exercising like a maniac. She looks more beautiful than ever. Her lips are pink and full. And her tits are bigger—a lot bigger—than they usually are.

There's a knock at her apartment door and then the sound of keys jingling. The deadbolt turns and Ryan comes in from the sunshine and the rain.

"Magpie! You home?" he calls out as he rubs the raindrops off his shaved scalp.

"Just a second, sweetie. I'm exercising." Maggie scrambles for her sweats so she can cover up her disappearing waist.

Ryan ignores her and continues walking into her room. He catches her struggling to get her tennis shoes through the leg of her sweat pants. Her eyes are big and scared.

"What the hell are you doing?" He grabs Maggie by the hair and jerks her head back.

"I-uh-I was trying to put on my sweats." Maggie strains to talk.

"Yeah, no shit." He jerks her hair tighter. "What are you trying to cover up?"

"I was cold."

He pushes her head away, throwing her on the floor. She lies there, all tangled up in her sweat pants.

"Look at how fat you're getting. I mean, Jesus! Look at you!"

"Sorry." Maggie whimpers and rolls over on her side.

That bastard stands over her and rears his foot back to kick her in the stomach. Maggie shuts her eyes tight and curls up into a ball. As Ryan swings his foot forward to kick Maggie, he catches himself and stomps his foot down, just in front of her belly.

Maggie flinches.

"Come on, get up," Ryan offers her his hand, "You're not going to make me do this. Not today."

Maggie opens her eyes and starts breathing again.

"Come on. Get up." Ryan grabs Maggie by the arm and jerks her off the carpet. Maggie is dazed. She doesn't know what to do. Ryan has never pulled a punch like that before. Not ever.

"You'll just have to get on a diet. That's all." He smiles at Maggie and then hugs her. "Hey, sorry for losing it. So what if you're getting a little fat. Right? I can handle that. I still love you."

"Sure." She can't look him in the face.

Ryan squeezes her closer and gives her a kiss on the lips. Maggie shuts her eyes.

"So what are you fixing me for lunch?" he asks.

"What?" Maggie tries to catch her breath.

"I said, what's for lunch?"

"I don't know . . . I can, uh, maybe grill some chicken. I'm not sure."

"Hey, don't worry about it. I'll fix us something. How's that sound?" Ryan gives Maggie another kiss on the cheek and then leads her out of the bedroom and into the kitchen.

"So where's the room-bitch?" Ryan looks around the empty apartment for Maggie's roommate, Erica.

"I think she's out shopping with Billy."

"She still dating that faggot?"

"Yeah, I guess." Maggie mopes into the kitchen and pulls an icy brick of chicken breast and Styrofoam out of the freezer.

"I've got this chicken we can cook." Tears hang in Maggie's eyes as she holds the chicken up.

"Hey, I said I was going to do that." Ryan walks behind Maggie and slaps her on the butt. "Go sit down."

Maggie walks out of the kitchen and glares at Ryan.

"Now what was that look for?" He cracks a smile.

She folds her arms and looks at the floor. "Nothing."

"Are you pissed off because I said you'd gained a little weight?"

"No, Ryan." Maggie starts to cry.

"What?" Ryan puts the chicken down.

"You just hurt me."

"Maggie, don't. Come on." Ryan walks out of the kitchen.

"Why, Ryan, why?" Maggie sobs.

He grabs Maggie and hugs her. She shakes and cries in his arms.

"Sh-shhhhh." Ryan holds her like a child and smoothes her hair.

While Maggie cries in the arms of a murderer, the rest of the campus is crying in the arms of one another. They're weeping for Sarah Jane Bradford because today is her funeral. They arrive at the First Baptist Church in wrinkled khakis or flowery dresses because most of these kids have never faced death before and nobody told them that Abercrombie and Fitch and Urban Outfitters aren't the places to go for funeral clothes.

Sarah Jane's sorority sisters show up en masse. They've caked on their makeup, so they sort of look like circus clowns as they pile out of their Beetles and Cooper Minis. They scramble to console one another, wailing and carrying on something terrible. And when the squalling reaches a fever pitch, they all huddle up into a giant group hug and then try to walk through the tall church doors together. This big amoeba of hysterical girls expands and contracts its way into the church and up the narrow aisle. People pull the girls apart, one by one, to seat them. And the sorority sisters holler even louder because their young hearts are coming undone and they do not know what to do.

Sarah Jane's parents are sitting in the front row. But not together. Sarah Jane's dad, a big-time Baton Rouge doctor, is here today with his twenty-three-year-old wife, Jessica. She's wearing a black mini-dress, and her implants jiggle up and down as she sobs into her hanky. Dr. Bradford and his sexy young piece look straight ahead and try to avoid eye contact with the first Mrs. Bradford, who is sitting across the aisle from them.

Sarah Jane's mamma looks nice. She looks like a good mom—the kind of mom who's soft and warm when she hugs you. She's wearing a heavy black church dress and bawling her eyes out—convulsing with grief and despair, totally unable to keep it together because she's lost her baby girl. Sarah Jane's dark-eyed grandmother is holding Mrs. Bradford and cutting the good doctor dirty looks. Sarah Jane's brother, James, sits next to them, staring up at the white lilies on the shiny mahogany casket. This is the stuff that nightmares are made of and I wish that I could do something to let them know that things aren't as bad as they seem, but I can't. Because things are worse than bad.

As the choir lady sings "Amazing Grace" and the organist shakes the stained glass with a long, slow white folks' remix of the hymn, I wander the church looking for Sarah Jane's ghost. But I don't see her anywhere. I guess she was on God's A-list and got to go straight to heaven. However, it seems to me she could have at least gotten a day pass to come to her own funeral.

By now, the church is packed. Standing room only. Ashley and Kimbrough get here late and end up standing in the back of the sanctuary. They're holding hands and it's enough to make me want to take over Tucker so I can punch Kimbrough in the glasses. Ashley's crying into a Kleenex and it reminds me of how she was at my funeral. All stoned on Valium and weepy while her new boyfriend held her close. Now she's got herself another new boyfriend and another person to bury.

All this makes me so homesick for my life that it hurts. I'm jonesing for my body, for my Porsche, for my pot-smoking days and cat-chasing nights. Life is ripe with possibility when you're nineteen. But that possibility rots pretty fast in a grave.

As freaky as Sarah Jane was or I guess is, I do feel sorry for her. Actually, I feel real sorry for most everybody here. I really do. This hurts like hell. My mamma cried every morning for a year after I bought the farm. In fact, my parents were so screwed up by my death that they had my body cremated. I reckon it was their way of healing my broken neck. But what it did was leave no evidence behind to prove that I had been killed. Not that it would have even mattered. The police never suspected that I was murdered. Not by Ryan, at least. Besides, I had a glowing reputation as a spoiled-ass, liquor-sloshing screw-up, so my death didn't really surprise anyone. People were always talking about how reckless and stupid I was. At my funeral, my parent's friends consoled them with the fact that they were lucky that I wasn't behind the wheel at the time.

When you are young and rich and drink a little too much, people almost always think you're some kind of screw-up when you die. Like you did something to bring it on or that you were just fated to die. But I've got news for all those self-righteous bastards: They're not any safer than I was. When the shoe drops, the shoe drops. It doesn't matter if you dot your i's and cross your t's, you're still going to be a dead motherfucker when it happens.

I guess you could say I'm a little bitter. But look at what's going on here. Ryan is carrying on, business as usual. And nobody thinks a thing about it. Well, I take that back. Detective Watkins knows something is up. He's sharp. I guess that's why he just showed up at the funeral. Everybody turns around to look at him. People whisper back and forth as they try to figure out what a black man is doing at Sarah Jane's funeral. Watkins politely smiles back at the gawking faces and takes a seat in the very back. He pulls out his small spiral notepad and starts taking notes as the eulogies begin.

To help Maggie shed those extra pounds, Ryan fixes them both a low-carb, high-protein lunch. After the silent meal, he gets in his freshly repainted Jeep and drives over to Power Dorm. He has some unfinished business to take care of by the name of Alex Trudeaux. Ryan's got this freakish, serial killer sixth sense and he "knows" that Alex is the one who called the cops. So Ryan carries his backpack with him as he walks down the hall of Power Dorm and he looks at the room numbers, trying to find Alex's room. He finds the room and knocks on the door very politely. But there is no answer. He knocks again, a little bit louder this time, but still no answer. Ryan puts his ear to the door. He can hear movement and the faint songs from a stereo. Alex sees Ryan through his peephole so he hides behind his bed and prays that Ryan doesn't break down his door.

"Alex, open up. It's me, Ryan." Ryan knocks on the door lightly.

No answer. Ryan looks both ways down the hall and then knocks on the door again.

"Come on, Alex. Let me in. I have something real important to tell you. The chapter wants you back."

Alex shakes and holds his breath.

"Look, Alex, I'm going to leave you this DVD, and tell me what you think I should do with the other copies, okay?" Ryan pulls out a disc from his backpack and slides it under Alex's door.

"Call me when you're ready to talk!" Ryan slings his backpack over his shoulder, swaggers down the hall and back to his Jeep.

Nineteen

E ver since Sarah Jane Bradford died, Tucker Graham has been sober. And try as I might, I can't get back inside his thick head. He's really trying to get it together, trying to bring his grades up so that he can get initiated next semester. He studies all the time, and Ryan has been too busy dodging Detective Watkins to mess with him. So life for Tucker has been pretty quiet and normal.

I'm just going to sit back and wait. Might as well, I'm obviously not going anywhere. I'll let Tucker hit the books and pull his grades up so that he can get initiated next semester. Then when the doors are locked and the curtains are drawn that week, I'll take over and I'll throw Ryan down the stairs of Gamma Chi house, just like he did me. Then we'll see how Ryan likes being a ghost.

I know it's not that original of a plan, but I'm getting sick of waiting for the perfect moment. Besides, Ryan got away with it. So I figure, why can't I? That way, Tucker doesn't take the rap for doing my dirty work and I get my revenge. The funniest part will be seeing how everybody reacts to Ryan's dead body sprawled out at the bottom of that staircase. All those morons will probably say that those stairs are cursed after Ryan breaks his neck on them.

And for once, they'll be right.

At this point, I have no idea what's going to happen to me. But I figure if I have to walk this world for the rest of eternity, I'll at least get the satisfaction of killing Ryan and I'll be a much happier ghost for it. I'm here to tell you, forgiveness is highly overrated. In principle it sounds good, but in practice, revenge is the only way to pay the bills.

I follow Ryan around a lot these days, looking for a weak link in his armor, looking for ways to get to him. For once in his sorry life, he's worried. Detective Watkins follows him everywhere too. Every time Ryan turns around, the detective is right there stalking him, taking notes, in the quad, the bookstore, the library. Watkins has even started working out at Ryan's gym. He knows something is up with Ryan and he's become obsessed with the case. The only problem is there's no evidence. Sure, there's the whole doughnut-on-the-dicks story and Sarah Jane's run-in with Couvillion's naked ass, but those are all pretty much par for the course for college. Nothing points to a motive. Only thing is, Ryan never has motives. At least, not like normal people do. He's totally insane in the membrane and all you have to do is piss him off or catch him on a bad day and that's motive enough for him. However, if Watkins holds his net out there long enough, he's bound to catch some shit. But I'm not holding my breath. Everybody knows the longer a case stays open, the less likely it is to ever be solved. Blood trails run cold over time and murders fade into just freak accidents.

Ryan has been awfully neglectful of Maggie ever since she gained a few pounds. Besides, with Detective Watkins snooping around, he can't knock her around. So he figures, what's the point? She's too fat to screw and too important to his alibi to bruise up. So he works off his frustrations at the gym and with hookers like Cherie-Elise because just being around Maggie makes him want to slap her, and Ryan knows he can't afford that luxury right now.

As for Maggie, she's not doing so well. She's all weepy because she's pregnant and Ryan never calls or comes by. But I guess the bright side—if you can say that there's a bright side to any of this—is that Ryan hasn't laid a hand on her in over a month.

Without Ryan's abuse, Maggie really doesn't know what to do with herself. She's built her entire life around covering up all the bruises and shame. So to make up for this black gap in her life, she eats—a lot. Tubs of Blue Bell ice cream. Zapp's Crawtators. Marshmallows dipped in chocolate icing. Marie Callender's peach cobblers. Whole pans of Stouffer's lasagna. She eats tube after tube of Slice and Bake cookie dough. She swallows pinwheel rolls by the dozen, dipping them into half-melted sticks of butter.

As a result, Maggie plumps up in just a matter of weeks and becomes even more depressed. She turns into a recluse who never showers and never leaves her apartment. She's got over five hundred dollars worth of fines to Tri-Phi because she's missed so many chapter meetings. But she doesn't care. She's pregnant and desperate and getting fatter by the Blue Bell gallon. She thinks about getting an abortion, but the very thought drives her right to the freezer section of her nearby Albertson's. Maggie stuffs herself every day until she is full and numb, to the point where she can't think or feel anything. And when she's not eating or crying, she stays strung out on daytime television, trying to find redemption in Oprah's pep talks and book lists.

One sunny afternoon, Maggie pulls herself together and actually takes a shower, and while she's in there, she looks down at her swollen stomach and breasts. She cries hard and washes her tears down the drain with the shower spray. I have to say that my heart is breaking for her. I am a complete bastard; after all, I did this. I took advantage of Maggie at her weakest hour and I took what I could and this is what I left her with: a baby without a father.

Maggie stares at her naked body in the mirror and to be completely honest, she looks better than she ever has. She's not fat. She looks like some kind of water nymph or fertility goddess—with dewdrops on her belly. But what she sees is a different story, and she mourns deeply for her disappearing waist. Her weight was the only thing she could control and now that's gone. She sobs as she puts on her nightgown. She takes a couple of deep breaths and whimpers herself back to sleep. She can't face the day being this fat, no matter how sunny it is.

Maggie's weight is a very minor symptom of a much more major problem—her being pregnant. I know that women have babies by themselves all over the world and nobody bats an eyelash, but this is Louisiana and Baton Rouge debutantes don't get knocked up. Maggie Meadows is the closest thing LSU has to a celebrity. She's God's little gift to the sorority alums and socialites in this town. Maggie is the golden cookie cutter for every sorority girl on this campus. She is who they all want to act like, look like, even talk like. They completely adore her and they absolutely hate her. And as soon as all those girls and their mothers find out that the sweetheart of Gamma Chi is pregnant, they'll throw elaborate showers and teas full of evil gossip about her. And for someone like Maggie, who lives for people's high opinion of her, the very thought of this kind of rumor-fest is worse than a fiery hell. So she just keeps eating, sleeping, and skipping class. And praying for some kind of miscarriage.

Meanwhile, Detective Watkins and his partner, Detective Boudreaux, sit outside on the red brick patio of Highland Coffees, enjoying the sunshine and waiting for Alex Trudeaux. A rare Gulf breeze rustles the palmettos next to the detectives' iron table as Watkins reads the sports page and Boudreaux tries dipping a scone into his coffee.

"I hate these scone things." Boudreaux shakes his head. "Why doesn't this place serve beignets? We should have met this kid at the Coffee Call. Now, they got the beignets." Boudreaux munches on the soggy end of his scone.

"This is where he wanted to meet, okay?" Watkins folds his newspaper up and puts it on the table.

Boudreaux looks at his watch and growls, "Well, he's late."

"Be patient. He'll be here." Watkins takes a sip of his coffee and looks around at all the college kids with their bed heads and backpacks, walking from campus to order double tall skinny lattes and triple shots of espresso.

"Ugh! This ain't fit to eat." Boudreaux throws his scone back on the plate and pushes it away. "Anyway, if you ask me, I think this Trudeaux kid is yanking your chain. There's no way that Ryan Hutchins set that girl on fire. No way. I thought we'd already established that."

"Look, Trudeaux says he knows something. I want to talk to him."

"You're wasting my time with this frigging bullshit. The chief wants this case closed. And you're off chasing goddamn ghosts. I'm telling you. I got instincts. I can smell a killer a hundred miles away, and Ryan Hutchins ain't your man."

"We'll give Mr. Trudeaux ten more minutes and then we'll go. Okay?"

"Then what?" Boudreaux asks.

"Then we stop by his dorm and ask him why he stood us up."

"Give this frat-boy conspiracy a frigging rest. Ya heard me?"

"Do you have any better leads?"

"No, because my ass has been sniffing around frat houses and fairy-ass coffee shops." Boudreaux slurps his coffee. "Look, here's the profile: probably some swamp rat. A pyro or something. Probably lives in a stilt house with his mamma, slicing up animals and shit for the devil. That's who killed that little girl. Not Senator Hutchins's nephew."

"Well, I've got to hand it to you. You have yourself some instincts, all right." Watkins shakes his head.

"Instincts or not, bubba, Trudeaux ain't showing. That's all I'm saying." Boudreaux picks up his discarded scone, takes another bite, and spits it out. "Ugh, nasty!"

"That scone didn't get any better by sitting there."

"Come on, now. I'm hungry. How about we go down the street to the Chimes and get some real food, huh?" Boudreaux grumbles as he wipes the scone pieces off his pitted cheeks and mustache with a napkin.

"You can do whatever. I'm waiting right here for the kid to show." Watkins folds his arms and offers up his best fake smile.

"Yeah, you go ahead and do that, bubba. I'm going to get some lunch." Boudreaux gets up from the table and walks over to the Chimes without his partner.

* * *

As much as I hate to say it, I'm with Detective Boudreaux on this one. I don't think Alex is going to show and if he does I don't think he'll spill it, not after Ryan left that DVD on his doorstep. So I float down Chimes street, past the Chemical Jesus graffiti, past the Bayou, the Gap, past the Chimes and the Varsity, and down the alley to the Gamma Chi house where Miss Etta is cooking red beans and rice for lunch. I follow three barefoot pledges inside; each one is wearing a dirty baseball cap and carrying a suitcase of cheap beer. This is what I call classic Gamma Chi study skills. See, it's too beautiful a day to be in class, so these three fellows are going to soak up the sunshine on the roof and get drunk after lunch. They'll get the notes from some straight-A scholarship case who wants to go through Rush next year. Or better yet, they'll just look off his paper for the test.

I touch down in the kitchen so that I can talk to Miss Etta, but she's busy serving up the red beans and doesn't seem to notice me.

"Miss Etta." I wave my hand in front of her face and smile. "Hey, Miss Etta."

She just keeps serving the plates, acting like she doesn't see or hear me.

"Why are you ignoring me?"

She keeps slopping the beans on top of the rice and stacking a piece of cornbread on top of the plastic plates.

"Why are you acting like this?"

But no matter how I plead, Miss Etta acts like she can't see me. Actually, I don't think she's ignoring me. I honestly think she can't see or hear me. I think maybe she's lost her shine, so I tap her on the shoulder. She doesn't turn around. I scream in her ear and she doesn't even flinch. She just keeps on making the plates and passing them through the kitchen window to the hungry brothers standing in line for lunch.

I wonder what I did to cause this. Why now? Why all of a sudden can't she see me? This really blows. So I stay on Miss Etta's heels trying everything I can to get her attention. After she serves up all the red beans and rice, she walks over to the fridge and pulls out a big vat of banana pudding. The good kind with vanilla wafers and whipped cream and sliced overripe bananas. She pulls off the Saran Wrap and then starts slopping it into little baby-blue cafeteria bowls. I stand by her hoping—okay, praying—that she will see me and then she looks at me with one eyebrow cocked.

"You should try praying a little more often and you might not be standing in here watching me sling this pudding. You be up in heaven where you supposed to be."

"You can see me."

"Of course I can see you, baby." She puts her wooden spoon down and stares at me. "I just had my radio station tuned off, that's all. I get sick listening to your ass and the static in your attic."

"What?"

"I said"—she picks up the spoon and slaps it against my ghostly head—"I get sick of you running your lip in my ear. I'm sick of listening to you whining and cursing and carrying on. I need some peace." She continues scooping out the pudding and soggy cookies. Lanky-ass McCallahan comes up to the window and grabs a bowl.

"Mmmmm, pus-pocket surprise. My favorite." He winks at Miss Etta.

"Don't make me baptize your skinny ass with this hot grease back here." Etta brandishes her spoon at him.

"You know I'm just kidding with you, Miss Etta."

"Miss Etta don't play. She too old to be taking lip from some Big-Bird-looking white boy."

"Hey, now. I said I was just kidding."

"I told you I don't play! Now grab you two puddings and try to fatten your bony ass up and get out my face!" Miss Etta lowers her head and shakes her jowls.

McCallahan grabs a second bowl and sits down. Miss Etta has a way of putting people in their place.

"And now you." She turns around to me. "You could learn a

lesson or two from that boy right there. He does what he's told."

"Yeah, hot grease has a way of making people listen."

"Your ass is going to be in something hotter than grease if you don't start walking with the Lord, baby."

"Well, I guess I'm a lot like you. I don't play."

"Baby, God don't play either."

"I haven't seen him so I wouldn't know."

"Oh, Lord. You hopeless," she sighs. "Hopeless."

"Hope is overrated, especially when you have nothing to lose."

"Nothing but your eternal soul."

"Look, I have reasons for what I'm doing."

"Vengeance is mine sayeth the Lord. It don't say it's Conrad Sutton's." She puts her hands on her hips and bobs her head. "Your ass need to be praying for forgiveness—not plotting and planning to murder folks."

"Look . . ." I try to explain.

"No! You look! I have told you and I have told you. But you don't listen. And I'm tired of it. I try to be a good Christian. And I try to have patience with you. But you full of hate and I'm sick of it."

"So what are you saying?"

"I'm saying it's time for some tough love."

"What?"

"Tough love as in tough, T-O-O bad. Too bad, I ain't talkin' to you no more. I ain't gonna stand around talking to no murderous spirit no more."

"But you're all I got."

"No more!" Miss Etta shakes her head and shuts her eyes.

"But, please."

"No more." She points her finger toward the service window with one hand and rubs her gold cross with the other. "No more!"

And as she says those words to me with the fieriest of convictions, I am pushed away from her and out the kitchen service window. She pulls down the metal screen behind me and locks it—leaving me and about fifty small bowls of banana pudding sitting on the counter while the brothers sit at their tables, enjoying their lunch. They're all yucking it up because Ryan and Couvillion aren't here. Even the pledges are laughing and having a good time. I walk around the room feeling sorry for myself, looking at how lucky and alive everyone is. I get a heaping helping of jealousy and envy as they all fill up on Miss Etta's red beans and rice. And then, just when I'm at my lowest, Kimbrough stands up and yells, "Food fight!"

He slings a handful of banana pudding at Sammy Blanco, hitting him right in his midget face. Blanco retaliates by chucking his cornbread muffin, but he hits McCallahan in the mouth instead. In just a matter of seconds, the beautiful Gamma Chi dining room becomes one big slippery war zone with muddy red beans and yellow pudding snot everywhere. It's all over everybody, the table, the walls, and the floor. The guys are smearing it in each other's faces, slipping and falling down in the shit, throwing it and laughing— laughing hard because this is what life is all about. Food fights. Being big overgrown kids and enjoying this big mess of a world and everything that it throws at you—laughing even when you get stung by a cornbread muffin.

But all this happiness is just too much for me. I'm glad and all that they can be alive to enjoy things like food fights, but watching this just puts me in a bad mood, a real bad mood. I'm so jealous right now that I can't see straight. That should be me throwing that cornbread. That should be me laughing and wiping pudding out of my eyes. It makes me mad and lonely all at the same time. How can Miss Etta not see what Ryan took away from me? How can she not understand? I'm hurting here. Hurting deep. How can she just cut me off ? I have to get out of here. I have to leave. I go where I know happiness can't be found. I go to Alex Trudeaux's.

Alex doesn't bother to watch the DVD that Ryan left him; he knows what's on it. Instead, Alex breaks the silver disc with his bare hands. Then he very calmly takes the shards of the broken disc and starts cutting himself with them. He begins to bleed but he doesn't cry. I guess you could say he's messed up about doing the deed with a goat. Maybe even a little crazy from it. Can't say that I blame him. Ugh. I don't know how he did that in the first place. The smell alone is enough to make you gag. How he caught wood for a goat is beyond me.

The end result has taken Alex down, down far and deep into a very bad place. His innocence, that stupid-headed boyishness about him, is gone. There's nothing in his eyes except an empty craziness that he fills with compulsively counting everything: his footsteps to and from class, the letters in his name or in words spoken to him, the number of cracks on the stucco walls of the quadrangle. And the real topper is his grades. The bastard studies night and day, filling his head with as many facts and figures as he can. I reckon he's trying to somehow crowd out his memories of the goat. Whatever the reason, he's setting the curve in all of his classes. Plus, all of a sudden, he's keeping his room spotless like a museum, like he never did before. Poor Alex has become this soul-broken overachiever, and since he lives by himself and none of his Gamma Chi pledge brothers will speak to him, he's falling fast and there's nobody to catch him. The only person who ever calls him is Tucker Graham. But Alex never answers his phone; he just counts the rings until his answering machine picks up.

But as crazy as Alex may be, he still has the wherewithal to stop talking to the police. Ryan's threat is enough to keep anyone's mouth shut. Can you imagine if Ryan sent copies of Alex and the goat to everybody on campus? To Alex's mamma and daddy? That's some serious blackmail. And lucky for Alex, he still has the sense not to tempt Ryan.

It's situations like this when I know I'm right in killing Ryan. He's broken Maggie. He tried raping Ashley. He's murdered Sarah Jane. And now he's driven Alex completely insane and useless. This has all got to stop.

Everyone here is too damn young to be crying this damn much.

Twenty

The clouds of late November have descended on South Louisiana, bringing with them a gray and bleak Thanksgiving Day. The air is full of humidity and dishwater feelings. And since I'm stuck in Baton Rouge, I spend this day of thanks watching Ryan and his family eat turkey. It's a real joy. Ryan is an only child, and I see where he got all his charm. His dad is a nitrous-oxide-sniffing kiddy dentist, and his mother's a fifty-five-year-old anorexic. Lovely family. In fact, they're very highly thought of in Baton Rouge, especially among the state politicos—being that Dr. Hutchins's brother is a U.S. senator and all. I reckon they'll throw one hell of a funeral when I finally do kill Ryan. They'll probably get the governor to give the eulogy.

The Hutchinses sit in their Acadiana fortress with its antique bricks, iron gates, and gaslights, all nestled back in the sprawling tarantula oaks of Beau Cage. Mrs. Hutchins has her maids dressed in starched black uniforms while they serve the family this big-ass spread of Cajun-fried turkey, oyster stuffing, cranberry relish, and sweet potato pie. Mrs. Hutchins very delicately picks at her food as she runs her mouth all through dinner.

"Ryan," she drawls, "you said you shaved your head for what now?"

"Gamma Chi, mom. We've already been over this."

"And what does Maggie think of your shaved head?"

"She's fine with it."

"Well, I guess I gave her more credit than she deserves." Mrs. Hutchins balls her hand into a fist full of diamonds and liver spots and shakes it at Ryan. "If I was a young lady, I wouldn't be seen dead on the arm of some skinhead . . ."

"Can we change the subject?" Ryan drops his fork on his plate.

"All I'm saying is, I don't see why a handsome young man would do that to himself." She smiles graciously. "Don't you agree, Henry?"

"Sally, leave the boy alone." Dr. Hutchins chews on a piece of turkey skin and covers his mouth with a napkin. "Hell, could be worse. Could be a nipple ring." He winks at his son.

"Hen-ery, please." She pushes her food around her plate. "I will not have such common language used at my dinner table."

There's a long silence broken up with silverware clinking against the fine china. And then Mrs. Hutchins starts in again.

"It's really too bad Maggie couldn't join us. Where did you say she was, dear?"

"She's got family obligations. Her grandparents are coming in from Slidell."

"Oh my. Her people are from Sly-dell? Ryan, you never told me that."

"So what?" Ryan cuts his turkey and dips it in cranberries.

"In two words: White. Trash," Mrs. Hutchins whispers carefully. "You know, I always thought it strange that Maggie's mother wasn't in the DAR, but now I know. Trailer trash from Slidell. It's a wonder they let her debut. Honey, we might have to rethink this one. Got to keep those bloodlines clean."

Ryan looks down at his plate and shakes his head. A quiet rage builds up in him, and all he can think about is decking Maggie square in the jaw. Funny thing is, Maggie's grandparents are long dead and Ryan has no idea where they're from. The truth is, he refuses to be seen with Maggie in public, or at home, until she drops some poundage.

So instead, Maggie spends her Thanksgiving at home with her parents and two younger sisters. She deflects their questions about her weight and tries her best to conceal her morning sickness. It's just as well that Maggie's not with Ryan today, because Mrs. Hutchins is worse than Maggie's own mother when it comes to body-fat obsession. Mrs. Hutchins is like some kind of weight-guessing carny. She can tell you, to the ounce, how much weight you've gained and where you've gained it. It's a real talent.

I reckon Maggie's fragile ego probably couldn't have handled that kind of scrutiny, but Ryan uninviting her to his family's Thanksgiving dinner definitely took its toll on her. The price she pays is exactly five Burrito Supremes from Taco Bell and one pecan pie, eaten late that night after Thanksgiving dinner.

Other than supper with Ryan's family, my Thanksgiving is just another fun-filled day in ghostland. Just more time spent waiting for next semester's initiation. However, I am curious as to how my family spent the holiday. I bet you Daddy took Mamma out of the country, to maybe Greece or Spain.

It's really weird; I know every move that Ryan Hutchins makes, every shit that he takes, but I have no idea if my parents are even stateside.

Alex Trudeaux comes back from Thanksgiving freakier than ever. While he was on break, some younger kids from his high school made baa-baa noises at him when he was at the Mall of Louisiana. Obviously, the word is out about why Gamma Chi balled Alex. And now everywhere he goes, cute little sorority girls turn up their noses at him or they whisper and giggle.

Today, Alex is back in his dorm room. He's trying to count every word in the dictionary. But the counting doesn't work anymore. Everything he had is gone. And that awful funk-smelling memory of goat flesh stains his every thought. The Gamma Chis hooting and hollering bleeds in his ears—"Go-baby-go!" So he turns up his stereo to drown out the pain. Eventually, Alex cracks up. A single tear runs down his cheek and then he starts to cry like no human I've ever seen. Weeping and wrenching his body, trying to squeeze that dirty-ass memory out of his eyes and through his tears. And you know what, I don't blame him. I know I joke about him and I make fun of him for doing it, but he just wanted to be-long—so much so he was willing to do anything, even betray him-self. Poor bastard.

However, before Alex can get himself so down low that he'll never get back up, the phone rings loud, and Alex grabs it off the hook just to shut it up.

"Hello," he sniffles.

"Mr. Trudeaux?" A voice, deep like Barry White, burps through the phone at him.

"Yeah. Who is this?" Alex sniffles.

"Detective Watkins. Are you, uh, crying?"

"Uh, no. Just a second." Alex grabs Kleenex off his bedside table and blows his nose. "Allergies."

"Oh." The detective waits for him to finish.

"Sorry, sir. I've got really bad allergies."

"So you're a hard man to get in touch with."

"I was gone. It was Thanksgiving."

"I realize that, but we had an appointment."

"Appointment?"

"Wednesday. Highland Coffees. Eleven o'clock."

"Oh, man. I totally forgot."

"You forgot?"

Alex can feel Detective Watkins's breath exhale through the phone, full of exasperation and coffee halitosis.

"Do you think that Sarah Jane Bradford's mamma forgot that her daughter was burnt to death? Do you think she forgot that her daughter's killer is still out there walking around, eating leftover turkey and dressing? Do you think she forgot that?"

"Uh, no sir. I'm sorry. It's just that . . ."

"Look, I'm about two minutes from your dorm. I'll be right over."

"Sure." Alex's face goes blank.

"Okay then, bye."

"Bye." Alex hangs up. He looks down at the knotted phone cord and thinks dangerous thoughts.

* * *

Alex Trudeaux isn't the only person having dangerous thoughts. Now that Maggie is back at her apartment, she is too. However, before she can do too much thinking, she saves herself with a bag of Doritos and some hot Velveeta and Rotel. This or a can of cream cheese icing has been her solution every time she starts to think about how royally screwed she is. And as much as I hate to say this, she's really starting to get big. And I'm not being an ass-hole when I say this. It's just the facts.

Maggie's getting fat has done something weird to the emotional calculus of her relationship with Ryan. It's majorly upset the equation. In fact, he's lost all interest in her. Maggie is invisible to him now. A nonperson. I guess in Ryan's mind, a fat Maggie doesn't even exist. And this has totally devastated her. He never returns her calls and he never comes by to see her.

But this is probably the best thing that ever happened to Maggie. Lord knows, Ryan never would have let her leave him, not when she was so hot that she melted butter just by smiling. Maggie, on the other hand, doesn't really see being fat and pregnant and having lost her boyfriend as a blessing. She's ready to open up her wrists. She's desperate for love and redemption, even if it comes with a smack or two. Today, Maggie's pain is growing so big that there's not enough cookie dough in the world to spackle the holes of her broken heart.

Maggie flips the channels on the TV to find solace in E! gossip or the Home Shopping Network. She scans the recesses of her memory for happier times and all she can remember is the only guy who ever showed her love: me, or rather, me inside of Tucker. So she gets herself together and she calls Tucker Graham. The phone rings and rings, and Maxwell Bonecaze picks up.

"Hello."

"Hi, is Tucker there?" Maggie asks.

"Sawee, he's gone. Can I take a messidge?"

"Uh, no. I mean, yeah. Just tell him Maggie Meadows called."

"Maggie who?"

"Mag-gie Mead-dows."

"*The* Maggie Meadows?" Maxwell asks with total disbelief.

"I guess." Maggie sort of laughs. "I'm in his geology class. Just tell him that I called. He's got my number."

"Yeah. Sure. I mean I would be gwad to. I mean it's real nice talking to you."

She can almost hear Maxwell's face turning red.

"Okay, thanks." Maggie hangs up the phone and smiles a real smile for the first time in about two months.

Detective Watkins drives up to Power Dorm in an unmarked white Chevy Caprice Classic. He's wearing his gym clothes: a BRPD muscle shirt and shorts. He grabs his pen and note pad and gets out of the car. All the kids in the parking lot, carrying in their clean laundry from the break, watch Detective Watkins; they breathe a collective sigh of relief when they see that he doesn't have a drug-sniffing dog with him.

The detective walks down the pale green cinder blocks of a hallway to room two-fifteen. The smell of piss and industrial-strength citrus overwhelms him and he covers his nose. He knocks on Alex's door and before he can knock a second time, the door flies open and Alex grabs Watkins by the arm and pulls him inside.

"Hello, Detective. Come on in." Alex quickly shuts the door behind them.

"Hey, what's the rush?" Watkins asks.

"Oh, no rush." Alex grins. "I just didn't want to leave you waiting."

Watkins looks around Alex's room. It's spotless.

"So what can I help you with?" Alex pulls out this orange plastic chair from his study desk. "Here, have a seat."

Detective Watkins sits down while Alex remains standing and fidgeting.

"Sit down, Mr. Trudeaux." Watkins pulls out his note pad and pencil. "You're bugging me standing over me like that."

"Oh, sorry." Alex plops down on his bed.

"Okay, Alex, how well did you know Sarah Jane Bradford?"

"Oh yeah, Sarah Jane. See, I only met her once at an exchange so I didn't 'know her' know her." Alex nods his head.

"Okay." Watkins scribbles that down in his pad.

"What was that?" Alex cranes his neck. "What did you just write down?"

"I'm taking notes. Is that okay with you?"

"Uh, sure. I mean, nobody's going to see them, right?"

"Who you worried about seeing these notes, Mr. Trudeaux?"

"Uh, nobody. I mean, I don't want Ryan to, you know, think that I'm trying to get him in trouble."

"Are you?"

"No, of course not. I think I probably just . . ."

"He did it?" Watkins looks deep into Alex's eyes.

"No . . . maybe I jumped to the wrong conclusions." Alex bobs his head up and down, looking everywhere but in the detective's eyes.

"Weren't you and Ryan fraternity brothers?"

"I don't know." Alex looks down at the floor and then at the ceiling tiles. "I just don't know."

"What do you mean, you don't know?" Watkins squints. "Has he threatened you?"

"Who, Ryan?" Alex is caught in the headlights of the truth. "No, no, I haven't talked to Ryan since I got—since I dropped out of Gamma Chi."

"Why'd you drop out?" The detective chews on his pen.

"I needed to concentrate on school. Too much partying."

"Did they haze?"

Alex hears the bleating of the goat in his head and the banging of jungle drums in his heart.

"Uh, not really."

"Not really? So you just quit?"

"Yeah, I just quit."

There's a long, stale silence. And the detective lets out a sigh.

"Why won't you level with me, Alex?"

"Look, sir, I told you I made a mistake. I don't know anything. I really don't."

"Has he threatened you?"

"No, nobody's threatened me!" Alex stands up. "I think that's about all I have to say. Okay?"

"I'm not leaving until I get some answers." The detective stands up.

Alex takes a deep breath and musters up all the courage he has to ask, "Do-do you have a search warrant?"

"What? No. Are you kidding?"

"Okay, then. My dad's a lawyer and I could get you in big trouble if you don't leave right now."

"Look, kid, I don't need no search warrant to question you. Calm down."

"I think you need to go." Alex's voice cracks.

Detective Watkins puts his hand on Alex's shoulder.

"I can help you."

"I don't need any help." Alex pushes him away. "Please, just leave!" Alex looks down at his feet.

"Mr. Trudeaux, I don't know why this is so hard for you. But there's a girl, your age, and she burned alive. Do you know how much that must have hurt?"

Alex looks up at the detective; his eyes are swollen and red like two bee stings. He hears Sarah Jane's screams over the goat and the words start gathering up in his mouth, like they might just jump out.

"I'm giving you a chance to do right by this girl, Mr. Trudeaux. Tell me why Ryan would want her dead."

Alex tries to catch his breath and he wipes the tears from his eyes. He takes a couple of breaths and he sings like a gospel choir.

Maggie's phone call with Maxwell was like a double dose of Prozac. She's actually putting on makeup and fixing her hair. She puts on a long black dress and a big gray sweater. She looks pretty. I don't know where she's going, but at least she's not crying in her bed eating little buckets of sugar and lard, waiting for Oprah to save her.

Maggie's roommate, Erica, is in the kitchen on the phone, talking to her boyfriend, Billy, and smoking a cigarette. Erica hasn't slept at the apartment in over a month. She shacks over at Billy's and only uses this apartment to keep her clothes and to call her folks from. However, it's getting close to dead week—the week before finals. And like the rest of the campus, she's moved back to her own apartment to start ramping up to study.

She says good-bye to Billy and hangs up the phone. Maggie walks into the kitchen to get a Diet Coke.

"Don't you look cute." Erica blows her smoke away from herself and then fans it.

"Hey sweetie," Maggie kisses her on the cheek. "Long time no see."

"Yeah, I know. Don't even start." Erica checks Maggie up and down.

"So how's Billy?"

"Fine. I guess. He just pissed me off. He's all in a bad mood because he's got a D going into his organic chemistry final, and I'm forbidden to see him until after finals. Can you believe?"

"Like it's your fault he didn't study all semester." Maggie plays along.

"Exactly." Erica takes a long dramatic drag off her cigarette.

"So what's going on with you?" Erica asks.

"Oh, nothing much. Just trying to get ready for finals."

"So has Prince Asshole been over here a lot since I've been gone?"

"Who, Ryan?"

"There are like all these stinky lasagna trays and ice cream buckets in the trash. I mean, does that boy ever stop eating?" Erica exhales and fans it away.

"Oh yeah, he's a bottomless pit." Maggie sort of laughs.

"Really? I thought he was like Mister Healthy." Erica inspects her French manicure. "Well, whatever. It's a good thing he works out because he would be a total fatty if he didn't."

"Erica, you crack me up." Maggie grabs her purse and keys. "I'll see you when I get back. I've got some errands to run."

"Okay, Magpie. I'll see you when you get back." Erica turns on the kitchen faucet and puts out her cigarette before she throws it in the disposal.

As soon as Maggie shuts the door. Erica picks up the phone.

"Charmaine, hey girl." She lights a fresh cigarette. "Yeah, I'm back at my apartment. Maggie just left. Get this—there are like a thousand lasagna trays and ice cream cartons in her garbage. No, I'm not kidding. Her butt is humongous. She's gained at least fifteen, twenty, thirty pounds easily. We're talking major eating disorder . . . Yeah. No wonder nobody's seen her in the past month."

Detective Watkins is smiling and singing to the car radio. He got exactly what he needed from Alex, and now he's driving in the stop-and-go traffic on Dalrymple Drive to the Garden District, to Detective Boudreaux's house. His brain is on fire, tying up the loose ends and clarifying motives. He knew Ryan was the one, and everything that Alex told him about the Jeep and the doughnuts and the hazing is the strongest lead yet. He's just got to organize his thoughts. There's a coherent thread there somewhere. He's just not sure where.

He turns on Boudreaux's street. It's full of quaint little fifties-style houses, some fixed up, some not. Boudreaux's house is one that's not—with its mildewed pink paint and burglar bars. There's a group of shirtless boys chasing and hitting each other in Boudreaux's driveway, so Watkins parks on the street and walks up to the house. The kids stop their cussing and punching to stare at Watkins as he approaches. The oldest boy, a chubby twelve-year-old in need of a training bra, hollers, "Can we help you or sumptin?"

"Yeah," Watkins smiles at the boys, "I'm here to see your daddy."

The boys freeze and stand there with their mouths gaping.

"Wait right here. I'll git 'em." The boy runs inside the house, slamming the screen door behind him, forgetting to close the real door. His voice echoes out onto the front lawn. "Diddy! There's some black man out here to see you!"

The other three boys huddle together and stare at Watkins as if he might be here to steal their birthdays.

Boudreaux comes outside dressed in his New Orleans Saints sweat suit; his chubby son slips out past him and runs back to play.

"Oh, it's you." Boudreaux furrows his brow and then smiles. "Whaddya doing here?"

"I got what we needed. That Trudeaux kid sang like a canary."

"What?" Boudreaux pauses as if he's actually thinking. "Come on inside. We gotta talk about this." He waves him up to the house.

Watkins walks up the crumbling cement steps and then Boudreaux holds him in place.

"Wait just a sec." Boudreaux turns his head and yells inside. "Tempy, you dressed? We got company!"

"What? Company!" a high-pitched woman's voice shrieks back. "I ain't got no clothes on! I'm breast feeding da baby!"

"That's why I'm telling you we got company! Go git in the back da house and git ya'robe on!" he yells.

Once the coast is clear of naked housewives, Watkins follows his partner into the house. The smell of fried food and dirty diapers is everywhere. He walks with Boudreaux into the wood-paneled den where he sits down on their green leather couch in front of a big-screen TV. Boudreaux sits in "his" chair and picks up the remote and mutes the television.

"All right, now let's talk." He pulls out the footrest on his La-Z-Boy.

"I got Alex Trudeaux to tell me everything. I mean everything." Watkins grins.

"What exactly is everything?"

"That Ryan knew Sarah Jane. He lied to us. She spray-painted his Jeep. There was this ongoing hostility between them. He sent her doughnuts after he and the rest of the fraternity put them on their penises."

"You're shitting me. That's pretty damn funny."

"What's wrong with you? A girl is dead because of all that."

"So you're telling me that Ryan Hutchins torched this girl because she vandalized his Jeep."

"Well, yeah. I think there was more going on. But yeah, I think that was part of it."

"Let me get this straight. We've got this kid, Mr. Big-Man-on-Campus. And he—in front of an entire crowd at Tiger Stadium—catches this lil' gal on fire and you're telling me nobody recognized him."

"It was Halloween."

"Ryan has an alibi—his girlfriend. And you ain't got nothing but this pissed-off Trudeaux kid, who wasn't even there, who's talking smack about this guy because he probably kicked his little wussy-butt."

"I know Ryan did it. What about the spray-paint on his car? What about the doughnuts?"

"That's not a case. Hell, that's not even a lead. That's a college prank."

"So what are you saying?" Watkin's eyes narrow.

"I'm saying that we close this frigging case. I'm saying that girl was wearing cotton balls. Cotton balls sprayed on with flammable glue, for chrissakes. And I'm saying that it was probably an accident. An open flame. A cigarette ash. And poof! She went up. I mean, hell, those stupid kids were up there playing with rattlesnakes."

"But I'm telling you, I've got this gut feeling. There's more to all this."

"Look, bubba, you might have yourself a gut but you ain't got yourself a case. Least not where I'm sitting."

Now you see why my own death never got investigated as a

murder. Boudreaux or some lazy-ass like him was probably on the case. It's like I said, people always chalk up young deaths—especially ones on a college campus—as freak accidents brought on by the very person who was killed. There's a lot of psychobabble involved as to why most people want to believe this. However, in Boudreaux's case, I don't think it's a fear of death. I think the whole reason why he wants to close this case has more to do with keeping himself parked in front of the TV so he can watch Sports-Center.

While Detective Boudreaux couldn't care less about Sarah Jane's murder, it is all that Alex can think about. He's horrified that Ryan will somehow find out that he talked to the police again. He's afraid that Ryan will send the goat movie to every sorority house, to his church, or maybe even to his parents. Alex just knows all the Gamma Chis are sitting around watching the DVD and laughing. And you know what? He's right. Jeff Couvillion has about worn that disc out showing it to any and everybody who will watch. So whether or not Ryan burns copies of it and sends them out doesn't really matter, because the whole campus already knows every nasty last detail. I mean, that's just too good of a story for it not to spread like wildfire. Hell, they're probably even talking about it at Tulane and Ole Miss by now.

There's a knock at Alex's door; it's the Domino's pizza man, but Alex checks his peephole just to make sure. He opens the door and it's actually a pizza person. But with her Indigo Girl haircut and big man arms, you can't really tell that he's a she through the peeper. In fact, you can't really tell too well standing face to face with her.

"One cheese pizza. That'll be ten-oh-seven." She pulls the pizza box out of the giant red vinyl envelope and smiles.

"What's that smell?" Alex starts to freak. "What's that smell?"

"What do you mean? It don't smell like nothing but a pizza"— the woman sniffs the box—"see?" She shoves the box in Alex's face.

"Ugh!" He pushes the box away. "Get that out of here!"

"Hey, man. What's your problem?" The pizza lady opens the box and shows him a perfectly normal, steaming cheese pizza. "See, ain't nothing wrong with it. It's still hot, even."

"What kinda cheese is that?"

"Cheese?" The friendly lesbian makes weird eyes at Alex. "You know, pizza kind of cheese. Mozzarella."

"It smells like goat cheese." Alex stares at it.

"No, this ain't goat cheese. Maybe at other places, but Domino's ain't all fancy like that."

"It's goat cheese. I can smell it. Get it out of here!"

He slams the door on the pizza lady and locks it. The big woman knocks insistently on the door, but eventually she gives up. Alex ignores her. He's stoned on that horrible night. All Alex can think about is that horrific pizza full of goat cheese, blood, and sex; he curls up on his bed in a fetal position and rocks back and forth.

I'm sick of watching people go baby and cry. So I leave Alex's room, and I go to another wing of Power Dorm to Tucker Graham's.

And lo and behold, Maggie Meadows is standing outside knocking on his door. She's got on dark sunglasses and a baseball hat along with her big sweater and long black dress. It's obvious that she doesn't want to be seen. Tucker eventually stumbles to the door; he was busy choking his rooster. He spies Maggie in the peephole. So he runs around and gets all cleaned up. Finally, Tucker opens the door acting like he was asleep. He reeks of hand lotion.

"Hi, can I come in? I think we need to talk." Maggie tips her sunglasses.

"Uh, yeah. Sure."

Maggie walks in. The beds are all unmade and there are papers and dirty clothes everywhere. Tucker hurries to pull out a chair from his desk.

"Here, have a seat."

"Thanks." Maggie takes off her shades and looks around. There's a bottle of Lubriderm on Tucker's bedside table.

Tucker catches her looking at it. His face turns a few shades redder than his hair; Maggie just smiles and acts like she doesn't know what it's for.

"So how have you been?"

"Uh, fine." Tucker plops down on his bed. He kicks a pair of skid-marked grippers under it with his foot before Maggie spots those too.

"I haven't talked to you in a long time." She forces a smile and her eyes keep darting to the lotion.

"Yeah, you never come to geology anymore." Tucker is reeling with embarrassment.

"I know." Maggie looks away.

"So do you want my notes or something?"

"Why are you acting like this?" Her eyes begin to tear up.

"Like what?" Tucker's mouth drops. "What's the matter? Are you okay?"

"No, Tucker, I'm not okay." She begins to cry. "I'm pregnant."

"Oh, shit." Tucker lunges for the Kleenex next to his bed and hands it to her.

"Thank you." Maggie pulls a couple of tissues and blows her nose.

"So what are you and Ryan going to do?"

"It's not Ryan's." She stops her crying and looks straight at Tucker.

"Then whose is it?"

"Yours."

The memories of him tangled up with Maggie rev their engines and slam his hood. They run over Tucker like an eighteen-wheeler, and he actually faints. Maggie clutches her Kleenex and tries to revive him. I, on the other hand, take this opportunity to dive right on in. I push Tucker's jilted consciousness out of the way and I take the driver's seat. I open his eyes and see Maggie hovering by my head, gently slapping my face.

"Wake up, Tucker. Wake up."

I reach up and kiss her full on the lips. She pushes me away.

"Stop that!" She stands up and wipes her mouth as she backs away from me.

I sit up and smile.

"Just thought I'd steal a little kiss while you were down here."

"That's what got me in this mess to begin with. Remember?"

"Yeah, I remember." I stand up.

She keeps backing up toward the door.

"Stop looking at me like that."

"Like what?" I wink at her.

"Oh, I don't know. Just stop smiling like that." She looks down.

I get right up on her and we lock eyes.

"Like what?" I sort of whisper.

Her eyes are big and green and full of pain. I put my hand on her cheek and she closes her eyes. I reach over and very softly touch my lips to hers. And that's about all it takes to melt her. She grabs onto to me and she hugs me like she's holding on for dear life. I push the dirty clothes and crap off Tucker's bed and we kiss. It's sad kissing at first, like we just need to hold on to something to keep from falling in to something sadder. But then Maggie's tears mix with our lips and our tongues, and we start to forget about all the pain we're in. We tug and pull at each other's clothes. We kiss and rub and strip each other. And before we can get there all the way, the door flies open and in walks Maxwell. Maggie pops up and covers her naked breasts.

I turn around with my pants around my ankles.

Maxwell drops the books he was carrying.

"Get out of here!" I shout at him.

"Sorry, dude. Sorry." He turns around and shuts the door behind him. You can hear him singing to himself down the hall. "Tuckay gettin' some bootay!"

She jumps up and puts her bra back on.

"Hey, where are you going?"

"We just got busted by your roommate." She pulls her dress over her head. "I'm not waiting for the rest of Power Dorm."

"I can lock the door. Come on. I mean look at me here."

"I said, no."

"Okay, okay, calm down." I pull my pants up and walk over to her. She lets me put my arms around her swollen waist. "I guess there's plenty of time for that when we get married."

She pushes me away. "I hope you're kidding."

"Kind of kidding. Kind of not."

"I'm not marrying you."

"Why not?"

"Tucker, I don't even know you."

I feel like someone just filled me full of buckshot.

"I don't even know what I'm doing here." She puts on her sweater and her baseball cap. "We'll have to talk about this later. I can't handle you getting all crazy about this. Not right now."

"But I thought . . ."

"Thought what? That because you knocked me up that I'd have to marry you?"

"No. It's just that I thought . . ."

"Tucker, I don't know what we have here. No, wait. Actually, I do. We had sex. And that doesn't mean that you love me any more than I love you. It just means I got pregnant."

"That's not true. I love you." I can feel the heat of tears burning these eyes.

"No, you don't, Tucker." She looks at me with an icy stab. "You don't even know me."

She storms out of the room and slams the door behind her.

I stand there stunned from the pain, like I just got punched in the nose. It hurts so bad that I jump out of Tucker's body to get away from it. Tucker wakes up with his whole body aching, not knowing why. I stand beside him feeling the same because the pain didn't go away. It's the kind that hurts whether you're dead or alive.

Twenty-One

O n the night before the last exams at LSU, there is a stench in Power Dorm that has grown so rank and so terrible that the whole dorm has to be evacuated. The stink is everywhere. And it's worse than the nastiest fart you've ever smelled. It smells ungodly. It smells like death—a long-forgotten death. And it's coming from room two-fifteen, Alex's room. He killed himself at the beginning of dead week, after he wigged out about the pizza. And since he never had a roommate, his body has been hanging in his dorm room going on a week. Now, he just hangs there with his tongue sticking out and maggots everywhere. He's stinking up the place with this scream of a smell, begging people to put him to rest. I wander around his room looking for his lost soul. Maybe I can offer him some consolation, some company. I sure could have used some when I croaked. But I can't find him. I guess that's what they mean by lost soul. Come to think of it, I guess that's what I am too.

Lost.

The campus police come to investigate the odor, thinking that it's a stink bomb—some end-of-the-semester prank. Boy, are they surprised when they find Alex's rotten body hanging from a noose of neckties. The Baton Rouge coroner is called in and a small army arrives in biohazard suits, goggles, and masks. They run in and examine the corpse. They do their deal: tag it and zip it up in a black body bag. As they're strapping the corpse onto a gurney, Detective Watkins shows up. He maneuvers through all the dorm residents in the parking lot. Everybody is crowding against the yellow crime scene tape, holding their noses and hoping to see some real blood and guts.

Watkins flashes his badge to a campus cop and walks under the tape. He runs down the hall to Alex's room. They're wheeling the body out by the time he gets there. His eyes water from the stench. The coroner, a little man with a comb-over, is supervising the investigation.

"How'd it happen?" Watkins flashes his badge to the coroner, who is busy taking pictures of the room.

"Suicide. Probably lost it over finals. Maybe his girlfriend broke his heart. Who knows?"

"Are you sure it was a suicide?" Watkins covers his mouth and nose.

"Positive. He hung himself." The coroner takes another picture of Alex's closet with its straight rows of starched shirts and spit-polished shoes.

"I want to see the body."

"Look, Detective." The coroner puts his camera down. "It stinks pretty bad in here in case you haven't noticed. So I'm taking the body out of here so these kids can get back to studying. If you want to take a look, you can follow me to my office. Or you could follow procedure and wait for my report. But right now, I'm getting this place cleaned up."

"Sorry, didn't mean to overstep my bounds. It's just that I knew the kid."

"Well, I'm very sorry about your loss. I really am. And I don't mean to be rude, but I have a little girl at home who's having a birthday, and I'd really like to get out of here. How about we talk tomorrow?"

"Sure. I'll call you. Thanks."

"No problem." The coroner walks over to Alex's medicine cabinet, opens it, and snaps a picture.

Watkins catches up with the coroner's team outside as they roll the body into the parking lot. He stands there as the body is loaded into the coroner's van. He watches his only real lead drive away as the tiny red taillights of the minivan disappear down Highland Road.

I sort of feel sorry for Detective Watkins, but really he has nothing to worry about. He needs to go home and spend time with his pretty new wife. Because little does he know, I'm taking care of business. If I have anything to do with it, this case will be closed. Soon.

While Alex's body is being locked away at the morgue, waiting for his parents to come claim it, Ryan is waiting on a body himself: Cherie-Elise's. Ryan has always been one of her best customers, but ever since he stopped seeing Maggie, he's become a daily trick.

Cherie-Elise always runs late, so Ryan takes the opportunity to do a couple of lines of coke, to get ready for his all-night fuck-fest. Before Ryan can get it all up his nose, there's a knocking at the door.

"Open da do-ah, shuga!" a voice sweet and dirty like molasses calls out.

Ryan snorts up his last line and stands up all red faced and squinty eyed. He sneezes and then staggers through his head rush to the door and opens it.

There's Cherie-Elise in all her hooker glory. She's dolled up in a tiny black miniskirt with nothing else on but a gold Wonderbra and spiked high heels. The mole over her lip is darkened and her lips are a sticky red.

"Ew-wee, look at you, ché bé." She tongues his ear and bites it. "Are you ready for some sweet, sweet shuga pussy, baby?" she purrs.

Ryan grabs her ass and pulls her inside, locking the door behind them. He licks and fondles over and under what little clothing she's got on. Cherie wiggles and gasps for an Oscar; she's quite the actress. But Ryan—like most guys who believe they're actually getting a hooker off—always thinks that the hooker is moaning for what's in the front of his pants and not what's in the back, like his wallet.

Cherie-Elise starts in on Ryan. And before long the whole room smells like canned tuna and Calvin Klein Obsession. They get into all sorts of acrobatics and what have you. Cherie-Elise gives her best porn-star performance ever and after they're done, they cuddle naked in Ryan's bed. He holds his head to her enormous plastic boobs and hugs her in the gentlest way.

"Now how was that?" she coos.

"It was good." Ryan nuzzles her chest and plays with her silver dollar nipples.

"How about you let Lil' Miss Rumpshaka have a lil' toot, den?"

"Sure. The bag is over there." Ryan points to the cocaine sitting on his desk. "Help yourself."

Cherie-Elise gets up barebacked and cuts herself some lines with the razor blade sitting next to the bag. She rolls up a twenty-dollar bill and sucks the coke up like some kind of big-tittied anteater.

"You ah da sweetest thang!" She rushes back to bed and kisses Ryan all over the face. He grins. There are big red lip prints hickied all over his cheeks and forehead.

"You dis sweet to all da goils?"

"Hell no. Only with you."

"Shuga, you ain't gotta flatta me. You payin' my ass."

"Treat a lady like a whore. And a whore like a lady."

"Ain't you's a hort breaka," she growls in his ear.

"More than you know."

"Well, shuga, goils love a dangeriss man."

"Tell me about it." Ryan lights a cigarette and lies back to stare at the ceiling. Cherie takes it from his mouth and takes a drag. He slaps her hand and snatches it back. She giggles.

"So whaddizz-ya lil' prom queen think about being treeded like a whora?"

"Maggie?" He blows a steady stream of smoke and then puts the cigarette in Cherie's mouth. "She needs it. Keeps her honest. Keeps her from being a whore."

"Baby, I thought you said you liked whores?"

"I never said that." Ryan puts his smoke out in the ashtray next to his bed and rolls over onto to Cherie-Elise. "Bitches like you are only good for one thing." He grinds.

"Baby, this time'll be extra, okay?" She bats her crumby black eyelashes.

Ryan grabs a handful of her hair. "That coke you just snorted—I'm takin' it out of your ass."

"Look, shuga!" Cherie's eyes turn catlike and angry. "Lil' Miss Rumpshaka don't give no free pussy. Now get offa me!" She digs her square, red fingernails into his arm and tries to push him off, but he smacks her in the mouth and holds her down. She slaps and spits and cusses.

"Fuck-king co-operate!" He grabs her by the throat. "Or I'll burn your skank ass like I did that little Bible bitch!" He chokes her and hits her in the face with his closed fist.

"Okay, baby, okay." She shakes her tangled head of dyed hair and tries to catch her breath. "Just no more hittin', okay? Okay?"

Ryan doesn't say a word. Instead, he sticks his tongue in her mouth and humps her as hard as he can. Cherie-Elise sniffs up her bleeding nose and swallows it. She knows what to do. She's a pro at this. She starts her growling and back-scratching to get Ryan off so she can get the hell out of there. Like the rest of Louisiana, Cherie-Elise knows all about Sarah Jane's death and now she knows she's being ramrodded by the psycho-bastard who did it.

Finals ended today. Tucker went home to Vidalia. Ryan picked up his guns and coke and moved into his parents' house. And Maggie went home to her parents' house as well. She calls Ryan all the time, begging him to come over to see her. But when she calls there are only two things he wants to know: a) Has she lost any weight? and b) Has a black cop come by asking her questions about where he was Halloween night? Since the answer to both questions is "No," Ryan refuses to see her. So Maggie keeps herself company with chicken potpies and Jerry Springer, forcing her frantic mother to buy her an after-the-holidays weight-loss program from the Jenny Craig for Christmas.

I do my best not to think about Ryan. The idea of having to

spend Christmas at his house is unbearable. So I occupy my time floating around the city. That way it takes my mind off my revenge and I won't be pulled to him.

Since I am stuck in Baton Rouge with nothing to do for a month, I try to make the best of it. I try to enjoy the holidays. Tonight, I fly over the state capitol to look at all the lights that Al Copeland, the Popeyes fried chicken millionaire, donated to the state. His neighbors complained about this monster Christmas display being in his front yard because it caused traffic jams for miles. So he "donated" it to the state to avoid lawsuits. Anyway, the whole front lawn of the capitol is now full of tiny colored lights in the shapes of giant teddy bears, candy canes, and other Santa Land displays. The trees and hedges are draped in strands and strands of twinkling lights. There are speakers hidden all over the lawn, blaring Zydeco Christmas music. And hanging from the front of the capitol itself is a huge pink neon sign that reads HAPPY HOLIDAYS YA'LL.

There's quite a crowd here tonight, young and old, black and white, strolling across the lawn, taking pictures of the lights and animatronic reindeer. Everyone is ga-ga over these stupid decorations. It's weird; people are smiling and pointing like they've never seen an electric light bulb before. I will admit, though, as ridiculous as $100,000 worth of Christmas lights is, there's something magical about this place. It just makes you happy to be around all the glistening and shining.

Among the crowds of families and couples holding hands, I see Ashley. She's with that double-dealing bastard, Jay Kimbrough—all cozied up to him. They're watching the robotic elves in Santa's workshop. She looks up at him and smiles.

"Doesn't this make you feel like Christmas?"

"Imagine what a trip all this would be if we had some acid right now." He flips his hair and grins.

"Uh, no you don't. Not with me."

"Hey, I'm kidding."

"You better be."

"I told you I quit. I was just reminiscing. That's all."

"You're not even allowed to do that."

He sighs and she kisses him on the cheek and he hugs her.

"I'm just glad the semester's over," he says.

"Me too." Ashley squeezes Jay's hand. "I want to ask you something."

"What?"

"I want you to quit Gamma Chi."

"Do what?"

"Jay, there are too many drugs."

"Look, I don't know what you've heard, but it's not that bad. It's no big deal. Trust me."

"Your fraternity brother drugged me and tried to rape me!"

She pushes him off her and walks away. He just stands there shaking his head, wishing he had a bong hit about now. Dumbass.

Well, I'm glad she finally saw what a backstabbing loser Jay is. Serves him right for trying to steal my girlfriend like that. Ashley gets in her car and leaves Jay at the capitol. And I can't help but laugh my ass off at him. I start laughing so hard that I float upward to the top of the capitol tower. I can't stop laughing. I couldn't have asked for a better Christmas present. And then way up there in the sky, I notice that Capitol Park looks like my sister Shannon's LiteBrite from when we were kids. The memory of it all twists my laughter into sadness. I begin to wonder what Shannon and my family are doing this year for the holidays. And all of a sudden I feel real homesick.

To get away from all these heavy memories, I fly away from these stupid, twinkling lights to Miss Etta's house, in hopes that she can cheer me up. I land on her porch. She's got her own little light show going on with a wrinkled strand of blue lights hanging on her small wood-frame house. By her front door, there's one of those plastic Santas all lit up and glowing, except she's painted his face brown. On her screen door, she's hung a foil tinsel wreath that says "Joyeux Noël." I try to walk through the door, but I bounce off. I guess she put up her whammy to keep me out.

It's the holidays, for God sakes, and she refuses to take me in. Now that's real Christian of her. She knows I'm stuck here. Oh well, I just sit on her front porch and watch the cars go by. She knows I'm out here. I'll just wait.

Eventually, all of her lights shut off inside and the door creaks open. Miss Etta walks out onto the porch in her ratty housecoat and long johns. She unplugs the blue lights and black Santa. She looks down at me and whispers, "Get!"

She hisses and scratches her hand in the air like a cat clawing.

"Hey, Merry Christmas to you too," I pop back.

She shuts the door and I hear the locks clicking.

And then I start to itch so bad that I have to get up off that porch and leave. I don't stop itching until I get a block away from her house. Man, I can't believe her.

I've decided that I just need to be alone for the remainder of the break. I stay at the empty Gamma Chi house because I can't stand watching Maggie pine away for Ryan anymore. And watching him unwrap an automatic deer rifle with his sick-ticket family isn't my idea of holiday cheer. So here I sit in my library, trying my hardest not to think about any of them. I spend my Christmas morning with a stray tabby cat that's wandered in the house. He mews at me. I reckon the little fellow can see me. I reach down and pet him and he purrs. I name him Jingle Balls because he hasn't been neutered yet. We both sit here and look out the window. Then there's the squeak and scratching of a mouse on the hardwood floors, and so much for my little Christmas companion.

I pass the rest of the morning snooping in and out of the brothers' rooms. I find a stack of *Big Fat Nasty Butts* magazines hidden in Jeff Couvillion's underwear drawer. After that, I'm done snooping. I glide down the stairs that I died on and hover back to my library. And I'm blown away by who I see:

It's Ashley Sonnier standing here alone.

She's holding a poinsettia and she's talking to the air. I walk right up to her face, but she doesn't even blink.

"And then, Sarah Jane died. But you probably already knew

that." She wipes the mascara-stained tears from her face. "I just wanted to wish you a merry Christmas. And to tell you about me and Jay. I know he was your friend and all." She starts to smile. "And I think you'll be happy for us. I've finally found someone who loves me as much as I loved you. He makes me laugh like you used to. Anyway, these are for you." She puts the flowers on the table. "I know you don't really care about flowers, but I thought you could use a little Christmas. I don't know. I just hope you have a merry Christmas wherever you are, Conrad. I love you." She waves good-bye as she backs out of the room and shuts the library door. Out the window, I see her run down the front walkway into Jay's arms. She hugs him and he holds her, rocking her back and forth.

For the first time since I've been dead, I realize that there will be no second chances with Ashley. I can't be jealous of Kimbrough taking her away because, for all practical purposes, I don't exist— at least not in any fashion that could ever make her happy. It's time I let her go. So I do. It hurts like worse than when my neck broke, but I let her go.

Twenty-Two

The Gamma Chi pledges return from Christmas break the day after New Year's to clean up and repair the house from last semester. It's "workweek" and it's no small task. Their pledge trainer, Jeff Couvillion, is here yelling and slapping them around. He makes them all wear the exact same thing: blue jeans and plain white T-shirts. With their fuzzy heads and uniforms, they sort of look like a chain gang. The only things missing are the big black numbers and shackles.

Couvillion makes sure that there's no monkeying around. He's got them doing everything from fixing broken windowpanes to whitewashing the giant columns of the grand old mansion. It's like watching the Bob Vila show. The pledges pull out wood saws and repair broken banisters. They replace sheetrock and rusted pipes. They retile bathrooms and put broken doors back on their hinges. They polish and shine all the brass and wood. They bring Couvillion cold beers and Taco Bell.

Tucker Graham is on painting detail. Which means painting everything—every column, every eave and window seal on the three-story house. It's Wednesday morning and the air is crisp and nice, but it's sunny enough for Tucker to already be getting a sunburn. Tucker is sitting up on the steep roof, painting the third-story window trim.

Clay Weaver comes up the ladder with a bottle of Jim Beam in his hand.

"Mind if I join you?

"Sure."

Clay picks up a brush and starts painting.

"So how was your break?"

"It was okay." Tucker keeps moving his brush up and down, but doesn't look at Clay.

Clay opens the Jim Beam and takes a swig. "Here." He hands it to Tucker.

Tucker chugalugs the whiskey like it was milk.

"Dude, don't drink it all."

Tucker sighs, shakes his head, and moves his brush in long, wet strokes of white.

"So have you talked to Alex's parents?" Clay's face is soft and full of compassion.

Tucker puts his brush down in the paint tray and looks over at Clay.

"No, have you?"

"I wonder if they know about the goat . . ."

"Trudeaux was my friend. Keep talking shit about him and I'll sling your ass off this roof."

"Jesus. I was just curious. Sorry." Clay puts his brush down.

Tucker stands up and walks to the top of the roof.

"Okay, just sit down, Tucker."

Clay fumbles and drops the Jim Beam bottle. It slides off the roof and explodes onto the concrete walkway below them.

Tucker looks down at the broken bottle. Then suddenly, his foot slides a little bit on a broken tile.

Clay flinches.

Tucker catches himself.

"Get down. You're gonna fall."

Tucker slowly lowers himself down at the top, with both sides of the roof falling away from him. He puts his head in his hands and looks out over fraternity row.

Clay mountain-climbs very slowly and very carefully, on his hands and knees—scared as shit—up to where Tucker is.

"Tucker, man. I didn't mean to be a dick. I'm serious." Clay takes a place next to Tucker. He grabs hold of the shingles as the ground and sky swirl around him.

"He was a good guy." Tucker stares off into the space.

"Yeah, yeah, he was." Clay carefully pats Tucker on the back.

The two pledge brothers sit up there, high on Gamma Chi's roof. Tucker looks out over the trees and rooftops while Clay holds on for his own life.

Christmas break was hard on Maggie. She's about eleven weeks pregnant and she's got the classic symptoms: the aching boobs, and the endless need for a nap. Only thing is, her morning sickness has been replaced by this voracious appetite and she keeps eating everything in sight, just like she did before the semester was over. Her parents are real worried. Maggie is getting very large and she sleeps all the time. Maggie's mamma has diagnosed her with depression from the symptoms she saw listed on a Humana Hospital commercial for mood disorders. She called the 800 number and has set up a screening for Maggie. Mrs. Meadows doesn't plan on telling Maggie's daddy. She'll just put it on her secret credit card.

Today, Maggie sits in her bedroom in her parents' house and, instead of calling Ryan, she calls Tucker Graham. But there's no answer because he's at workweek and there's no answering machine because Maxwell took that home during the break. So Maggie gets in her little black Bug and goes to the grocery store. She finds comfort in the baking aisle. She buys pudding mixes and cake mixes, cans of icing and buttery shortening, pecans and cocoa. To her mother's dismay, she spends the better part of her day baking elaborate cakes full of hazelnuts, dark chocolate shavings, or raspberry filling. She eats them all, every last slice, with big glasses of milk with ice cubes. And when she's not eating or baking, she sits in bed and watches TV. She's not thinking about the future or what's growing in her belly. She's going to sleep and eat it all away.

By Saturday night of workweek, the house looks amazing. Everything is polished. The carpets are cleaned. The broken doors and windows replaced. The columns and trim painted an astonishing white. And the front yard is neatly carpeted with fresh blocks of brilliant green sod laid down over the winter mud. Now all the pledges are hanging out, drinking beer, acting like they own the place.

There's nothing like having your identity and self-dignity stripped away to bring you together with your pledge brothers. Tucker and Clay Weaver used to hate each other; now they're thick as thieves. Jeff Couvillion got bored with the whole week and ended up skipping out by Wednesday, since he couldn't really haze anyone because the real purpose of the week is to fix up the house. Couvillion had quarantined the pledges from going out and drinking. But since he's gone and the house is sparkling pretty, they decide to rebel. The entire class goes to the Chimes. They've got this beer club called "Drinking Around the World," and the Gamma Chi pledges are ready to set sail.

They start off in America with a round of flaming Dr Peppers and then go south of the border with tequila to warm up before conquering every beer in the world. The goal of tonight is to get completely shellacked. It's their last chance to enjoy themselves before hell week, which starts Monday. And every ounce of alcohol helps you forget what you're heading into.

Tucker slams a Guinness and then a Foster's. He and Clay toss back a Corona and St. Pauli Girl and then a Samuel Adams. They get all sloppy and start singing their little Gamma Chi ditty with their arms around each other's shoulders and suds sloshing in their fists: "Got fists like anvils because I've seen the Gamma Chi candles. I can eat razor wire for dinner. And then I'll make your own mamma want to be a sinner. I can drink the meanest poison and spit it in your face. 'Cause I ain't got no taste. Then I'll take your girl and show her my blue steel rod. And make her call me God. That's because! That's because! I'm a Gamma Chi! Gamma Chi! Gamma Chi! By Lawd!"

It's lame, I know. But when you're drunk and with twenty guys who you're about to go to hell with, it's a moment.

Tucker is really enjoying himself and I sort of feel bad about taking him over. I feel bad for about five seconds and then I get over it. I take hold of him while he's slamming some funk-ass ale that has strawberries and hops still floating around in it. The jolt makes him spit his suds out of his mouth and nose. He shuts his eyes from the beer burn in his nostrils and when his eyes open again, I'm seeing through them. Granted, it's a little blurry, but I'm here.

I've got Tucker and I'm here.

Twenty-Three

G amma Chi's hell week begins at the end of God's most holy of days—Super Bowl Sunday. The fraternity house windows are covered with cut-up garbage bags and the porch lights are shut off. There is a piece of typing paper taped up with duct tape on the front door. It reads in angry black marker:

Initiation in Progress!!! BROTHERS ONLY!!!

As the blood-orange sun drips down into the Mississippi and the cricketless night rolls over the campus oaks, the worthy brothers of Gamma Chi hole up in their big old house and they wait.

They wait for us.

We all show up together, just after sunset, in coats and ties with our duffel bags, pillows, and sleeping bags in tow. We silently line up, putting our heads down and shutting our eyes. Most everybody is quiet with fear—and they should be. They should be deaf-mute with fear because for an entire week their lives will be in the hands of boys—boys who are fueled by hot, raging hormones and cheap, cold beer. This week will be brutal and everyone knows it. But each and every pledge brother is here on time and ready to do whatever it takes to be a worthy Gamma Chi.

The actives come outside, smoking cigars and drinking beer. They're actually very friendly. Couvillion and Ryan are nowhere to be found. Instead nice-guy actives, like Kimbrough, Trey Cordova, and Matthew McCallahan, are all here, patting us on the backs and telling us how excited they are to get our initiation under way. Cordova keeps saying, "Don't worry, boys, it's a cakewalk. Nationals are here."

Everybody sort of chuckles with Cordova when he laughs, grasping onto the hope that maybe the guys from the national fraternity headquarters really are here and they won't allow any hazing, like they promise in their pamphlets.

Kimbrough lines us up into rows under the golden cross that hangs over the front door. Somebody turns on the porch lights from inside and Cordova snaps our picture. Then the lights go out again and they file us into a line with our heads down, eyes shut, and our right hands on the shoulder in front of us. The front door opens and I feel the pull and tug of the line jerking into motion. We are herded inside. The TV is blaring and brothers are talking and laughing over it. They're probably sitting around cutting farts and watching the big game. The pledge line is pulled into my library and we're allowed to open our eyes. The lights are dimmed and Cordova stands at the door. We take a seat at the study tables while trying to act like we are very serious about all of this.

"Pull out your pledge manuals and get to studying. No talking. Start with the creed. Pledge Master Couvillion will be in here in about an hour to check on you."

He shuts the door behind him and everybody breathes again. I roll my neck. Keeping your head down for that long sucks. I look around the room at all the pledges and try to guess who is going to get reamed the worst this week. I reckon Tony Audoin will get it. The actives still haven't forgiven his arrogance about not wanting to shave his head. Speaking of which, Tucker's head full of hair is a waving red cape this week, just asking for abuse. It should get very interesting. Then there's Charlie LaPrairie; he can barely remember his own name much less all the actives' first, middle, and last names along with their major, hometown, and big and little brothers. So my money's on Audoin, LaPrairie, and myself for the biggest ass chewings. Last year it was me and Jason Cefalu. Jason fingered Brad Domingue's drunk ex-girlfriend, and that didn't set too well with a lot of actives—especially Brad Domingue. It's a wonder Jason's not the one haunting the Gamma Chi house. The entire chapter hazed the shit out of him. I only had to worry about

Ryan. Funny how Jason's the one who made it through initiation and I didn't.

Everybody sits here and memorizes the pledge creed. I already know it. I can still say it backward, even. I'm sitting next to Robby Romero and Clay Weaver. They're whispering the creed to themselves over and over. I try to sit still but can't. So I try to strike up a conversation with Romero.

"Hey, Robby," I murmur.

He whispers back, all pissed off, "What?"

"Do you know this?"

"Do you?"

"Yeah, I learned it months ago."

"Well, good for you." He nudges me with his elbow.

"I heard they make you eat a bucket of sick if you don't memorize this."

"Who told you dat?" He looks up at me with his lip curling under his nose.

"Ryan."

"You serious, brah?"

"You have to say it perfect."

"Perfect or not, I ain't eating no vomit."

"Tell that to Ryan and Couvillion."

"Why don't you shut da fuck up? I gotta study!"

"Just trying to help."

"Shut up! Both of you!" Clay shushes us.

"Butt-munch ova here is telling me we gotta eat puke if we don't memorize dis. You know anything about dat, Clay?"

"Robby, just shut up and study. God." Clay shakes his head.

"All I know is I ain't eating no vomit. That's all I know." Robbie puts his head back down and shuts up.

For the next fifteen minutes or so, the room hisses with everybody reading to themselves. Romero starts and stops reading out loud and then he shakes his head. He nudges me.

"Tucker," he whispers, "who told you we hadda eat vomit if we didn't know dis?"

"Ryan."

"Really?"

"Really."

"Then I'm hosed."

I make gagging and vomiting noises. Romero shuts his eyes and shivers. I know he's a pledge, but he's a total ass and I can't resist. I just can't.

While the rest of the pledges are memorizing the creed, I daydream about knocking Ryan down the stairs. I think I'll do it Thursday night while all the pledges and actives go out to the woods to prepare for the ritual. That was the night that Ryan got ahold of me and forced me to shoot Everclear. It was the night that he broke my neck. This year it'll be his turn. I just have to figure out how to keep him here without too many people asking too many questions. This could be trickier than I thought. But I'll figure it out.

Time totally drags its fat ass and everybody starts to get stircrazy. Whispers and hushed laughter take the place of the studying. None of us is allowed to have a watch, so I have no idea how long we've been sitting here. I would guess that it's been at least four hours, though.

The doors to the library rattle; everybody puts their heads back down and acts like they're studying. Ryan and Couvillion bust in with big McDonald's bags. They're all laughing and cutting up. Ryan tosses cheeseburgers out to all the pledges and Couvillion drops a bag of fries and a small Coke in front of each of us.

"Eat up." Couvillion grins as nice as you please.

Everybody tears into their burgers and crams the fries down their pieholes like they've been on a thirty-day hunger strike. The pledges eat fast and nobody's really sure what to make of Ryan and Couvillion's generosity. I know what's up, but I have to act like I don't.

Ryan walks around smiling like he knows something. He walks behind me and kneels down while I'm eating.

"Is that burger good, Tucker?"

"Yes, sir." I nod.

"I'm impressed. 'Yes sir.' You've learned some manners."

Ryan picks up my half-eaten cheeseburger off its yellow paper. "You enjoying this burger, Tucker?"

"Yes, sir!"

"That's good. So have you been studying?" He puts my burger back down.

"Yes, sir."

"Have you learned the creed yet?

"Yes, sir."

"You sure? I mean, you can tell me if you haven't. It's okay. You've got until tomorrow."

I look up at him—straight in his eyes—and I recite the pledge creed backward, like I used to do for him at dinner back when I was still alive:

"Worthy forever be will I that myself behave so and myself shape so to venture will I that, eternal is trust our of pledge the that; regard and reason me given has Chi Gamma that; earnestness all in promise this say I. Brethren our by respected genuinely and worthy more and people all by revered Fraternity Chi Gamma the make to try will I. Manners fine and decency, justice embrace I."

Ryan stands there, breathing through his open mouth like a retard. He's blown away. It's written all over his face. I look back down like nothing just happened.

"Uh, that was, uh, very good, Tucker. Very good." He pats me on the back and gets the hell away from me. "Just don't be such a show-off next time." He huffs and shakes his head like he's disgusted. "Come on, Couvillion. Let's let them study."

Ryan grabs Couvillion's arm and rushes him out of the library. Once we're alone again, all of Tucker's pledge brothers lift their heads and gawk at me.

"Man, where did that come from, Tucker?" Clay grins.

"Yeah, Tucker, way to make the rest of us look bad," Charlie LaPrairie bitches.

Clay turns around. "Tucker's obviously been studying. If he looks good, we all look good."

"Yeah. Sure. Whatever." Charlie puts his nose back in his book. There's some commotion outside the library doors; it's probably brothers horsing around or something. But it scares the shit out of the pledges, so everybody follows Charlie's lead and studies their manuals.

We continue studying for what could be three hours or thirty minutes. Boredom has a way of distorting time, and not having a watch or clock anywhere doesn't help. Eventually, Couvillion pops his head in.

"Pull out your sleeping bags and lights out!" He shuts off the lights and leaves.

We fumble for our sleeping bags and everyone wrestles to get in them. We all go to bed with our ties, coats, shoes and everything still on. Nobody makes a move without permission—even if that means taking off your coat and tie to go to bed.

There's some random coughing and yawning. And then everyone starts whispering.

"Hey, Tucka," Romero breathes through his teeth, "you awake?"

"Of course I'm awake. They just shut off the lights."

"Tonight was pretty easy, huh?"

"Yeah, cake."

"What do you think tomorrow will be like?"

"Probably the same. I heard Nationals is here."

"Nationals ain't here, bruh."

"I heard it was true. I heard this initiation is going to be the easiest one ever." I lie to him.

"Great. Then we'll never get no respect. We'll be a buncha pussylip bastards compared to da rest of da chapta."

"So then you want it to get bad this week?"

"Shit, yeah. I don't want no half-ass initiation. Bring da shit on. I can take it."

There's a loud banging on the doors and Couvillion yells, "Don't make me come in there! I said lights out!"

After that nobody mutters another word. For the rest of the night—with the exception of a couple of random farts and muffled laughs—the only noises made are the wheezing and light snoring of everybody sleeping. I roll over on my back to get comfortable.

Which is impossible when you're on this hardwood floor. I can feel every bump of wood and every bone in my spine. I couldn't sleep here if I wanted to. But I don't want to. I can't afford sliding out of Tucker during sleep. So I keep my eyes wide open. I worry about Maggie all night and what she's going to do with that baby growing inside her.

Wake-up for us comes within a couple of hours after lights out. The day begins with Couvillion blaring an air horn and shouting. This is the only way we know that the day has started since the black garbage bags cover all the windows, blocking out all sunlight and reality.

"Wakey-wakey, ladies!" he hollers.

Some of the pledges jump up like Pop-Tarts out of a toaster while others stay curled up in their sleeping bags. Couvillion goes around and kicks those dead weights in the sides.

"Come on, girls. Get up!" He bleeds the horn in their ears.

The sleepers jerk and pull themselves awake. They yawn and stagger to their feet. Eventually, we're all standing next to our sleeping bags. Everybody is all wrinkled and puffy-eyed. Couvillion walks around the room, blowing that stupid horn and making me want to cram it up his ass.

"Okay, roll up your bags and get to studying!" he barks, and then leaves the room, slamming the door behind him.

We do what he says and take our places at the tables and we study. Everyone chants the creed quietly to themselves. Except now everyone's rotten-ass morning breath is filling up the room and making me sick. I close my eyes and imagine the sun rising white rays through the frosty oaks and morning mists. My daydreaming is interrupted when Couvillion comes in carrying two boxes of Daylight Donuts, a stack of Styrofoam cups, and two big plastic jugs of milk.

"Don't just stand there," he snaps at Clay as one of the jugs starts to slip out of his grip. Clay quickly catches the jug along with the cups; he puts both on the table.

"Don't eat until I say when." Couvillion goes around placing one doughnut in front of each brother. "Clay, start pouring your pledge brothers a glass of milk."

Everybody devours their doughnuts. Everybody but me. I mush mine up into a ball and put it into my pocket. No telling where those things have been and I'll be damned if I'm putting some dick-nasty doughnut in my mouth, or rather Tucker's mouth.

After breakfast, we sit on our butts and study. I read this stupid pledge manual because there's nothing else to do. As the day or night or whatever time it is creeps by, my toes start to feel cold and stiff. And so do my hands. I think they cut off the heater in here.

In fact, everybody's breath is turning to frost and their noses are runny and red. This cold is what I hate the most. I can stand the yelling and even the hitting to some degree. But the silence and the cold is torture. It really is. It makes me wish the hazing would start just so I'd have something to think about. I'm tempted to get my sleeping bag out and wrap up in it. However, that would throw all these scared pledges into a tailspin and make me seem oddly unafraid of Ryan and the actives. And I can't have them thinking that Ryan is going to die this week. This just really pisses me off, sitting here like this. When you have a body, you're meant to move it. It rots your mind doing this. It's making me sleepy and it pisses me off because I can't afford to let this body sleep no matter how badly it needs the rest.

This is pretty much the whole story for Monday: cold and butt-numbing. We are left to ourselves all day. No actives come by to even see if we're doing what we're supposed to. All of Tucker's pledge brothers act like they're studying, but we're all too bored and too tired of sitting here to even fake it very well. Finally, Couvillion shows up. The actives are having their chapter meeting and Couvillion wants us to go upstairs and wait on the third floor until it's over. So we march up the stairs, and he has us line up down the long hall of the third floor. The Gamma Chis' house speakers and party sound system are at the end of the hall.

"Sit down. Cross your legs and put your head between your knees!" Couvillion shouts.

The pledges drop, me included, and we assume the position. The lights go out and the sound system goes on. They play this horrible loop of the Beatles' "Number Nine" from the *White Album*. For those of you unschooled in this piece of music history, it's a bunch of screeching and water drips and crazy-ass noise interspersed with some English dude saying, "Take this, brother, it will serve well." It is complete mind-erasing, brainwashing noise. Couvillion turns the system up loud along with the upstairs heater. Before long the entire third floor is hotter than a sauna and everybody's necks and butts are aching from sitting all balled up like this. If you try to raise your head or stretch your neck an active brother comes by to push you down and maybe box your ear. The seconds pass like seasons. I reckon that song is about five minutes long. So I count how many times it plays. So far, I calculate we've been up here for going on three hours. Robbie Romero is shaking and whimpering next to me. Can't say that I blame him. The cramping gets pretty bad. Couple that with the sweating and this ear-bleeding song, and you really do think you might go crazy if they don't let you out. The worst of all this is you have nothing to think about. All you have is this disturbing chaos in your ear pushing out your thoughts. What I really want to do is teach these actives who keep pushing my head down a lesson or two. I mean, this was bad enough going through it the first time.

I take a deep breath, hold it, and then let it out. I have to save all my venom and black deaths for Ryan if my plan is going to work. So I keep my head between my knees and try to think of what it will feel like to kill Ryan.

By the number of times this song has played over and over, I reckon we've been up here for five hours by the time they stand us up and bring us down the stairs. There are bright strobe lights that make me seasick and white bedsheets hanging all over the place. It's all happening in a flickering slow motion and the sheets make this place look like some kind of ten-dollar haunted house. I hope none of these pledges are epileptic because those strobe lights will get to you even if you aren't.

We're shoved downstairs while the actives scream, "Are you worthy?" in my face and Ravel's "Bolero" blares from a big black boombox sitting by the library door. I am having major déjà vu. This was exactly how it was when I went through this last year.

This whole room is one big flash and fury with actives shouting and popping us upside the heads. Once inside the library, we're greeted by a whole gaggle of Gamma Chis that are my dad's age, in business suits, smoking cigars. These old men are here to haze us. They're violently pissed off over stupid stuff—like pledges not knowing what year Gamma Chi was founded. I mean, who cares?

The good thing is that nobody's really reaming me so much. Which is good because I'm really not in the mood to get yelled at or bitch-slapped because I don't know the Gamma Chi Sweetheart of 1956. What's cool is even the alumni are intimidated by Tucker's size. I don't care how old you are, it takes some balls to yell at a six-ten farm boy with hands the size of baseball mitts. The only actives who think they're bad enough to go head to head with Tucker are Ryan and Couvillion. However, Ryan has gotten all caught up in the moment and he's ripping Charlie LaPrairie a new asshole. Couvillion is helping him.

I just stand here and look around the blinking room. Each pledge has about three guys, up close and in his face, yelling in slo-mo. And the pledges try their best to take it while these peepaw alumni ream them. Romero and LaPrairie have already broken down. They're sniveling and crying.

My lack of hazing doesn't go unnoticed. A group of alumni in business suits who have been huddled together and smoking cigars point at me. They laugh. Two of the alums with their backs to me turn around to look. And it's my own goddamn father and uncle. What are they doing here? I guess I'm about to find out because here they come with their buddies to haze me. Great.

My Uncle Jack and my daddy walk up. My dad has that look

on his face like he used to get right before he took his belt off to whip me. This is definitely not going to be fun. My uncle is the first to start in on me.

"So what's your name, son?"

"Tucker Joe Graham, sir." I stand at attention and look straight ahead.

"So what year was this house finished?"

"1924."

"Wrong! It was rebuilt in 1974!" Uncle Jack gets all up in my face. "Don't lie if you don't know the answer. You say, 'I don't know and I don't care and I don't want to be your brother, sir.' Got it?"

"Yes, sir."

"Who is this library dedicated to?" My father chimes in.

Those words don't even hit my ears. They hit me in the face like shrapnel. I want to cry out loud. I want to tell him it's me. I want to grab him around the neck and hug the old man. And then I want to ask him what he's doing this for. But instead I answer in the most hurtful way possible. I answer like I'm supposed to.

"I don't know and I don't care and I don't want to be your brother, sir."

"What do you mean you don't know? It's my son's room!! Conrad Avery Sutton the Third!" he explodes.

My uncle puts his hand on my daddy's shoulder and tries to calm him down.

"This room was dedicated for his son, my nephew, you piece of shit. Do you even know when Conrad died? Do you even know what he meant to this chapter?"

I have to look away.

"Look at me when I'm talking to you!" Uncle Jack shouts and then puffs on his cigar. "Do you even know who Conrad was or why this library was built for him?"

I look him straight in the eye and instead of giving him the mandated "I don't know and I don't care" spiel, I say this:

"Look, Jack"—I hold Tucker's bowling ball fist up to Uncle Jack's face—"I know who Conrad Sutton is. Trust me." I give him a look with Tucker's face that's so mean and feral that I think he and my daddy both shit their pants.

"What kind of crap are you trying to pull, you punk?" Jack steps back from me, horrified, his cigar hanging on his bottom lip.

I shake my head and point at my dad with Tucker's big dull finger. Then I jerk the cigar out of Uncle Jack's mouth just to be a wiseacre and I push them out of my way, knocking Jack on the ground. I walk out of that library to get away from all the strobe lights and chaos and mangled feelings. I go out the front door and stand on the porch. I look out onto the cold starless night and smoke that cigar. Tastes pretty good. I look at the label. It's a Balmoral.

Uncle Jack always did like good tobacco.

I try to figure out how I'm going to go back in there and face my daddy. I don't think I can. This is way too much for me to handle. I mean, what the hell is my dad doing here? He's using my death to screw with these guys. How can he do that? How can he reduce my memory to some kind of head game? My own father has sold me out just like Uncle Jack sold out my cousin Barrow when he got kicked out of this house.

I stand out here and puff on this cigar and try to figure out the best way to get my revenge, to get this all to end. Couvillion and Uncle Jack swagger outside to get me.

"What the hell are you doing, Tucker? Get back in here!" Couvillion looks around to make sure that nobody outside can see what's going on. My uncle just stands there all pissy, with this lip dragging the ground. The screaming and the Bolero music echo out the door and onto the porch.

"Look," I point my cigar at them. "It's a little too intense in there right now. I'll get back in as soon as I can calm down. Okay?"

Uncle Jack looks at Couvillion. "This never would have happened, not back when I was here."

"That's just the problem, Jack. You're not in college anymore now are you, old man?" I stare him down through the ribbons of cigar smoke.

"What?"

"I didn't stutter." I wave the smoke out of my way. "Look at you. You're a grown man with a son. A son this place rejected. And yet you're here."

"Look!" White foam collects in the corners of Uncle Jack's mouth. "I don't know who the hell you think you are! But we do not have to initiate you!"

"Tucker, you are buying yourself a houseful of pain," Couvillion barks at me.

"I'm the last pledge on earth you want to fuck with, Jack. Trust me."

And with that said, it gets so quiet out here you can hear the oak trees growing.

Uncle Jack turns around without saying another word and goes back inside.

"Get your ass back in here. You are in such deep shit it's not even funny." Couvillion grabs me by Tucker's arm, and I let him lead me back inside.

Twenty-Four

onight's festivities have gone from the alumni and active brothers merely yelling at the pledges to a full-on ass kicking. The old geezer alums are putting the pledges in chokeholds while the actives punch them in the gut or burn them with a cigar. I, on the other hand, am being taken back to the chapter room so that I can apologize to my uncle and my daddy in private. I am sure Couvillion has some real spiteful punishment in store for me since I just dissed the high and mighty alumni of Gamma Chi.

And I am right:

The room is candlelit and full of broken glass—how imaginative. And my father and uncle are in here too, standing under the colossal Gamma Chi crest. They're busy looking mad and very waspy. Then, as soon as the door shuts, an avalanche of actives steps out of the shadows and tackles me, swinging beer bottles and fists. There are four of them and their weight alone drops me to my knees. My father stands there and watches. He winces as blood from my busted nose sprays across the floor. But he does not try to save me. My Uncle Jack laughs, "That'll teach you. You jackass."

I see red and then white sparks moving out into space like a supernova. I completely lose it. I throw those four actives off me. I go straight for Uncle Jack. I grab him by the throat and I lit into him.

My father tries to pull me off, but this forest fire rages inside of me, and it lays waste to everything that was green and beautiful. It incinerates me, destroying what was left of whatever might have been good in me. I am a demon, spitting out hate and breathing in fire. I can't be stopped. I'm going to kill this old man, and then we'll see if he still wants to talk shit after he's dead. I bet you my cousin Barrow will even thank me. After all, the only thing Uncle Jack ever gave him was money and I'm about to break the piggy-bank for Barrow; I'm about to make him an heir to half the Sutton fortune.

The actives claw and pull and punch me, but there is no stopping my attack. I'm about two blows away from braining the old man.

And then, pop!

There's a gunshot.

I turn around and Ryan stands behind me holding his smoking pistol over his head. I let go of Uncle Jack almost automatically. It's like Tucker's body knows it doesn't want a bullet in the head, so survival instincts override my possession. I step away from my uncle and put my hands up. My daddy walks over to Uncle Jack and takes care of his bloodied mess of a face.

Ryan points the gun at me.

"Okay, Tucker, put your hands behind your head and drop to your knees."

I stare at him and the gun. I do as he says. I do it very slowly and carefully because if he shoots me this is all over. I can't be blowing through bodies like Kleenex. I need to take Ryan down this week, and I can't very well do that if Tucker Graham buys the farm. So I take a deep breath and try to calm down. I can feel my heart beating away in my throat and I try to swallow it.

"Don't move." Ryan walks over to me, keeping his gun steadily aimed at my head. He puts the barrel to my temple and I look straight ahead, not wanting to tempt the psycho.

"Is Mr. Sutton okay?" Ryan asks my daddy.

"We need to get him to a doctor." My daddy soaks up my uncle's bloody face with his own suit coat.

"Looks like we might have to put crazy Tucker to sleep."

"I think you need to put that gun away, son." My daddy holds my Uncle Jack's bloody head.

"Hey, just keeping the peace, Mr. Sutton. This gun saved your brother's life. Isn't that right, Tucker?" Ryan nudges the barrel into my temple. I don't give him the satisfaction of a response. I mean what's he going to do, blow Tucker's brains out in front of all these people?

My daddy takes Uncle Jack to the emergency room, and Ryan puts the gun in the waist of his jeans and drags me by my ear into the library with the rest of the pledges. They're all bruised, broken, and burned. It's a pitiful sight. Their eyes are hollow and with their buzzed heads, they look more like concentration camp victims than college boys. I take my seat next to Clay Weaver while all the actives go into the chapter room to discuss what they're going to do with me.

Clay's got a big cigar burn right in the middle of his forehead. It looks nasty, like it will leave one ugly scar. From the looks of all the pledges, this was a particularly gruesome Monday night. The actives took it way too far with the cigars and the choking.

"It'll be okay, buddy." I pat Clay's shoulder to console him.

"They burned my face," he sobs quietly.

"Hey man, you're going be okay."

"I don't think I can do this."

"Yeah, you can, Clay. Come on. Here, listen. This is what we're going to do."

He tries to suck up his crying.

"We're going to fight back."

He wipes the snot from his nose with his coat sleeve.

"Next time they come at us. We all fight back."

"We can't do that."

"You seriously think they're going to kick all of us out?"

"You're nuts, Tucker."

"It's a test. They want us to fight back. They want us to rise up and act worthy."

"There's no way, Tucker." Clay shakes his head. "That's not why they're doing this."

"Then why else would they?"

"I don't know. It's just part of it."

"I'm telling you, Kimbrough told me that's what they want us to do. Most classes don't fight back until Friday and so that's why initiation doesn't start until Saturday night most times. But we can speed this up if we just do it."

"Are you sure?"

"Look, we have to fight back if we're ever going to get initiated."

"Okay. It sort of makes sense." Clay nods.

"Exactly. Jeez." I roll Tucker's eyes.

Now you and I both know this isn't true. I'm totally lying here. The last thing actives want a pledge to ever do is strike back. But when you've just gotten the life beat out of you and you're sporting a cigar burn on your head, you're likely to buy any fish story. And Clay's pledge brothers buy my lies just as eagerly. After a quick little pep talk from Clay, they're ready to fight. I mean, after all, it is a logical thing to do—defending yourself, that is.

Couvillion comes back alone.

"Tucker. You need to come with me!" he bellows.

I stand up slowly and look straight ahead.

Couvillion struts over to me.

"Come on, you crazy shit. There's a bottle of Tabasco with your name all over it."

"Now!" I shout, and the pledge class attacks. I take off my blue blazer and gag Couvillion with it so he can't scream for help. The pledges rip into Couvillion. They unleash a semester's worth of pain on him. It's quite a feeding frenzy, and if I don't do something fast they're going to beat him to death. They're lost in it. Mad with the moment.

"Okay! Okay! Stop! Stop!" I hush and shove them away. But they don't hear me over their own rage. They just won't stop. They keep coming at him, delivering blows to his face and ribs, kicking him hard in the shins. I jerk Couvillion away from them and I hold him in a full nelson. Clay Weaver continues hitting and slapping Couvillion's head even after everyone else has stopped. Eventually, Clay gets his hate off and he pulls himself together. I'm here to tell you there's an anger that swells from being abused, and woe be it to whoever unleashes it.

The pledges are breathing heavy. Smiles start to crack across their bruised and swollen faces. They feel good about standing up for themselves and they start to laugh and high five each other. I look at Couvillion and he's TKO'ed and bloodied. Two broken and bloody front teeth dangle from his busted lip. I lay him down on a study table and he starts to moan and come to. That's when the panic rises in the pledges.

"What did we just do?" Charlie LaPrairie freaks.

"Exactly what we're supposed to do," I whisper. "Now be quiet."

"Look at him. He's like in a coma!" Charlie chimes in.

"You're the one who went medieval on his ass. The plan was just to fight back. Not to kill him," I say.

"This went too far." Charlie wrings his hands. The rest of the pledge brothers get all wide-eyed and quiet, like we just murdered someone or something.

"Look, the last time I checked, Gamma Chi wasn't a sorority, so if you want them to initiate you, I recommend you grow some balls. God, what's the matter with you guys?" I shake Tucker's red head. "You're a bunch of scared little girls. I'm telling you this is part of the test."

"Tucker's right." Clay steps forward. "We can't back out now."

The pledges get quiet. They know what must be done. They know that whether or not they were supposed to fight back, they did. And now they have to pay the price. They have to face one hundred worthy brothers of Gamma Chi and they have to win. This is enough to even put a lump in my throat. Because it's a tall order to fill—especially with psychopath Ryan packing heat. But we all stand together and agree to hold fast to ourselves and each other. Even cowardly little Charlie swears to protect himself and his pledge brothers. And that's when Couvillion comes to.

"Easy does it." I help him sit up.

"Get offa me!" He pushes me away.

He holds his head and he tries to get his bearings. He's in a world of hurt right now, but somehow he manages to stumble to the doors of my library.

"You pledges are fucked." That's all he says as he walks out. I smile at Clay, but he doesn't smile back.

It's not long before Couvillion comes back holding an ice pack over his left eye and pointing his finger at me. Ryan is with him and so are Jason Cefalu, Derrick Cazayoux, and Sam LaCroix.

"So this is how it's going to be?" Ryan glares at each and every one of us. "You pukes have no idea what kind of trouble you've just made for yourselves. No idea."

Some of the pledges back up against the wall, like Ryan might just all of a sudden lunge at them. But I stand my ground and grin at him.

"Pledges, you will have your brother Tucker to thank for all this. I know he put you up to this, and you were stupid enough to listen to him."

Before Ryan can get into a real hellfire and brimstone speech, there's a knocking at the frat house's front door. The actives ignore it at first but whoever it is, is insistent.

"Jason, go tell whoever that is to go away." Ryan rubs the bridge of his nose.

Everybody holds their breath until the stranger at the door leaves. I try hard to listen to who it is. All I can hear are the deep mumbles of some man. The mumbles get louder and more insistent and Jason keeps repeating, "I'm sorry. We're in initiation. You can't come in."

Then the front door slams and Jason starts yelling, "Stop! You can't go in there!"

Detective Watkins comes busting into the library door waving his badge in one hand and his gun in the other.

"Detective Watkins. Baton Rouge Police. Everybody put your hands in the air!"

Swell, it looks like the cavalry has arrived, and just in time to take Ryan to jail and save his life.

"Ryan Hutchins. I'm here to arrest Ryan Hutchins." Watkins scans the crowd of shaved heads. "Where is he?"

Then I feel the cold steel of Ryan's revolver at my neck and his arm across my chest.

"That's him." Romero points at me and Ryan.

The pledges and actives huddle away from us. Detective Watkins points his gun at Ryan, and Tucker's heart flutters instinctively.

"Okay, Ryan. Put the gun down. You don't want to do this."

Ryan doesn't say anything. He just spits and looks crazier and crazier.

I try to act like I'm scared. I keep my eyes wide and my mouth gaping, like I just can't believe that this is happening.

"Son, you already got one murder charge. You don't want two. Come on, now. Drop the gun and put your hands up."

Ryan drags me across the room, to the crowd of cowering pledges and actives.

"I'll fucking put a bullet in his brain if you don't back off, man." He brings his arm up around my neck, putting me in a chokehold.

"Ryan, just calm down."

"No! You calm down!" He pulls me to the door, his trigger hand trembling and his heart thumping against my back. "I'm telling you to back away. I'm not kidding. I'll kill him, and then I'll do myself. I'm not kidding!" He growls and twitches.

Watkins keeps his gun on us, as Ryan pulls me up the stairs.

"Stay there. Or I blow his brains all over these fucking stairs!"

Watkins keeps his gun on Ryan, but stays put. He wasn't really expecting a hostage situation and I guess he's a little slow thinking on his feet.

Ryan pulls me up into his room and locks the door behind him. He makes me move his dresser and his bed in front of the bolted door. He keeps his gun on me while he rummages through his ski parka to find his stash of blow.

"Sit down on the floor and keep your hands where I can see them!"

I do as he says as he pulls out a Ziploc bag full of coke. He cuts himself three very thick lines on his footlocker with one hand while he holds the gun on me with the other.

"You're toast."

"Shut up!" He shakes his gun at me as he wipes the white powder from his top lip.

"They're going to fry you."

"Do you fucking want to die? I just said shut up!"

"You remember me?" I stand up and square my shoulders.

"Sit down!" he shouts.

"Go ahead. I'll just keep coming back."

"Conrad?" Ryan freezes. He knows who he's talking to now.

I look into Ryan's eyes, and I can see an opening, a way into his body. It must be the cocaine and fear. So I take it. I jump out of Tucker and into Ryan. Everything's all hot and gooey. It's a bloody mess in here. This heart is beating way too fast, and his brain is all lit up and buzzing like a tilted pinball machine. It's hard to get my bearings. Everything that's coming in these eyes is fuzzy, but then I focus and I see Tucker's clueless face staring back at me.

"Get out of here!" I slur at Tucker as I shake Ryan's gun around, trying to get control of all these tight and over-tweaked muscles.

Tucker just stares at me all bleary eyed and half asleep.

"Go on! Get!" I shout at him.

He stands there bigger and dumber than ever.

"Open the door and leave. Now!"

I move all the furniture out of the way while Tucker stands with his head wobbling, and then I open the door and push his heavy ass out of it.

"Go downstairs and tell the police I give up!" I shout; Ryan's voice rings in my ears.

I shut and lock the door behind Tucker. This is seriously creeping me out. I'm inside Ryan breathing with his lungs, talking with his tongue. I look down at the hands that killed me and I tremble.

And then I remember why I got inside this son of bitch in the first place—to kill him. I am going to make him suffer. I am going to pull the trigger and right before the bullet hits, I'm going to jump out of Ryan's body so he can feel the full impact of his face being blown off his head. The blood is going to gush and I'm going to laugh.

I walk over to the mirror and look at Ryan's reflection. I feel his stomach acids rise. And I put the barrel of Ryan's gun to his prized face. And then in the mirror, I see the two angels, the ones I saw arguing in Sarah Jane's room, standing behind me, watching me. I turn around.

"Jesus. What do you two want?"

They don't say a word. They just glow and shine and stand there with their arms all akimbo. The guy angel flutters his big white wings and the girl angel looks at him knowingly. They both shrug their shoulders and smile at me.

"What?"

Nothing. They just shine.

"Look, I'm going to do this."

Still nothing but big sad eyes and pure love smiles.

"You're not going to stop me. He's evil."

The girl angel speaks in a smoky voice, "Evil is live spelled backwards."

"What? That's the stupidest thing I've ever heard."

The guy angel holds the girl angel's hand and speaks like a trumpet, "Evil destroys the order of life."

"No shit. Evil took my life, Sarah Jane's life, and Alex's life. That's why Evil's gonna die."

"Evil destroys life," the girl angel says again.

"Yeah, look what it did to me."

The angels start to laugh at me and they fly off into a bright nowhere, leaving me holding Ryan's gun to his face.

Then I realize what I just said: Look what it did to me. Look what Ryan's evil has done to me. I've changed. I'd actually enjoy killing him. I would get off on it. I would. I want his blood, his pain, his death. Nothing would give me more pleasure than killing him violently like some whack-job. I've become evil. I've become Ryan. And all of a sudden I feel sick and dizzy. I feel claustrophobic, like I'm breathing through mud. I put the gun down and I look in the mirror. I see Ryan's scared blue eyes looking back at me. This can't be me. I have come face to face with the devil. And it's not Ryan. It's me. This evil, this hate lives in me. It's taken me over. I've become what I hate.

Ryan will have completely killed me if I pull this trigger.

I sit on the bed and I take a couple of deep breaths. I should get out of Ryan right now. I shut my eyes and try to leave. But I can't seem to find a way out. I am in here. Jesus Christ, I am Ryan and I'm stuck. I look at the gun and wonder if maybe that's my only way out now. And then it dawns on me: I may be inside of Ryan but more importantly I'm still me. And yeah, I may be wrong in the eyes of the Lord, but I am not evil. Ryan will not take that away from me. I was a good enough guy. A little drunk, a little spoiled, but I was essentially a good person or at least a decent person. And maybe I'm not big enough or strong enough to forgive Ryan, but I refuse to become like the monster who killed me. So I put down the gun; I unlock the door. I put Ryan's arms in the air and I walk down the hall shouting, "Okay, I give up. I give up. Just don't shoot me!"

Twenty-Five

I wake up in Ryan's body, alone in the Baton Rouge Parish jail. I've been here for going on three weeks. Ryan's connections made sure that he is—or rather I am—kept safe in a private cell. I reckon they figure pretty-boy Ryan will be eaten alive once he gets tossed in with the rest of the prisoners. But I got news for them; they don't know the real Ryan Hutchins. However, if he was ever to meet his match, I guess it would be in prison.

Anyway, I plea-bargained a confession so Ryan wouldn't get the chair. I told the DA and Ryan's lawyer everything—and then some. It took the better part of a night to tell my story, in fact. I talked for good ole Ryan Hutchins, and I made that glorious confession that he never would. I let the truth spray like a fire hose all over the place.

I told them about how he beat the shit out of Cherie-Elise after he paid her for sex. I told them how he smacked Maggie Meadows on a daily basis; how he drugged Ashley Sonnier and tons of other girls with roofies and GHB. I squealed about the cocaine in his ski parka. I accidentally let it slip that Couvillion also had two kilos of crack in his room. Oops. I told them how Sarah Jane Bradford had to die because she spray-painted his Jeep and how he forced Alex to have sex with a goat. I told them how he murdered a pledge named Conrad Sutton. And then I mocked them for not having caught Ryan sooner.

Then for good measure, I told a couple of white lies—like how Ryan liked to dress up in women's undergarments and pretend he was Michael Jackson.

My confession, or rather Ryan's beautiful confession, made the front pages of the Baton Rouge *Advocate,* New Orleans *Times-*

Picayune, and *The Shreveport Times*. The *Picayune* has drawn comparisons between Ryan and the Columbine psychos, while the *Advocate* led readers to believe that the murders were part of a fraternity drug ring. All three papers described Ryan Hutchins as the cross-dressing, bad-seed son of Baton Rouge high society.

And get this: The local TV news did a huge exposé on Gamma Chi, causing LSU to shut them down. I've got to say that I'm eating this up. I actually cheered when I heard the news and everybody looked at Ryan like he was crazy. Imagine the guards watching Ryan stand up and cheer when he hears these horrible news stories about himself. My tragic tale of woe went national the next week with a cover story in the *New York Times Magazine*. It was a picture of Ryan with a big black bar over his eyes. The title read "Beware of Greeks: The Fraternity Murderer."

That feature prompted *60 Minutes* to do a story also. Mamma and Daddy were interviewed by Morley Safer. They filmed at our house in Shreveport. Mamma and Daddy sat on the couch in our living room and talked about how horrible it was to have lost their son to such an ugly, senseless act. Mamma went on about how she felt sorry for Ryan and what a lost soul he was and how she prayed for his mamma and daddy. Mamma always was a good Baptist. Anyway, Morley asked Daddy if he had ever taken part in Gamma Chi's hazing rituals and he confessed that, yes, he had. Mamma wept openly on national television when she heard this.

Part of me feels sorry for my daddy. Actually, a lot of me feels sorry for him, but after all, he's sort of to blame for my death. So he can spend a few years crying on the lecture circuit, telling kids and parents about how much he misses his dead son.

But the truth of the matter is, right now I'm not completely dead. I'm stuck in Ryan's body, and no matter how I try, I can't get out. From the looks of things now, I'm going to have to suffer the consequences of Ryan's actions. I mean, isn't that the perfect ending to a bad life? First, I get cut down in my prime, and then I get stuck in the body of the psycho who killed me, only to have to suffer his punishment. Talk about some screwed up karma—if you believe in that crap.

This really isn't what I had in mind when I didn't blow Ryan's head off. I was thinking I would confess and then I'd let him rot away in prison. But I guess there's one thing I've learned about life from being dead: There are no guarantees. Maybe Miss Etta was right. Maybe the best revenge is just getting on with things and letting go of it all. Oh well, live and learn. Or in my case, live and die then possess a couple folks and then learn.

Aside from Ryan's attorney, I haven't had a single visitor. Ever since I gave my confession for Ryan, his parents have been nowhere to be found. So it's kind of weird that the guards are here this morning to take me to the visitors' room. I can't imagine who could be coming up here to see me.

Two prison guards grunt at me and put this plastic wrap on my wrists and shackles on my legs. They push and shove me out of my cell and past all the bars and rough scowls of my prison mates. With this stubbly head of Ryan's and this baggy orange jumpsuit, I look like your classic psycho ready for the electric chair.

The guards lock and unlock bars and doors in front of and behind me as we move through the prison. The last door leads into a sea-foam green room with a wall of Plexiglas windows, old telephones, and plastic school chairs. Miss Etta holds her red Bible up and waves it at me. She's smiling and flashing me her bright gold tooth like she just can't wait to tell me something real important. The guards undo the plastic string around my wrist and seat me across from Miss Etta.

"You have five minutes," one guard mutters.

I pick up the phone that's to my left. Miss Etta picks up her phone.

"So what do you want?" I ask.

"Your soul, baby. Actually, that's what the Lord wants, your soul."

"Well, He can't have it. I'm busy using it."

"Baby, you stuck in here. If you let me, I can deliver you like the good Lord sent me to do, but I ain't going to argue with your dead ass."

"Deliver me to where? Hell?"

"Shuga-child, you already in hell. You all caught up in Ryan and you in prison fixing to be somebody's girlfriend." She shakes her head and chuckles, "Shoo, it don't get much worse than that, baby."

"Yeah, I guess you're right."

"Shit. I been right since you first met me. You just too stupid to listen."

"Okay. Okay. Okay. Just get me out of here."

"See, that's the hard part. You got to eat a bite of this lemon pie I baked you and then we got to pray together."

"What? Are you crazy? They're not going to let you feed me pie."

"Well, then I guess you stuck." Her creepy blue-brown eyes widen at me.

"How am I going to get the pie to even eat it?"

"Baby, you got to trust in the Lord. If He wants to save your soul, He's going to save it."

Miss Etta pounds on the Plexiglas to get the guard's attention. The guard smiles at her, and instead of yelling at her, he delivers a slice of lemon pie to me wrapped in a paper towel.

"See, the Lord works in mysterious ways." She grins ear to ear.

"That's a miracle. How'd you get the guard to do that?"

"I did it the old-fashioned way. I paid him."

I laugh and she laughs too. I have to admit, crazy old Miss Etta is pretty funny when she wants to be.

"So now what do I do?"

"You eat that damn pie. And shut your mouth while I do some praying. And you need to pray too."

"What do I say?"

"Just talk to God, that's all. I'll take care of the rest."

"Okay." I put the phone down and take a bit of the pie. And contrary to what I thought it would taste like, it doesn't taste like a miracle. In fact, it doesn't taste that good at all. It's kind of sour, but I keep eating it and smiling back at Miss Etta, acting like I like it.

Then after I finish the pie, we both bow our heads. Miss Etta does some heavy-duty praying. She's all talking in tongues. I shut my eyes and find that I'm at a loss for words. I mean, what do I say to God? Especially after I talked so much smack about Him.

Then right when Miss Etta gets all feverish with prayer, the guard taps me on the shoulder.

"Time's up."

"Okay. Just ten more seconds, please. We're praying here."

"Now!" The guard grabs my arm.

Then all of a sudden the rolling sounds of thunder fill the room. The guard backs away from me and points up at the black maelstrom brewing inside the room. The storm clouds roll across the ceiling, and pea-size hail starts falling all over the place, pinging everyone and jumping on the floor like popcorn. We're talking about two inches of hail in just a matter of seconds.

That's when I hear this whistling like a teakettle and I feel this vacuum, and then, pop! I'm standing outside of Ryan and he's covering his shaved head from the falling ice. The guards, prisoners, and visitors are all going crazy. At first everybody tries to look up at the ceiling to see where the hail is coming from, but it starts falling so hard and fast they have to bury their heads under their arms. The visitors run out screaming. And the guards start huddling the prisoners together. And then suddenly it stops. The black clouds recede, and all that's left is a floor covered with ice pellets and a roomful of half-crazed guards and prisoners. Ryan's head is bleeding from the hail dings and he stands there in his cubicle, all wide-eyed and confused. Miss Etta taps on the window and holds up her receiver. Ryan picks up his phone.

"Hello, Ryan. How you doing, baby?"

"What's going on? What am I doing here? What the hell are you doing here?"

"You in prison, baby."

"Huh?"

"Look, visiting time is ova. You gotta go. But I'm going leave this Bible for you. There's this part in here about Thou Shalt Not Kill. You probably should read it. Learn it real good."

"Come on." The prison guard grabs Ryan and pulls him away. Miss Etta laughs and waves at him as they pull his crazy ass back through the ice to his cell.

I walk through the wall over to Miss Etta's side of the room.

"Lord. Look at the mess you done made." She shakes her head.

"You did that. I didn't."

"Boy, if you weren't all up in here possessing folks, I wouldn't have to be doing no exorcisms. Especially in front of all these innocent peoples," she laughs. "Shoo, they probably all needs therapy after all that crazy shit."

"They're in prison. I wouldn't exactly call them innocent."

"Don't start your sassing with me. The time has come, Conrad."

"What do you mean the time has come?"

"Your time. Your time has come, sweet baby."

Then these two angels blister out of this flash of white light. It's the same angels from before—the guy and the girl—and they shine like gold. Except this time instead of being action-figure-size they grow into these giants. Their wingspan alone must be eighteen feet. They've got to duck their heads just to fit in the room.

The guy angel whispers, "Let's go."

"Where?" My voice shakes, giving away how absolutely scared shitless I am.

"Now!" The girl angel trumpets and the Plexiglas room divider shatters.

"Say Hello to the Lord for me, baby. Give Him all my loving. Hug His neck for me." Miss Etta waves to me as I am whisked into a brilliant nowhere by these giant things with wings.

"So where the hell am I?"

"This is not hell." The girl angel pats my back. "Hell is where you create it."

"It's a figure of speech."

"Oh, sorry. Words are not my providence." She smiles.

"You mean province?"

"You know what she means." The guy angel rolls his eyes at me.

"So who are you two anyway, and where are you taking me?"

"We're taking you to The Eternal Now." The girl angel flutters her wings and looks heavenward. "And my name is Muriel. I am an angel—in case you haven't noticed. And my province is Wisdom and Justice."

"I'm Michael. Archangel of the Fiery Sword of God."

"Oh-kay. So I guess I'm in trouble now?"

"Depends on what you consider trouble." Michael winks at Muriel.

"Yeah. Trouble is as trouble does." She giggles.

"What's with the Forrest Gump act? I thought you said you were the angel of Wisdom."

"I have infinite wisdom. I'm so smart you think I'm dumb. You cannot fathom me."

"Sounds like a good excuse to me."

"You are so rouge!"

"Rude. The word is rude."

"Okay, Conrad. You want to fight? Is that what your soul is all about?" Michael turns dark and ominous like a thunderhead moving over the sun.

"Look, I'm dead. Bowing up on me is sort of pointless, don't you think?"

"He's not trying to fight you. He's just trying to reflect you." Muriel puts her arm around me. "See, you want to fight—I think that's the word, 'fight'—and that's what you get: a fight."

"Now, that's where you're wrong. I'm tired of fighting. I'm tired of all this. I'm tired of stealing people's bodies. I'm tired of being dead. And I'm tired of watching everyone go baby and die."

"Look, Conrad." Michael walks over to me. "We're here to bring back what you've thrown away. It's a gift or it's a punishment. It all depends on what you make it."

"What is it?"

"Life!" Muriel beams.

And that's when the dumb angel touches that crease right under my nose and above my lip. I feel this whip, and then the roar of the ocean fills my ears. All of a sudden, I am small, very small, and then I realize I am under warm, soft water, all curled-up fetus style.

I'm in a baby. A baby that is growing inside of Maggie Meadows. Maggie Meadows Graham. She married Tucker and they're expecting me in about three months. The angels whisper in my little ears and this is what they tell me: They tell me that Tucker and Maggie both dropped out of LSU and have moved to Tucker's parents' rundown plantation in North Louisiana. They tell me that Maggie saw in Tucker the only person who ever loved her for who she was, not what someone thought she should be. They tell me that this—that this impulse marriage—will be their life. This will be my life.

I guess I have some karma to burn off and God and his angels have seen fit to put me here. The angels show me pictures of what the future will be like and this is what I see:

There will be arguments about finances and dirty clothes. At times Maggie will look at her *Vogues* and her *Cosmos*, and she will grow wide-awake bored with her country life and with big old Tucker Graham. The grind of the cotton farm will wear her out. But there will never be any hitting or yelling and no one will expect her to be perfect. Tucker will praise her beauty even though she's fifty pounds overweight. He'll say he likes a woman with a little meat on her bones. He'll mean it too. He will be gentle and kind to her. And Maggie will love him for it. She will bake him chocolate sheet cakes and rhubarb pies for it. It'll be far from perfect—with all their hick neighbors, gravel roads, and the seasons that bring with them too much or too little rain. Money will be tight. There will be no Mercedes or debutante balls in their future. Maggie and Tucker will live the Louisiana farm life full of pesticides, tax forms, and church meetings.

I will grow up on that farm, strong and redheaded like my

father. And they will call me Elijah. Elijah Delaney Graham. It's a name that came to Maggie in a dream. And like a dream, I will forget all about who I used to be and all the pain that rode with me. And you know what? I'm glad. After all, who needs the past? Especially when you've got a future.

MISS ETTA'S TRANSLUCENT LEMON π

2 cups of sugar
1 cup of Crisco
4 eggs, separated
3 tablespoons of apple jelly
4 tablespoons of fresh-squeezed lemon juice
1 teaspoon of salt
1 uncooked pi crust

Cream the sugar and the Crisco. Add egg yolks. Add jelly, lemon juice, and salt. Beat egg whites until medium stiff. Fold into above mixture. Bake in uncooked crust in slow oven at 250 to 300 degrees until firm.

3.14159265358979323846264338327950288419716939937510582094944592307816406286208998628 03482534211706798214 80865132823066470938446095505822317253594081284811174502841027019385211055596446229489549303819644288109 75665933446128475648233786783165271201909145648566923460348610454326648213393607260249141273724587006606 3155881748815209209628292540917153643678925903600 11 ...

Acknowledgments

Michelle, I can only repay you with my heart. Thank you.

Thank you, Cornelia Bolen, my second-grade teacher who taught me the magic of words and myths.

I wrote *The Worthy* when I was twenty-six. And on the very night that I typed the last period at the end of the final sentence, I dreamed that Stephen King congratulated me for signing with Simon & Schuster, and then he gave me a ham sandwich. Almost ten years later, this dream came true—not the ham sandwich/Stephen King part obviously, but the Simon & Schuster part.

My dream of publishing has paled compared to the reality of it all, mostly because of these fine people:

Denise Roy. Your editorial sleight of hand is astonishing.

David Rosenthal. You are King of the Super-Ninjas.

Kristan Fletcher. You rawk! at concert volume.

Annie Orr. The only thing that outshines your kindness is your future.

Michael Accordino. If people judge my books by your covers, I will be a very lucky man.

Tracey Guest and Victoria Meyer. You two rock louder than Sleater-Kinney.

Aja Shevelew. Thanks for saving me from myself and the hideousness of my sloppy typing.

The S&S sales armada. Thanks for fighting the good fight for me and my books.

Jenny Bent. You kick ass in ways that most people have yet to invent. Holly Henderson Root and Jessica Pazlas, you too.

Thanks to: Mom and Dad, Grant and Heidi (the party was the best), Dan and Karen, Josh and Denise, Aunt Margie Ann and

Uncle Jerry, Modena and Leon Henry, Ann Reed, Aunt Nancy, Cynthia, Kevin and Jayme, Nicole and Scott, Prue and Gary, the entire Titus clan, Kevin, Amy and Thad (thanks for all the free steak dinners). Thank you all for putting up with my tours, listening to me say things you've all heard before, and for buying way too many of my books.

Thanks for the hook-ups, freelance gigs, and the traveling mercies that have made it possible for me to follow my dream of ham sandwiches and publication: Ann and Randy Asprodites, Olga Arseniev and Bruce Johnson, Jimmy and Cindy Bower, Jennifer and Coty Rosenblath, Jodie and Chris McJunkins, Justin Lundgren and Kiersta Kurtz-Burke, Grant Morris, Coert and Molly Voorhees, Gina Cotroneo, Jeff Stayton, Ashwinnee Bhatt and his wonderfamily, Mick Weisberg, Meredith and H.O. Maycotte, Dale Wootton and Garden Café, Candy and Jeff Peterson, Matt and Kristin Klug, Ann Pearson, Lisa Deatherage, Bill Kreighbaum, Kathy Leonard, Matt Savage, Ray Graj, Simon Graj, Eric Gustavsen, Leslie and Corey Murphy of Legal Grounds fame, Erica Helwick, Sara Straubel, and the Texas Book Festival gang: Clay Smith, Andrea Prestridge, and Mary Herman.

My writers group.

Bob Bookman. Wow.

God.

About the Author

WILL CLARKE doesn't want you to know where he lives or what he's doing next. However, he is not opposed to you buying his other book, *Lord Vishnu's Love Handles: A Spy Novel (Sort Of)*.

Reading group guide

Discussion questions

1. *The Worthy* is filled with startling scenes; some are violent, some are outlandish. Which scenes were most shocking? Overall, did you find the violence or the fantastical elements of the plot more surprising?

2. Conrad says that the one perk of being dead is that "the living are like open books that you can read without turning the pages" (2). How does this new perception change him? Are there sides to his personality that we see when he's ghost, but wouldn't have seen when he was alive?

3. The novel is set in Louisiana, and the author incorporates many details and observations about Southern culture. What aspects of his portrayal of the South are most realistic? In what ways does the author play with stereotypes of the South?

4. The pledges come to Gamma Chi looking to become part of an elite group. How does the pressure of measuring up to their peers influence them? Why do you think they are willing to put up with so much misery?

5. Discuss the character of Tucker. What does Conrad think of Tucker? Does he relate to him or care for him at all, or does he just use him? How is Tucker affected by Conrad's possessions?

6. How does Conrad's postdeath perspective change his feelings about Gamma Chi? What does he miss? If he could go back to being a part of the fraternity, do you think he would?

7. Maggie Meadows and Sarah Jane Bradford are both sorority girls, but they are almost polar opposites. How does each one adapt to or reject the social customs of the LSU campus? What knowledge about Ryan and, more important, about himself does Conrad gain from each girl?

8. Conrad says "it's really weird; I know every move Ryan Hutchins makes . . . but I have no idea if my parents are even stateside" (175). Why doesn't he try to see his parents? How do they deal with his death? Why does Conrad react so strongly when he sees his father and uncle during hell week?

9. How would you characterize Miss Etta's powers? Discuss the influence she has over Conrad and the role she plays in shaping his fate.

10. Clarke highlights the contrasts between our fantasies and reality. What kinds of fantasies do the characters have about fraternity life, love and relationships, or even human nature? Does being a ghost change what Conrad's most cherished fantasies are?

11. Clarke writes in a darkly humorous style, often finding comedy in the most serious of subjects. What are some key examples of this style?

12. Throughout the novel, Miss Etta urges Conrad to forgive and to stop seeking revenge on Ryan. Discuss what happens when Conrad possesses Ryan's body at the end of the novel. Does he forgive? Does he get revenge? Do you think he's content?

13. What do you make of the ending of the novel and Conrad's reincarnation? Why do you think he was given a second chance? Were you satisfied with the ending?

14. The brothers of Gamma Chi call themselves "the worthy" (and consider everyone else unworthy). In the end, can any of the characters truly be considered "worthy"? Do you think God is making that determination by singling out Miss Etta and Sarah Jane Bradford?

15. In *The New York Times Book Review,* Liesl Schillinger wrote, "the supernatural is more than a gimmick. It's a device Clarke uses to trick the cynical eye into taking a leisurely, evaluative look at the craziness of the mundane." Do you agree with her assessment? What do you think Clarke reveals about "the craziness of the mundane"?

16. What is your opinion of the Greek system after reading *The Worthy*? What do you think the author's opinion is? Is it a viable option for college students looking for social interaction?

Enhance your Reading Group Experience

To learn more about Will Clarke, the author of *The Worthy*, visit his website and blog at www.willclarke.com. Or to invite Will Clarke to speak to your book club in person, via the phone or video chat, email him directly, at willclarke13@mac.com.

Gamma Chi's violent hazing process is a significant element of *The Worthy*. To learn more about actual hazing and current efforts to prevent it, visit www.stophazing.org.

Further reading: For more of Will Clarke's black humor, check out his first novel, *Lord Vishnu's Love Handles*. Or for a true account of hazing and fraternities, read Brad Land's memoir *Goat*.

Author Q & A

1. Paramount won a heated bidding war with New Line for the film rights to your debut novel, *Lord Vishnu's Love Handles: A Spy Novel (Sort Of)*. Film rights to *The Worthy: A Ghost's Story* have also been purchased, this time by Sony. What's going on with that?

After Michael London set up *Lord Vishnu's Love Handles* at Paramount, I was lucky enough to sign with an agent at CAA. My agent is the kind of guy who really shepherds his clients. He doesn't mind pushing you out of your comfort zone. So even though I saw myself as strictly a novelist, he asked me to write the adaptation of *The Worthy*. To my surprise, I enjoyed the process, and the end result was actually something I was very proud of. My agent sent my screenplay over to Doug Wick and Lucy Fisher at Red Wagon Productions, and before I knew it they had set up the project at Columbia/Sony. Doug and Lucy have produced some of my favorite adaptations, like *Cider House Rules, Jarhead, Memoirs of a Geisha*, and *Girl, Interrupted*. I'm completely stoked to be working with them.

2. In *The Worthy*, Conrad Avery Sutton III's ghost has come back to earth to seek revenge against his murderer. How did you come up with this storyline?

I was enrolled in a fiction writing class at SMU when I was twenty-five. The first assignment was to place a character in conflict with his or her environment. Since my life experience at LSU had just been drenched in the Greek world and I was still trying to make sense of it, I set the story in a fraternity house. I made the character a kid who had lost his body in a hazing episode. The conflict that I began exploring was what it would be like to be dead at nineteen and to be stuck in a house where the people who killed you were still enjoying the carnality of their young lives. It was a short story that I couldn't finish. I kept working on it, and the story about a frat boy ghost became the first novel that I ever completed.

3 Do you believe in ghosts?

I do believe in ghosts. I think I might even have upset one once. My good friend Meredith bought this ancient, almost falling down house in East Dallas. She single-handedly restored this old place and then, to celebrate, had a bunch of us over for a dinner party.

After dessert was served, along with a few too many glasses of wine, the Ouija board was pulled out. We contacted a ghost named Natalie. Somebody asked Natalie if Tootie from *The Facts of Life* was with her. We thought this was hysterical and kept taunting each other and "the ghost." The only semiweird thing to happen at the party was that a fuse blew out and sparks flew everywhere in the kitchen, but we just laughed it off. After we had all gone home, in the wee hours of the night, three different people called Meredith asking for "Natalie." Mysteriously, the Caller IDs of the folks asking for Natalie were not from Dallas or related to anyone from the party. The next morning when Meredith woke up, her dining room and kitchen were flooded. The pipes had burst, probably about the same time the calls for Natalie came in.

A week later, I was over at Meredith's looking at the tile samples she had picked out. Meredith was excited about her selection and that her insurance would be covering the damage. I quipped, "You should thank Natalie for getting you a new floor." We both laughed, put the tile sample square in the middle of the kitchen counter, shut off the lights, and left. As Meredith was walking me to the door, we heard a crash in the kitchen. We went into the room to investigate, and there on the floor was the tile sample. Meredith ran out of the house screaming, and I went chasing after her.

4. You were in fraternities at both Louisiana Tech and Louisiana State University. Was the hazing really as bad as you describe? Or are you sworn to secrecy?

I was indeed sworn to secrecy. But I don't believe in keeping secrets.

However, before I muddy the waters with my own fraternity experience, let me point out that Kappa Chi, the made-up fraternity in my book, is not based on any one fraternity in particular. It's an amalgam of news stories, anecdotes, and my imagination.

With that out of the way, I can safely say that my first pledgeship didn't go so well. I pledged Teke when I was a freshman at Louisiana Tech and after a hazing ritual that they called "Three Fires," where I was taken out into the woods late at night with a burlap sack over my head, I depledged. The beating, yelling, and threatening really rattled me, and fortunately I had the wherewithal to quit. This was not a popular decision with my friends or the fraternity, and I spent the rest of the year at Tech as an outcast.

My sophomore year I transferred to LSU, and because I have always been slow on the uptake and pathologically desperate to fit in, I went through rush *again*. I pledged Sigma Chi. But this time, I had it easier because of my name. The worst hazers in Sigma Chi were huge fans of baseball great, Will "The Thrill" Clark. These actives had this weird misplaced affection for me and they focused most of their worst tirades on other pledges. And when I did catch the brunt of some active's wrath, I tried to remain as detached as possible, observing myself and the event almost like a journalist.

5. Have you ever known someone like Ryan Hutchinson, a handsome "rising star" who is, in actuality, the "darkest black hole you'll ever meet?"

While I belonged to a fraternity, both as a pledge and an active, I was often astonished at the cruelty and violence that normal guys—guys who were upstanding citizens in the outside world—

would perpetrate when it would be kept a secret. When the lights went out and the oaths were sworn, it really did feel like *The Lord of the Flies* a lot of the time. I think most of it was alcohol fueled, but the whole hazing dynamic creates this tempest in a teapot abuse of power. It's a dynamic that couldn't exist without pledge programs and secret oaths.

So, Ryan is a metaphor as much as he is a character. He's the Waspy epitome of this whole hazing psychodrama and need for secrecy. But no, he's not based on any one person whom I have known.

6. What is your writing process?

When I am working on a novel, I write two pages a day for six months. That's about 365 pages of a rough draft. I write in fits and starts really, and I just try to get it down on paper. I often like to write in a café, because the lure of a nap is just too strong if I am near a bed. Oh, and I must have coffee and my iTunes. I love to write while I am buzzing on caffeine and listening to good music.

7. You originally self-published both *Lord Vishnu's Love Handles* and *The Worthy*. What was that experience like?

I wrote *The Worthy* in my mid-twenties and landed a big time agent right out of the gate. She spent the next two years trying to sell *The Worthy* to no avail. To keep my agent interested, I wrote *Lord Vishnu's Love Handles* and completed that novel in May 2001. But it also got rejected across the board when I tried to sell it the first time. So, I decided I had nothing to lose and that I could live with the shame of self-publishing. I looked into what rock bands had done, like Ani DeFranco and WILCO, and tried to follow that model. I also took a lot of cues from Dave Eggers. My background in advertising came in handy: I designed the cover, typeset the text, worked with a printer and got worldwide distribution through Amazon. But self-publishing is still such a dirty word for most people, so I named my press MiddleFinger-Press. I now use the press to create fiction anthologies featuring new writers, and I donate the money to charity. But right now, while I am touring for my books, the press is on hiatus.

8. Both of your novels have been optioned for films, praised by critics, and received endorsements from the likes of Tony Hawk, Christopher Moore, David Gordon Green, *Rolling Stone,* and more. Are you ever surprised by your own success?

I am constantly surprised by any success that comes my way. Success isn't a word that was ever really bandied around with my name as a kid or even as a young adult. I was pretty much a failure in everything I did. I was always the bench-warmer on the football team, the D-plus student, the ADD spaz boy. So when something goes right, I am always surprised and extremely grateful.

9. What's the one thing you'd like readers to know about you that they may not already know?

I want my readers to know how grateful I am that they have given five to eight hours of their busy lives to read my books. This is such a huge gift to give someone, and I'm not sure readers know how much writers like myself appreciate this.

Author @ccess presents
a special offer for book clubs

CHAT WITH THE AUTHOR!

WILL CLARKE is available to speak with your book club via telephone!

A Ghost's Story

THE WORTHY

WILL CLARKE

author of LORD VISHNU'S LOVE HANDLES

Photograph by Sigrid Estrada

Email bookclubcall@simonandschuster.com for information. Please put the book title in the subject line, and include information about your club.

Sign up for our free monthly newsletter at BookClubReader.com

It's the best source for reading group guides, author Q&As, chapter excerpts, tips for your club or how to start one, contests and much more!

Visit www.willclarke.com

book clubreader

SIMON & SCHUSTER PAPERBACKS
A CBS COMPANY

16723

Also available from Will Clarke

"WRY AND INVENTIVE . . . A SPOOF THIS PROMISING IS WORTH CELEBRATING."
—MIKE SHEA, *TEXAS MONTHLY*

A Spy Novel (Sort of)

Lord Vishnu's Love Handles
Will Clarke

"[A] hot pop prophet. America's latest cult comic novelist is Will Clarke."
—*Rolling Stone*

"Will Clarke, a Southern frat boy-turned-adman, has burst onto the literary scene like a kid cannonballing off the high-dive . . . His plotting reveals a man who thinks like Will Ferrell and dreams like Samuel Taylor Coleridge . . . Surprisingly tender . . . [with Clarke], the supernatural is more than a gimmick. It's a device Clarke uses to trick the cynical eye into taking a leisurely, evaluative look at the craziness of the mundane."
—Liesl Schillinger, *The New York Times Book Review*

Available wherever books are sold or at www.simonsays.com

SIMON & SCHUSTER
PAPERBACKS
A CBS COMPANY

Printed in the United States
By Bookmasters